OPEN:

A TALE OF LOVE, MERMAIDS, BASSISTS, & CREEPY DUDES

OPEN
A Tale of Love, Mermaids, Bassists, & Creepy Dudes
Emilie Nantel

*Get yourself some boys who got your back
the way Bobby and François got mine.*

ONE

I've learned with time that the best pick-up line a girl can use is 'I'm in an open relationship.'

I'm sharing a beer with Hugo before his set and he's telling me about the year he just spent in Australia. His eyes crinkle with amusement and I find myself staring at him, not really listening. His hair is a bit overgrown — a wavy chestnut cloud surrounding his face. I'm hit with the image of these deep brown curls nestled between my thighs, his eyes looking up at me in earnest. I've always had a bit of a crush on that boy.

This is it. Time to do what I came here hoping to do.

I lean over the table, a mischievous glint in my eye. Hugo stops talking and cocks a keen eyebrow. My hand on his forearm, I whisper:

"Can I tell you a secret?"

His smile widens.

"Yeah?"

A knot forms in my stomach and my own smile falters. What if I read him wrong? I don't want to mess up three years of friendship for lust. Hugo notices my hesitation and puts his hand over mine, still on his arm.

"Amy," he says softly, looking straight into my eyes. "It's me. You can tell me anything."

I try a smile, clear my throat, and take a deep breath.

You can do this, I tell myself. *You're the queen of flirting.*

"David and I are in an open relationship." My confidence comes back as I say the familiar line, and I punctuate it with a smirk.

Instantly, I can see I wasn't wrong at all. Hugo's eyes widen; his smile goes from amused to tempted. I recognize all the signs; his thinking process is clearly along the lines of, 'This formerly off-limits girl just became available' and takes him to the conclusion that, 'She wouldn't be telling me this if she weren't interested in taking this to the next level.'

Hugo's face lights up; crinkles surround his eyes again as he beams at me, realizing I'm hitting on him. He opens his mouth to speak, but someone comes up to him.

"Soundcheck in five."

Hugo nods, still staring at me in a half-incredulous, half-aroused way.

"Wait for me after the show," he whispers in my ear, kissing me on the cheek before disappearing backstage.

The bar fills up during the soundcheck. Now that I'm left alone with my beer and my thoughts, I get almost giddy with anticipation. I can't stop thinking about what will happen after his set. How am I gonna be able to wait that long?

As soon as Hugo appears on stage after the soundcheck, however, my mind shuts up. I let myself become completely absorbed in him and his music. He's alone before the crowd with a stool and his guitar, all eyes on him — under a lone spotlight, he's never looked better.

Fingers on the strings, lithe and nimble, pull magic from a piece of wood. A warm, enveloping voice. His words speak to me the way poetry never could. Deep brown eyes fixed on mine, full of promises of things to come.

I've been to many of his gigs. He used to do a lot of bluesy covers of different genres: 70's classic rock, 90's R&B, 40's crooners, but now he's branching out and writing his own material. Never have I seen him so raw, so sensual. The crowd around me is cheering, swaying to the music, but I know in the way his eyes never leave mine that this show is intended for me alone. I can tell the wait is killing him as much as me, and that he makes up for it with the most animalistic, almost erotic stage presence.

I notice I'm gripping my pint of beer so hard my knuckles are turning white. I let out a long breath and hold his gaze. Sweat ripples down his neck, making his thin, battered Bob Dylan T-shirt cling to his lean frame. I swear I can see the outline of an erect nipple, but that might just be my hormone-addled mind hallucinating.

Hugo sits down on the stool and strums a bluesy number, stripped down and raw. His voice goes hoarse and he closes his eyes to feel the intensity. The mere passion animating his whole being would be enough to turn me on, if I weren't already. The way he throws himself into his art so completely is irresistible to me.

He plays the rest of his set with the same drive and dedication, feeding off the love and energy from the crowd.

At the end of his set, he disappears for a few minutes backstage, where, I notice sadly, he changes out of his soaked shirt. He joins me at my table bearing two beers, one of which he places next to my own empty glass.

"Perks of being in the show," he explains.

"Thanks. God, that was… incredible. One of your best sets," I say breathlessly, clinking my glass against his.

"The crowd was great. It helps." Something in his eye tells me that by *the crowd* he means me.

The conversation is light, small talk almost, but it only serves as a front, something to do while we finish our beer and let the tension rise, higher and higher.

It comes to a peak when, a while later, he drains the last of his beer and looks me straight in the eye, smirking.

"So, should we get out of here?"

That's usually my line when I'm trying to pick someone up, and hearing it used on me makes me weak in the knees.

I smile and follow him out of the bar, anticipation building in the pit of my stomach. The late August night offers no respite from the bar's sweltering air. The sun is long gone, but the heat wave that's been overwhelming us for a few days doesn't even let up at night. The last thing I should want is to press myself against another warm, sweaty body, but try telling that to my hormones.

"It's a ten minute walk to my new place," Hugo suggests.

"Sounds perfect." I slip my hand in his and he guides me down a quiet street.

Further down the block, he stops in his tracks and pulls me in, unable to wait. He buries his face in my neck and spreads kisses from my ear to my shoulder.

"God, Amy," he sighs. "You don't know how long I've wanted to do this."

My hands slip under his shirt, fingers mapping the small of his back. I press myself against him, closer than close, and breathe in his ear.

"Me too."

It's true.

I never did anything about it because, when I first met Hugo, David and I were still exclusive. I forced myself to see him as nothing more than a friend. When David suggested we try an open relationship, I immediately thought of Hugo, but he was in Australia at the time. I told David about it, of course. We tell each other everything — well, except for the juicy details, that is. When Hugo said he was moving back to Montreal, David wouldn't stop teasing me about it.

Needless to say, my past self and I are currently high-fiving in my mind. Hugo suddenly grabs my hand, and all but sprints down the street. He tries to dig his keys out of his pocket while running — not an altogether successful endeavour. I laugh, struggling to keep up. We finally get to his apartment building, wheezing and cackling. It takes him a good minute to unlock the glass door — he tries three different keys until he realizes it was already unlocked.

"Motherfucker," he mumbles. He retrieves my hand and leads me across the lobby to the elevator.

Of course, the doors take forever to open. Hugo and I alternate between awkward laughs, stolen glances, and rushed kisses. He pushes me in as soon as the telltale *ding* resounds in the lobby, pressing me against the back wall as the doors close behind him. I'm pinned between the wall and Hugo's slender, warm body; his leg wedges itself between mine. I stand on tiptoes, letting him support most of my weight, and my skirt rides up my thighs.

His head is buried in my neck, once again. He nibbles and licks at my skin, right under my earlobe, where it's the most sensitive, and I let out a moan.

"What floor?" I ask, suddenly noticing we're still immobile.

"Oh, right." He sets me down for a second, punches the 9 button, and hurries back between my legs. I wrap them around his waist. He groans and presses even closer — I can feel how hard he is.

We kiss as if we were trying to fit the entire act of fucking into one messy kiss, eager for release. My senses are on fire. For a second that feels like several blissful minutes, I'm hyperaware of him in every fibre of my being. His scent of sweat and fabric softener overpowers me, deepening the hunger growing in me.

His fingers, calloused by years of guitar playing, raise trails of goose bumps in their trek across my thighs. His laboured, desperate breathing has the same effect; shivers spread down my neck, down my spine, erecting the hairs at the nape of my neck.

The ride up is excruciating. Hours seem to pass between each floor.

His kisses taste faintly of cheap beer, but I don't mind — the way he uses his tongue is mind-blowing. I moan into his mouth, ready to let him take me on the spot if we don't reach his apartment soon.

I weave my fingers through his hair. An especially well-placed lick makes me gasp and I instinctively pull on his curls. He lets out a growl and moves to unbutton his pants.

The characteristic *ding* of the elevator shrills and the doors open at that exact moment.

"Fuck." Hugo groans. Again, he takes me by the hand and fumbles with his keys in the other.

At last, he manages to get his door open and we tumble inside, laughing in relief.

"First door on the left." The sound is muffled by the shirt he's trying to take off.

I rush in, settle on the bed, and wait for him with a seductive smile.

"Should I try that hair-pulling thing again, then?"

"Fuck yes."

TWO

Click.

I turn away from my bedroom window. David stands in the doorway, looking at the picture he just took on his camera. He smiles — that smile I fell in love with four years ago, the one that lights up his perfectly gorgeous grey eyes.

"You look beautiful."

I look at my reflection in the mirror. My hair sticks out; I'm in mismatched, tattered pyjamas, cradling a mug of tea between cold hands. But I know David has a knack for seeing beauty everywhere — in the curve of a hip, the light hitting a skyscraper, hidden graffiti — and to capture it just right. His photographs are part of why I fell in love with him. The world is a wonderful place when seen through his eyes.

"So do you," I tell him, and pull him closer. There's that smile again. I wish I had his talent so I could capture his smile and show him how amazing he looks.

David pushes me softly on our bed and carefully sets his camera, his glasses, and my mug down on the dresser. He joins me under the covers and, just as delicately, pulls up my shirt.

"You look like you're unwrapping a gift," I remark, amused.

"That's exactly what I'm doing." David's voice is low, enticing.

"You're so cute." I press myself against him, and even as we kiss, he keeps on smiling, bright as a summer day.

"I love you," he whispers as he pulls down my pyjama pants.

The look on his face is eager, but the way he undresses me is lazy, like he has all the time in the world. I know he doesn't — he has a shoot in an hour and a half — but it feels excellent to be relished so slowly.

His clothes disappear way faster than mine, and he finally presses his warm skin against mine. It feels like home, like a warm cup of tea. We revel for a bit in each other's bodies, rolling around in the unmade bed. We enjoy the warmth, the love, not in any rush to do anything in particular, even though we both know where this is going.

The early sun rays shining through the curtains light up the sheets and David's long expanses of skin, making his eyes even brighter, almost silver. Morning sex is my favourite. Everything is blurred, fuzzy in the first light of the day. Voices are hushed, breaths are shared, and the sun warms the skin. You create lazy, sweet memories to last you throughout the day.

The image of David holding me tight and a litany of I love yous and More pleases help me survive the long day shelving records at work, as do his loving text messages.

¤

"So… I went to Hugo's gig this weekend…" I intentionally trail off, building the suspense.

It works. David leans in, on the edge of his seat. "Did you tell him? How did it go?"

We're having our weekly dine-and-dish date, where we talk about the people we've met and our feelings, where we touch base about our relationship — this is what we found was best for us, for making the open relationship work.

Honesty, communication, trust.

Not always easy, especially when you're busy like us. Eventually, you forget things, and it's like, *If I forgot to tell him, is it cheating? I didn't mean to!*

So we set time aside each week. And, to be honest, it's one of my favourite parts of the week. It usually helps me understand what I'm going through, and it's also really great to share the fun stuff with someone who, no matter what, is happy you're happy.

And, damn, if that look on David's face right now isn't the cutest thing ever. He knows how long I've been crushing on Hugo, and he knows I went to the gig hoping something would happen.

"It went great, if you know what I mean…" I wiggle my eyebrows lewdly to make him laugh.

"Yes!" David actually pumps his fist like a sports fan when his team scores.

Which, yeah, that's pretty much what happened, I guess.

"Was it just a one time thing, or…?"

"God, I hope not." I hide my face in my hands — it's kind of overwhelming how into Hugo I am.

David lays a soothing hand on my thigh. "Hey, I'm happy for you."

His smile is gorgeous. I just want to kiss him.

So I do.

"What about you?" I ask when I break the kiss, a bit breathless. "Met anyone fun?"

"Well, there's this one girl…"

I raise my eyebrows, curious.

"She's gorgeous, and funny, and smart, and she's a redhead, you know how much I love redheads — "

I do know. It's one of the first things he complimented me on, when we first met.

"— and she's just… heads over heels in love with me…" He winks mischievously.

"Is her name Amy Evans, by any chance?"

"…Yes."

I fling myself into his arms and we share a giggly hug, completely forgetting the dinner on the table.

THREE

La Pharmacie, a gay bar in Montreal's Village, is our favourite place to hang out. It's got everything: drag queen shows, a poolroom, a dance floor, and overly friendly shot girls. Tonight, a rare occurrence in our busy lives, the whole crew said they'd come: Alex, Julia, Michelle, Cory, Georgie and I.

Julia and Mitch are straight, but they love the place because they don't get hit on by douchebags. Plus, who doesn't love drag queens and shots?

I'm downing a shot of something pink and sickly sweet when Cory walks in.

"Hey, where's your girlfriend?" Julia asks. "I thought you said you'd come with S — "

Everyone's head snaps towards Julia. She stops herself mid-deadnaming Georgie.

You can almost hear the sound of a needle scratching a record.

Slowly, deliberately, Cory grabs a shot from the table and drains it. He takes a deep breath and turns to Julia.

"*Georgie* will be late. *He* had to work. For fuck's sake, Julia, he came out two years ago. Can't you get it through your thick skull? Georgie is a *man*."

"Geez, I'm sorry." Julia rolls her eyes. "I forgot, it's no big deal — he's not even here yet."

I let out a long sigh. I'm so sick of trying — and failing — to educate her on queer matters. Julia and I have been friends since we were six. By now, we pretty much just stay friends out of habit. In your mid-twenties, 'Her parents have a pool' doesn't quite cut it as a reason to hang out with someone.

Luckily, I can always count on Alex to set the record straight — or should I say queer? — whenever Julia demonstrates just how out-of-touch with our identities she is. Alex calls her out about deadnaming and when is she gonna learn, for what seems like the millionth time since Georgie came out. Cory listens, an air of gratitude on his face — I know how exhausting it is to always have to explain these issues to people who just don't seem to care.

"Is that clear?" Alex finishes her rant.

Julia nods, taking as little space as possible in her seat. She tries hard to avoid Alex's gaze, who very much looks like she could kick Julia's ass in her combat boots and jean jacket adorned with queer and feminist patches and pins. Julia sends me a terrified look, eyebrows raised in a silent plea. What is she hoping, that I save her from the Angry Lesbian™? Not a chance.

No matter how much I agree with Alex, however, I've always been shitty at debating. I get overly emotional and end up picking fights, instead of calmly proving my point. I can't get into this with Julia again.

"Excuse me, can I get you a drink?"

Saved by the cutie.

Tall and muscular, with short, blonde hair, she flashes a gorgeous smile and nods toward the bar.

"Absolutely!" I follow her, heaving a relieved sigh.

She orders two beers and we sit down at the counter.

"I'm Taylor," she says, raising her glass.

"Amy." I click my glass against hers and take a sip. The bitterness is welcome after the round of sugary shots.

"One of my ex-girlfriends was called Amy. Crazy bitch, she was."

I let out an uncomfortable chuckle. What a weird thing to say to someone you've just met.

"What about you?" she asks. "Any crazy ex-girlfriends?"

"I wouldn't call them crazy, I mean, just — not the right fit, you know?"

"Sure, yeah — I guess I'm just sick of dealing with psychos, you know what I mean?"

Man, this girl is weird.

Don't get me wrong; I love getting to know people. That's the main reason I'm in an open relationship: I need to discover, to get a taste of all kinds of people and connect with them. However, I've gotten pretty good at sizing them up and this Taylor is giving me a very creepy vibe. I get the feeling that if this goes any further than getting a drink, she might latch onto me and hold on until she decides I'm equally as crazy as her exes.

"So, um, what do you do?" I ask, trying to get the conversation going for the duration of the beer she paid for — it's only polite.

She tells me all about her engineering studies. I'm careful to look interested in what she says — not that it's hard, it sounds actually pretty cool — but not interested in *her*, to avoid leading her on. After we finish our beers, I get up.

"Thanks for the drink."

"Another one?" she asks eagerly.

"I have to go back to my friends."

She nods, a sad smile on her face. "I guess it's no use asking for your number, eh?"

"Sorry." I shake my head.

Taylor shrugs. "Have fun, then."

"You too."

"So?" Georgie is here when I come back to the table. He and Cory are looking at me expectantly.

I hug Georgie hello and sit down next to him. "Weird vibe. Unloaded all her 'crazy-ex-girlfriends baggage' before the second sip of beer."

"Girl, I don't know how you do it." Cory says. "Dating and one-night stands." He shudders.

"Yeah," Georgie agrees. "It's just so exhausting — you have to play by the rules, or whatever… I'm just glad I don't have to worry about this anymore."

The two of them look at each other with so much love in their eyes, I'm surprised they don't get on one knee and propose on the spot.

I shrug. "I guess I don't mind it. The fun of discovering amazing people makes up for those bad experiences."

"Plus," Alex pipes up, "you're like, scary good at weeding out the ones that won't work out."

"One bad call a year, that's how I roll." Alex and I clink our glasses together.

"Sorry it didn't work out with Captain Phasma over there."

"Anyway," Julia points out, "the one who really needs to meet someone is Mitch."

Mitch rolls her eyes. "How did we get into this conversation again?"

"What about that guy?" Julia points at a guy two tables over, not even trying to be subtle about it.

"Julia, this is a gay bar. There's no way this guy is straight."

At this moment, Cory excuses himself to the bathroom, and said guy's eyes follow him.

"Proving my point."

"Then we need to stop hanging out here and go to a *real* bar! You'll never find a man by staying here. Won't she, Amy?"

"Ooh, that's my song!" I grab Mitch's hand and pull her to the otherwise empty dance floor.

"Thanks," she shouts over the undanceable techno remix of "My Heart Will Go On" blaring from the speakers.

We bounce up and down awkwardly until Julia stops peering at us suspiciously. Mitch pulls me outside to the terrace.

"Here, we'll be able to talk," she says a bit too loud, not yet used to the silence outside the bar.

We find a spot in a corner devoid of cigarette and vape smoke and lean against the brick wall.

"So, I got a second date," Mitch says in a conspiratorial tone.

"A second? When did you get the first one?"

"Last week. I didn't want to say anything so I wouldn't jinx it."

"Who is it?"

"His name is Justin. He plays guitar in a band."

"Sexy!"

Mitch giggles. "We met at school. He's in my German class and he complimented my Hufflepuff shirt."

"Potterhead? He's a keeper."

Mitch fiddles with one of the friendship bracelets she always wears on her wrists. After two years of single life, Mitch has become quite shy about relationship stuff. She was hurt pretty bad the last time.

"So, second date, huh?" I hold out my fist for a fist bump, trying to put her at ease.

She chuckles and bumps it. "Well, it's less of a date than a 'Come to my gig and we'll hang out afterwards' kind of deal."

"He wants to see you again? Totally counts."

"If you say so." Mitch's face is turning beet-red.

"Why didn't you tell Julia when she tried to match you?"

"Please. She'll think I'm making him up to get her off my case."

"Yeah, that does sound like her."

"I don't mind it that much, you know. As long as she's not setting up actual blind dates for me, it's not so bad."

"I'm glad you told me, though."

"Well, I wanted to know if you'd come to the show with me? I feel weird going alone."

"I'd love to." I hug her. "Dude, I'm so happy for you!"

¤

We leave the club around two in the morning, a good two hours after Julia left, to Mitch's relief. My brain is fuzzy from the shots; the loud thumping of the bass still echoes through my ears — the others aren't looking much better. Cory is hanging onto Georgie for dear life, eyes scrunched up as if the mere act of standing upright necessitated every last bit of brainpower. In the span of twenty minutes, he went from flawless death drops on the dance floor to freshly-born Bambi on ice.

Georgie wraps his lean arms around Cory's large frame and it's a wonder he's managing to keep him up — Cory's almost twice his size. Bowler hat askew, Georgie looks fondly at him, and trudges on as if the two hundred pounds of man draped across his shoulders were nothing more than a light backpack.

A gang of dudes turn the corner ahead and, as one, we all steel ourselves. Our two groups couldn't be more different. Them? A uniform gang of dudebros, all white, all wearing backwards baseball caps, all with their pants almost falling to their knees, and most importantly, all drunk and rowdy.

Us? A half-Black, half-Dominican man, as flamboyant as you can imagine, wearing a rainbow feather boa and singing "Born This Way" at the top of his lungs. Holding him upright, a trans black guy with a beard, bowler hat, and flamingo-patterned button-up shirt. Add to the mix a purple-haired, leather jacket-wearing lesbian, plus two chubby girls, one of which is of Filipino descent, both dressed for clubbing — easy prey.

Georgie pokes Cory in the ribs to shush him, but otherwise we try not to show we've noticed their presence, not to grab attention — although our entire appearance calls for attention. We collectively hold our breath as they pass us — we don't want any trouble. I can feel Alex tensing up next to me like a bowstring. I'd hold her hand to calm her down if it weren't just what the dudes were waiting for.

I let out a relieved sigh as they walk away — too soon.

One of the guys lets out a cough, poorly hiding a slur — one clearly directed at Georgie, which I won't bother repeating here. You get the idea.

The bow of Alex's body releases and she shoots after them, catching up to the gang in an alley out of view.

"Alex!" Mitch calls after her. "Fuck, this is the worst idea she's ever had."

"They're gonna kill her!" Georgie exclaims as I sprint after her, struggling to pull my phone out of my purse, in case something happens. The others aren't far behind me — Georgie dragging Cory along — but Alex soon comes back into view, running towards us.

"Run!"

We dash the way we came from, towards the subway station, Cory sobering up enough to run on his own. We dare to stop only when we realize we're not being followed. We pause before the turnstiles in the station, trying to catch our breath, when I finally get a good look at Alex. Her knuckles are bruised and bloody, her hair is messed-up from running, but she seems otherwise unharmed.

Georgie gingerly takes her hands in his, a mix of worry and admiration on his face. "Did you just punch a dude in the face for me?"

Alex grins. "Two dudes. They didn't expect it from a tiny girl, so I had time to hit two of them before they realized what's up."

"You didn't have to."

"Hell yeah, I did. You heard what they called you. They deserved worse, to be honest."

"Alex, sweetie," Mitch says, shaking her head in fond disapproval, "one of these days you're gonna get yourself killed."

"Fighting the queer fight? Worse ways to go." Alex shrugs, still grinning, bouncing up and down from the adrenaline.

Mitch digs through her bag and emerges with a few band-aids. "At least let me fix you up."

Alex's grins softens and her fists unclench. "Thanks, *Mom*," she snarks, but we all know she loves it.

Adrenaline receding, Cory slouches back against Georgie. "Can we do this every night?"

"The partying or the ass-kicking?"

"Both."

¤

The next Friday, I meet Mitch in front of Buzz, a tiny bar that attracts mostly cégep kids, but has a decent stage. She's so excited that she has to drain half a pint of beer before she manages to calm down.

A first act comes onstage and fails to hold my attention. Their pseudo-philosophical lyrics whine about the fleetingness of human life and the singer whispers into the microphone, instead of singing. I refrain from pulling out my phone out of politeness, but at least their set is quite short so I don't have to suffer too long.

The J-Walkers finally come out and all the over-excited eighteen-year-olds start screaming and crowding the stage like it's The Beatles or something. I roll my eyes and drain my pint, flagging the waitress for another. I have no opinion on the band yet, but I'll need to be at least a bit tipsy if I'm to tolerate their fans.

The beat is quite catchy, and I find myself tapping my foot as I pay for the beer. That's when the bass line comes in and the bassist starts singing harmonies.

I almost drop my glass.

The bassist is fucking gorgeous: floppy blond hair, tall and skinny. His voice makes me melt inside — soft, but deep — the kind that would be perfect for dirty talk. I'm majorly crushing on him, and I almost want to join the screaming fans up there, just to see him closer.

The rhythm picks up and the dude just starts humping his bass. His hips are gyrating and he's hitting every note perfectly. He's basically making love to his bass right there on the stage. I've never had the urge to be a musical instrument before, but *good god!*

In the short break before the next song, I ask Mitch who he is.

"His name's Jeff — he's Justin's brother," she yells above the applause.

"I want one," I say, fanning myself.

Mitch laughs. "You have a thing for lanky musicians, haven't you?" She's good friends with Hugo and nothing stays secret for too long with these guys.

"Will you introduce me?"

The next song begins before she can answer, and she takes out her phone to film Justin's guitar solo. I spend the rest of the show basically drooling. Even though we're at the back of the room near the bar, I'm convinced Jeff is looking directly at me and singing just for me. *What the fuck,* my brain pipes up, *you're a grown woman, get a grip!*

During a pretty fast song, Jeff starts jumping in place with his bass — you know, like punk rockers do. His shirt rides up and I'm filled with the urge to touch his skin — maybe taste it.

I quickly down the rest of my beer — if it doesn't lull my lust, maybe it'll at least muzzle the annoying, judgemental voice inside my head.

As the show comes to an end, the legions of fangirls scream — and so do I, *shut up*. The J-Walkers get off stage and Mitch is about to join them.

"Wait, aren't you gonna introduce me?"

She scrunches her nose. "Justin and I aren't there yet."

"To Jeff! I want that boy so much it's not even funny."

"Um, okay, well, I'll see if I can get you past security."

I roll my eyes. "It's not the White House!"

I finally manage to convince her — she texts Justin to ask for 'permission'. We go backstage, past the non-existent security — the bar is a hole.

The members of the band are all hanging out on couches with Seasons of Inertia — the boring band — and a case of beer.

Mitch introduces me and I manage to keep my cool when I greet Jeff, silently thanking my years of playing the flirting game. He scoots over so I can sit down, hands me a beer, flashing me a gorgeous smile as he uncaps it.

"The show was great," I say lamely, looking down at my hands, unable to find anything better to say or do.

I don't know what's going on with me. I have lost the ability to flirt. No one has ever had that effect on me.

"I'm glad you think so," he replies, looking straight into my eyes as though I just said the most meaningful thing he ever heard.

I'm so nervous that I drink almost all of my beer in one gulp. Jeff chuckles and hands me another. His hand brushes against my knee as he reaches for the case, igniting my entire body.

I have to get him alone. I know that one-on-one I'll be able to kick this blushing virgin thing aside. Right now, in front of everybody — total strangers, basically — I just feel pathetic.

Jeff is leaning closer now, his arm on the back of the couch behind me, his leg pressed against mine. I take it as a confirmation that this isn't one-sided, and it gives me the confidence I need.

I try my hardest to stop picturing him naked and I ask him about the band.

"We've been together for three years now. At first it was only Justin and I, but then some of our friends joined. You've got Justin and I, Joanna on keyboards, Jonathan on drums, and Phil the lead singer. They really helped us find our sound, we're a legit band, now." He beams, and I can't help but notice his dimples deepening the wider he smiles. "Did you see the crowd that was out there? There were people we didn't even know, and they weren't with Seasons either. We have a UK tour lined up for next year, and I'd say — knock on wood — that we're about six months from releasing our first LP." He knocks on the wooden coffee table and winks.

"Really? That's amazing!"

"Well, I mean, we're not about to play the Albert Hall or anything — just pubs here and there. Joanna knows a guy in Bristol. Man, I can't wait to see London. I've never been, but it's my favourite city."

Jeff's eyes are filled with stars. He's grinning like a kid on Christmas morning. It's adorable. He catches me staring at him and looks down in embarrassment.

"Sorry. I talk too much. When I get started about — "

"Hey." I put a soothing hand over his and look him in the eye. "You're passionate about this. It's wonderful."

"You think so?" He half-smiles.

"Absolutely. People are too blasé nowadays, like it's uncool to care. People who aren't ashamed to love stuff are rare, but you know what? They're the best ones."

Jeff's full smile comes back and he nods emphatically. "You get it."

"I'm so glad I came tonight. I was here as Mitch's moral support, and to see what the famous Justin was all about, but you caught my eye right away."

"That's what all the groupies say. They came for Justin, but stayed for me."

"I'm not a groupie!"

"You still wanna fuck me, though."

I look at him, unable to tell if he's joking. That guy really keeps me on my toes. I like that. I decide to play along.

"Should we get out of here?" I ask, with a well-practiced smile that never fails, before he grabs another beer from the case. He smirks and heads out.

I suddenly get the nagging feeling there's something I need to say, but I can't remember what.

Before I can dwell on it, I feel Mitch tugging at my sleeve. I turn to look at her. She makes huge eyes at me, eyebrows raised almost to the ceiling. She nods at Jeff, then at Justin, and then shakes her head.

"Please," she mouths.

It takes me a second or two to realize that Mitch is telepathically begging me not to leave her alone. I nod and raise a finger in a 'Just a sec' motion. I grab my purse and head outside to join Jeff.

"Mitch isn't feeling too well. I'll take her home." I scrunch up my face to show I'm sorry we have to cut this short.

"Justin'll do it," Jeff shrugs. "He's really into her."

"I think she'll feel better with someone she knows well."

"Oh. Alright, then." Jeff is already turning away.

"Wait." I lace my fingers through his. "This isn't some excuse I'm making up to let you down gently. I really want to see you again."

With a pen fished out of my purse, I scribble my number on the back of his hand.

"Call me." I press a soft kiss to his lips and walk away, just as Mitch exits the bar.

"You okay?" I ask her once we're out of earshot.

"Yeah." She lets out a long sigh. "When I saw you guys leaving, I kept thinking 'Oh no, is Justin gonna ask me home too?' and I panicked."

"Because you don't wanna go home with him?"

"No. Well, yeah, but not right now." She takes a deep breath and buries her hands in her short black hair. "I'm such a mess."

"You're not a mess, sweetie." I open my arms and she cuddles in close. "You're just not ready. If Justin is the right guy, he'll wait."

"You think so?"

"Of course. Maybe what you need is some alone time with him when you can really talk about what you want. A low-key evening, with no sex-crazed friends to pressure you," I add with a wink.

"I'm sorry I made you leave Jeff."

"Ah, don't worry about it. I know I'll see him again. I left him a 'better-luck-next-time kiss.'"

FOUR

The next day, after work, a few coworkers and I head to Buzz again. It's tiny, but it's right down the street from Quarante-Cinq, the record store where Georgie and I work, so it does the trick for a beer or two after our shift. Since it's so close to the cégep and the university, it's usually filled with queer, or at least queer-friendly, people.

I'm halfway through my first pint when Georgie elbows me and nods towards a girl standing at the bar with two of her friends. She has her back to us, which is fortunate, because Georgie wasn't exactly subtle.

From where I stand, she looks gorgeous: short, with black hair cascading down her back. Her light blue, curve-hugging sundress makes her look radiant, even under the dim lights of the bar.

"She's been totally checking you out since we got here," Georgie says.

As if on cue, the girl turns around and our eyes meet. She smiles and her whole face lights up. Her East Asian features are soft and, indeed, gorgeous. I return her smile and we both look away, lest we look too eager.

"Yeah, she definitely wants you." Georgie nods and adjusts his trademark bowler hat so it sits askew on top of his head. Paired with his round cheeks and curly hair, it gives him an impish look.

"She actually did a double take when you walked in," our coworker, Jude, pipes up, looking up from their phone for a second. Probably posting Instagram Stories again, if I know them.

I shrug and refill my beer from the pitcher. "Well, the night's still young. I'm here to spend time with y'all, not to hook up."

"Excuse me, can I get you a drink?"

So much for taking my time. The girl finally picked up the courage to come and talk to me. I flash her my patented flirting smile, the one that never fails to win me cute girls' numbers.

"Of course! Excuse me, guys," I gracefully tell the gang.

We make our way to the bar, where she orders two beers.

"I'm Natalie," she says, raising her glass.

"Amy." I click my glass against hers and take a sip. "Listen, I'm really flattered and interested — " Natalie smiles — "but I'm here with some friends and we haven't hung out in a while, so…"

"Oh, I completely understand, don't worry about it. What do you say you and I have this drink, exchange numbers, and then I'll let you go back to your friends?"

We settle down at the bar and drink our beers — slower than usual, I might add. We talk mostly about movies and books, and her recent trip to China to visit her family — knowing we have a limited time tonight puts a damper on long conversations and getting to know each other. Reluctantly, I drink the last drop of beer in my pint.

"So I guess this is it?"

She pulls me close, presses a kiss to my cheek and a paper napkin bearing her phone number into my hand.

"Don't forget to call me," she whispers in my ear. Her voice is so soft and sweet it's almost dirty. There's no way I'm going to forget. Good god.

Cory walks in at that very moment, dropping heavily into the empty seat next to Georgie.

"A'ight. Imma need three things. One, the tea on that new babe of yours — " he jerks his head in Natalie's direction — "Two, a shot of something strong," he flags a waitress, "and three, a whiff of your hair." He pulls Georgie in close.

Georgie sets his bowler hat on the table and Cory buries his face in the soft black coils, eyes closing in delight.

"Fuck," Cory exhales when he resurfaces. "A labradoodle threw up all over me at the clinic. I've had three showers and I can't get the smell out of my nose."

He waits until the waitress comes back with three tequila shots, knocks all of them back, and reclines in his seat, hand settling in the crook of Georgie's neck.

"Okay. Cutie. Dish."

¤

It's quite fitting that a sweet girl like Natalie would suggest a dessert date. We get to the café at the same time, and I can't take my eyes off her as we walk towards each other. She does this cute little wave and her shiny black hair bounces as she quickens her pace to meet me, a gorgeous smile animating her features. Her arms snake around my waist and she kisses me on both cheeks, almost at the corners of my mouth, leaving me wanting so much more. I'm about to die on the spot from too much anticipation. She takes my hand and it fits snuggly in hers.

She leads me inside the dimly lit café to a table in the back and we take a look at the menu. Everything looks amazing and I seriously don't know what I want more: her or cake. I know — or at least hope — I'm probably going to have both, so I choose cake for now: a raspberry-champagne mousse. She gets a slice of the biggest chocolate cake they offer: six layers, fudge, mousse, ganache, and shavings of white, milk, and dark chocolate. It looks amazing, but also kind of terrifying — the slice is bigger than her head.

"Mmm, you *need* to try this," she almost moans, pushing her plate towards me.

It is, indeed, delicious, but I could never eat a whole slice. One small bite was enough for me. I try a bit of my own mousse and like it way better. I push my plate across the table so she can sample it too.

"Wow, I should have ordered that one!" Natalie exclaims, but still goes back enthusiastically to her own plate.

"Listen," I say, "there's something I need to tell you, just so we're on the same page." She nods, her mouth full of cake. "I have a boyfriend. We're in an open relationship, so this isn't cheating. I just don't want you to expect anything serious, you know?"

Natalie cocks up an eyebrow when I say the word 'boyfriend'. For a split second, I get an almost judgemental vibe from her, but she quickly reverts to her bright smile — I probably just imagined it.

"Oh, absolutely! This is just for fun!" she adds with a wink.

¤

Lots of fun indeed, as I realize when we go back to her place after dessert. She pours some white wine, dims the lights and puts on soft, jazzy music — the kind that universally means sexy times are about to happen. She sways towards her bedroom and I follow her, taking a large gulp of wine.

She's already taking off her dress, making a deliberate show out of it, when I enter the room and set my glass on her dresser. Her skin looks so smooth, I'm inexorably drawn to it. My fingers, cold from the glass I was holding, almost get seared at the contact with her warm, golden skin.

Natalie stares at me, looking innocent as ever, but there's no mistaking her intentions as she pulls at the hem of my dress. I've never been undressed this slowly — I can feel every single one of my nerve endings exploding as she caresses my skin with feather-like fingers.

We stand in the middle of the room in our underwear, bodies almost touching, but not quite, just revelling in the tension filling the room. Our breathing is so laboured we can barely hear the music coming from the living room. She leans in and her hair brushes against my cheek. I let out a gasp. The atmosphere is so electric that the smallest touch will ignite everything.

Unable to resist any longer, I take a deep breath and pull her closer, until our bodies are flush against each other. Her breasts heave against mine as her breath quickens, the pink lace of her bra hinting at something still hidden. Our lips touch at last, allowing us to get lost in our flaming desire.

¤

I wake up the next morning to a dip in the mattress, the sound of bare feet padding on the hardwood floor and a door closing. I suppose Natalie went to the bathroom, so I roll over and go back to sleep.

When I come to again, the sun is out and Natalie is climbing into the bed and cuddling next to me. I yawn and stretch, rubbing the sleep out of my eyes so I can look at her.

Wow.

Somehow during the night I managed to forget how gorgeous she is. Glossy black hair framing her face, a bright smile and dark eyes that light up when she talks to me. Naked amber curves, warm and smooth, glowing under the first sun rays. She could easily be the lead in a romantic comedy.

I catch a glimpse of myself in the mirror across the room and almost hide under the covers. Hair sticking out at the top of my head, yesterday's makeup smudged across my freckled cheeks, blankets tangled around my legs.

The contrast between us is striking. How can she look this perfect when she just woke up?

But then I remember hearing her get up while I was sleeping. I excuse myself to the bathroom, and sure enough: there's a wet towel on the floor, her makeup case lies open on the vanity, next to a hair dryer.

Oh, come on. Everyone looks like shit in the morning, why pretend she's perfect all the time? Her cutie-but-sexy act, however effortless it looked, was probably just as calculated.

"Listen," I start when I get back to her room to pick up my clothes, "I had a really amazing time last night, but I have to go back to my boyfriend."

"We said 'Just for fun', don't worry," she says with a perfect smile. "You don't have to make up a fake boyfriend just because you only want a one-night-stand."

"I do have a boyfriend — "

"Oh, please. You clearly fuck like a lesbian."

"I'm bisexual."

She looks at me with a mix of condescension and incredulity, as if I had announced I was a Jedi or a unicorn. I know arguing with her would be a waste of time — I've had my fair share of biphobic lesbians; the best way to deal with them is just to steer clear.

I finish buttoning up my dress, grab my purse and leave without another word.

"Call me when you step out of the closet!" is the last thing I hear as I close the door behind me.

So, that's it. My one bad call of the year. September, pretty late this year.

FIVE

Café Le Trèfle is plunged in semi-darkness, lit only by the last rays of a chilly September night. The place is deserted except for Alex and me, perched on a stool at the counter, waiting for her to close up shop. She's mopping the floor and singing along to the radio. My eyes linger over her tattooed arms, the way they move as she works. Alex is gorgeous, incredibly sexy. I had a thing for her when we first met, but it never lead to anything, and we soon became best friends.

Alex suddenly stops in her tracks, her mop forgotten in the bucket, and turns to me.

"I met someone."

"You did?"

She looks away in a bashful, very un-Alex manner.

"Yeah, she's a regular customer and we've been checking each other out for weeks."

"*You* waited weeks before making a move?" She's usually so direct: when a girl catches her eye, Alex asks her out immediately and gets out before the slightest commitment can be hinted at.

"Well, actually, she made the move. I went to a roller derby bout and she was on the team."

"Ooh, nice! What's her name?"

"Emma."

"Derby name?"

An amused glint lights up Alex's eyes.

"Emma Sculation."

"Excellent!" I laugh. "So, she made a move...?"

"Yeah, she recognized me from the café and came over to ask me out."

"Score." I hold out my fist and she bumps it. "When are you going out?"

"Tomorrow. I'm so nervous."

"So how come you never made a move on her?"

Alex shrugs and resumes mopping to avoid looking at me. "I really like her. Didn't wanna fuck it up."

"You are the cutest!" I've never seen Alex this smitten with anyone. It's a huge change from her usual hit-it-and-quit-it attitude.

"Shut up."

¤

After Alex's shift, we go back to her place for her bi-weekly hair trim. There's nothing Alex dislikes more than small talk — except for bigots — so she goes to the hair salon as rarely as possible. Clipping is the extent of my hairdressing abilities, so she still has to go for her dye jobs, but, at least, she can maintain her side shave without having to deal with a chatty stylist.

Alex puts her purple hair in a top knot, wraps a towel around her shoulders, and stands in front of her bathroom mirror. I set the clippers to the second-to-shortest setting — Alex likes her buzzed side quite short, and any longer would mean we'd have to trim it every week.

As soon as the clippers touch her scalp, she's shaken with an all-body shiver, almost making me shave off one of her longest strands of hair by mistake.

"Stay still." I grip her shoulder.

"It's cold," she complains through gritted teeth.

"That's not very punk of you." I wink at her reflection in the mirror.

She rolls her eyes, but otherwise stays still and I manage to do my job without any other incident.

Once I'm done, I take off the towel to shake off the hairs from it. A few stray hairs are sticking to Alex's neck so I blow them away. Alex's skin instantly covers with goose bumps and she exhales a sharp breath, shivering under the thin fabric of her black tank top. Our eyes meet in the mirror. An unspoken, defiant truth engulfs us for half a second, like a pulse. The warmth of her thinly clad skin calls to me. My fingers tighten around the clippers to keep me from making the most dangerous move of my life.

Alex clears her throat and looks away, brushing a hand over the freshly buzzed side of her head.

"Looks good," she says matter-of-factly, and quickly busies herself with a broom, gathering stray hairs and shoving the towel in the washing machine.

I walk to her kitchen, calling over my shoulder, "Beer?" grateful that we both came to our senses.

This would have been a *bad* idea.

SIX

I'm in the break room at work when my phone chirps and lights up. I unlock it to find a message from Hugo: a screenshot of a magazine review. The critic is raving, saying *Gibson has never been better* and *The atmosphere in the venue was electric; Gibson gave himself heart and soul to his public.*

I smile and go back to Hugo's message: This is all thanks to you. Come to all my gigs? :D

A tingle travels down my spine and settles in the pit of my stomach. Our sexual tension was so intense, so tangible, that the entire crowd felt it. The critics felt it.

This turns me on so much I don't know what to do with myself. I reply hastily: Please tell me you have a gig tonight.

Hugo Gibson — La Brunante, 9:30

I arrange to get there at nine: early enough to grab a beer with Hugo, but not so much that the tension drops from all the chatting.

I spot him as soon as I enter. The bar is pretty packed, but my lustful hormones hone in on him at once.

He's leaning nonchalantly against the bar, talking to some guy. I freeze for a moment, taking in the way he uses his hands to emphasize his point; the way he gazes into the distance when he's thinking; the way his whole face lights up when he notices me.

He excuses himself and walks up to me. With every step, his joyful smile morphs further into a feral smirk. For all I know, he's about to throw me on a table and devour me.

Red-hot desire pools into my cheeks at the thought; I'm grateful for the dim lighting. I probably look like a fire hydrant in flames, what with my red hair.

"Hi," Hugo says as he pulls me into a hug. The sound, almost like a growl right in my ear, kindles the fire down in my core into a goddamn pyre.

"Hi," I reply, making sure to breathe into his ear just right.

I kiss him on the cheek, right at the corner of his mouth. My fingers linger on his waist for a few moments after we step apart. Every move, his and mine, is calculated to elicit as much excitation as we can before he walks on stage. We didn't plan it, but we both know that's exactly what we're doing. The game in itself is doing wonders for my arousal.

We sit down at a table and order beers. We make small talk for a while, but neither of us really pays attention to it. There's another conversation going on underneath the surface, one made of lingering glances, feather-soft touches and attempts to get as close as possible to each other.

Someone eventually comes over to ask him backstage.

"See you later," he whispers in my ear, then presses a kiss right at the corner of my mouth, using my own tactics against me — not that I mind.

This gig might be even better than the last one. This time we know what works, so we give it our all. Hugo spends his whole set looking deep into my eyes. We share looks heavy with promises of what comes next.

He also changed his set: he sings raw, bluesy songs, songs that are magnetic and sensual. The way he looks at me while he sings these irresistible lyrics damn near kills me.

Hugo is met, once again, with thunderous applause. He leaves the stage to the next act and disappears backstage. I finish my beer while the next band is introduced and my phone chirps.

Meet me backstage.

I make my way towards the backstage door, unsure whether I'm even allowed back there. I notice with relief that Hugo is waiting right behind the door.

"C'm'ere." He pulls me into a room. "It's empty."

We're standing in some sort of a green room, filled with two couches, several musical instruments, and equipment. Hugo closes the door and presses me against it. His whole body fits into mine and I wrap my legs around his waist. He buries his face in the crook of my neck.

"I just couldn't wait any longer," he sighs. "My place is way too far."

"Fuck me," I pant desperately into his ear.

I dig my hands into the cloud of his curls and pull. He lets out a groan and ruts hard against me. I want him so much it actually hurts, down into my core. We melt into a whirlwind of skin and moans. It's all over quite soon, but now the urgency is gone. Now we can slow down, get a beer, and go back to his place for Act Two.

"So, when's your next gig?"

"Whenever you want."

¤

"Here Comes The Sun" wakes me up around eight the next morning. It may be a quiet song for a ringtone, but let me tell you, after three hours of sleep, it's as jarring as a dubstep remix of a dozen cats in heat.

I peek at the caller ID, keeping my eyes as tightly closed as possible to keep the sleep in. I cuddle closer to Hugo with a groan. We were 'otherwise occupied' until five AM, I'm so not up for a talk with my mom.

"Hello?" I answer quietly, heading towards the door not to wake Hugo.

"Good morning!"

"What's going on?" Hugo mumbles, fighting with his duvet to sit up.

"My mom," I whisper. "Go back to sleep."

"Is that David?" Mom's overly-cheerful-for-this-hour voice pipes up. "Let me say hi!"

"Mom, David had a late shoot last night, I'm gonna let him sleep in, okay?"

"Oh, alright. It's been a while, though. Your dad and I were wondering when you were coming to dinner."

"How about this Sunday?"

"Perfect! You say hi to David for me, alright?"

When I come back to bed, Hugo is still awake. "What's up?

"My mom. She heard you and thought you were David."

"She doesn't know about your arrangement, does she?"

"Nah, I figure my family only needs to know who I love, not who I sleep with. Why upset them for something that's none of their business?"

"Makes sense."

"Can we sleep, now?"

"Or, we could..." He wiggles his eyebrows lewdly, hands already making their way to my hips.

"Let me sleep a few more hours first."

"Deal."

¤

"How did it go?"

"Not bad — a bit awkward, of course."

I hand David a beer and we settle on the couch for a chat. He just came back from Hugo's place. We figured they needed to talk — it's the first time one of us hooks up with someone we both know, someone who's quite close to David, and since it's not just a one-time thing, we all need to be on the same page.

"I mean," David says, unscrewing the cap of his beer, "you know us, we're both pretty chill guys, open-minded, but how do you start a conversation like that? *So, you're screwing my girlfriend?* Like it or not, this changes things in a friendship."

I nod, wondering for the hundredth time in my life why open relationships don't come with an instruction manual.

"I must admit," David continues, "it felt weird. I know we've been open for almost two years, I should be used to it, but this time it was different? Like, usually, I can't put a face on the people you're seeing, but now it's someone I know. I mean, I was rooting for you guys, and I like to think I'm above monosexism, but when I was placed before the fact, even though it goes against everything I believe in, I felt a bit jealous."

"Did you?" I'm not holding it against him, of course. You can't control what you feel; even when your brain says something is A-okay, sometimes your emotions will go in an entirely different direction.

"You're gonna think I'm crazy," David goes on, intently destroying the label of his beer bottle, "but I somehow convinced myself I could smell you? All over his apartment? And that hit me hard. I couldn't get the fact that you were there yesterday morning out of my head."

I give a gentle smile and sidle closer to him. "Of course I don't think you're crazy. You can't help what you're feeling — the important thing is that at the end of the day, you trust me well enough to tell me these things."

David takes a sip of beer, considering what I just said. "So, we had a beer, played Mario Kart for a while, until we couldn't avoid it any longer. Basically, I tried to make him feel comfortable and welcome? Like I assured him I was okay with it — because I am, no matter what my archaic instincts try to make me believe — and told him he could talk to me if he needed to, for any reason."

"What did he say?"

"That he was glad we got a chance to talk, cause he didn't want this to become That Thing We Don't Talk About and that would grow increasingly more awkward whenever we'd hang out. Then we had another beer and I beat him at Smash Bros."

"At least you asserted your dominance there," I joke.

He chuckles. "God, I love how we work. I love how we let our relationship grow and evolve with us, and we talk about it whenever something changes."

"Yeah, we're pretty great, aren't we?" I grin and straddle him, peppering kisses down his neck.

He sets his beer down and his hands wrap instinctively around my hips.

A great fit indeed.

SEVEN

October 6. Charlotte, my baby sister, turns eighteen today.

I can't believe little Char is an adult now. Her best friend Lily is throwing a big birthday bash to celebrate and get her drunk. It feels like only yesterday Mom and Dad took us to the zoo for her eighth birthday. Ten years have passed and now, instead of being harassed by ostriches for food, she'll be harassed by creepy dudes for her phone number.

That kind of douchey nightclub isn't my scene, especially with a bunch of drunken eighteen-year-olds, but I know Charlotte will be glad to see me there. I asked Alex to come along for moral support, but she's got a second date with Emma. Righteous cause, at least. David, of course, wouldn't come because he doesn't do clubs, but he promised he'd get tickets for her favourite band to make up for it.

I get to the club around eleven; I figure Charlotte and her friends will already be there, so I won't have to wait for them alone and get hit on by creeps. I follow the teenage shrieks to find them, crowded around the bar, knocking back shots.

Charlotte is wearing a lei and a tiara, so that no one can miss she's the birthday girl. The minute she sees me she jumps to her feet, lets out a scream and pulls me into a hug.

"Happy birthday, honey!"

"Oh my god! I'm so happy you're here, I had no idea!"

"Lily called me."

Lily walks by at this very moment with a tray full of shots and reacts pretty much the same way Charlotte did — luckily, she sets down the tray before hugging me. She hands me a shot and, call me old-fashioned, but I've known Lily since she was a baby — I even babysat her — so it feels super weird to do a shot with her and my little sister.

Still, I'm here to party, so I might as well get used to it. And they're both adults, so it's not like when I caught them drinking Dad's rum when they were fifteen. They go back to their table and I order a beer at the bar before joining them.

"Well, look who's here…"

I turn around to see a tall blonde holding a beer.

"Vanessa, hi! How have you been?" I try to sound enthusiastic, even though this is pretty much the most awkward thing I've experienced in a while.

Vanessa is a girl I hooked up with about a year ago. I don't think I ever called her back, although I can't recall why.

"Not bad. How do you know Charlotte?"

I almost choke on my drink, but manage to recover somewhat gracefully.

"You know Charlotte?"

"Yeah, from school," she shrugs. "What about you?"

"I'm her big sister. How old are you?" I ask, alarmed.

"Eighteen."

"Last year, you said you were nineteen!"

"Well, I lied, didn't I? Otherwise, you'd've turned me down."

"Shut up! Do you want everyone to know?" A shiver crawls up my spine. A glance over my shoulder reveals that Charlotte is greeting a few more friends who just got here. She's not paying any attention to us.

Vanessa shrugs. "All my friends know I'm bi, so it's no big — "

"As far as Charlotte and the rest of my family know, I'm in an exclusive, long-term relationship with my boyfriend," I say through gritted teeth.

"So you don't want them to know you go around screwing minors?" she asks with a sly smile, stepping dangerously closer to me.

"Be quiet, please!"

"You know I like it when you beg."

There it is: the reason why I never called her back. She sends out a weird vibe, like she'll get what she wants, no matter the consequences.

I turn and walk away. I need a stronger drink.

After a long wait at the bar for an overpriced scotch on the rocks, I make my way to the dance floor where Charlotte and her friends are singing at the top of their lungs along to a song I don't know. I join their circle and start dancing with them. They all yell *Wooo!* when I join them, even though I don't know most of them.

I dance and drink with them until the feeling of being a supervising adult dulls and I'm left with a partying mood. I'm starting to enjoy myself when suddenly I feel hands on my hips. I swat them away and turn around. Vanessa again. She looks at me with a cunning smirk, half- seducing and half-challenging.

"Come on, Vanessa, that's not funny."

"I'm not joking. It's called flirting, maybe you've heard of it?" she adds with a wink.

Trying to get away, I make Charlotte twirl so she ends up in the middle of the dancing circle and I take her place on the opposite side from Vanessa. Everyone cheers as Charlotte busts some moves in the middle of her friends.

I wish Alex were here. She'd get me out of this, either by flirting with Vanessa, or by threatening her.

I decide to stick with Char and ignore Vanessa. She can't know she's getting to me or else she'll just have more ammo. Unfortunately, Vanessa is not one to be ignored.

Charlotte and Lily go back to the bar for shots and I follow them. Of course, Vanessa tags along. She orders two shots and hands me one. I take it reluctantly.

"Oh my god, you guys know each other?"

The shrill voice of my drunken sister saves me. I push the shot back into Vanessa's hands, spilling half of it down her front.

"Actually, Char, I have to go — early day tomorrow."

Charlotte pouts, but someone behind her calls "Shots!" so she quickly hugs me before being pulled towards the bar. I turn away and make for the door. I take three steps before Vanessa blocks my way.

"You really wanna leave me here, *alone*, where I could say anything to your sister?"

I honestly doubt Char would remember this conversation at the rate she's drinking, but I don't want to take any chances.

"Okay, what do you want?" I sigh, dejected.

"You."

I roll my eyes at her.

"Look," she says, stepping closer to be heard above the music. "Give me a chance to convince you. If you give this a shot, I won't tell your sister."

I heave a sigh. "Alright, but not here."

Outside the club, Vanessa suggests a small, intimate pub down the street.

"So, how is it, being able to buy alcohol with your real ID?" I ask as she pays for her beer.

For a second she looks offended, but quickly recovers and plasters a smile on her face as we sit down. "Less thrilling. But don't worry, I got plenty of excitement tonight, watching you squirm."

She trails her fingers up my thigh and teases the skin underneath the hem of my dress. I swat her hand away.

She raises a doubtful eyebrow. "Now, you said you'd give me a chance… I can still call Charlotte, you know?"

"I'm here, aren't I?"

"I don't get why you won't tell your sister. There's nothing shameful with open relationships."

"I still struggle with seeing her drinking, I'm not about to show off my tumultuous sex life in front of her."

"Yet, you had no problem fucking me, a fragile seventeen year old…" Vanessa bats her eyelashes at me.

"I didn't know! And please, you are anything but fragile."

"Glad you agree. Now, what do you say we take this somewhere more… intimate?" She is now splaying her whole hand on my thigh.

I stand up and she flashes a victorious grin.

"Oh, no. Don't get any ideas. I'm heading home. And you're not coming."

"That's not what I call 'giving me a chance'…"

"Yes, it is. I came here with you. We had a drink together. I listened to what you had to say. And I still don't like you. My part of the deal is kept. I assume you'll keep yours. Goodnight."

I turn around and leave. I've had enough.

¤

When I get home, David is getting ready for bed.

"How was your date?" I ask after I kiss him hello.

"Not bad."

"Yet you're here this early."

"You know I don't like to sleep out." He pulls me closer. "How was Char?"

"Drunk and her friends are crazy." I tell him the whole story as we get ready for bed.

He laughs so hard he almost falls off the bed. "Told you clubs are the worst."

On the bright side, I might still have a chance to get some tonight.

EIGHT

"Has anyone heard from Alex lately?" Sailor Moon asks above her menu.

We attract a lot of attention in the Mexican restaurant — looks like none of the other customers realized it's Halloween. Sailor Moon is Mitch and she looks amazing — she made the costume herself for last year's Comic-Con.

"Not since she texted me that she's bringing Emma tonight," I reply, adjusting the crown of leaves in my hair — I'm Poison Ivy.

"She called in sick at the café all weekend," Mitch says.

"They're probably having a bed-in," Pirate-Cory suggests, with a wink. "You know, to make up for the two week wait."

"I can't believe *Alex* waited two weeks before hooking up with someone," Cheerleader-Julia pipes up.

"I know! Ms. One-Night-Stand taking things slow? This must be love," Georgie adds wisely, setting down his Mad Hatter hat on an unoccupied chair. This must be one of the first times I've ever seen him without his traditional bowler hat.

"Love is 'a myth created by our heteronormative, patriarchal society, supported by Hollywood to sell us movies,'" I quote Alex. "Think she fell for it anyway?"

"I guess we'll know when we see them together. I can't wait to meet Emma," Mitch says.

"You've never met her at the café?"

"Nah, she only comes in at night. I work the morning shift."

The waiter comes and we order a round of margaritas while we wait. Alex walks through the door at that moment, alone. She's wearing a blood-stained fedora and a 40's-style suit, tommy gun in hand. The atmosphere suddenly turns ice-cold.

"Hey, Clyde, where's Bonnie?" Julia asks, ever so tactful.

"We broke up."

"What? Why?" Georgie asks, worried.

"Let's just say we both wanted very different things. I need more alcohol in me to tell the whole story. Where's the waiter?" she asks, looking around as she sits down.

I put my hand on top of hers and give her a compassionate smile. I know she needs time, and she needs to know we'll be here whenever she decides to talk about it.

She drains her first pint. The waiter sensed the urgency in her order and brings another as soon as the first one is empty. Meanwhile, the rest of us sip our margaritas and try to make small talk so Alex doesn't feel like the spotlight is on her.

A beer and a half in, Alex decides to tell the story. She interrupts Julia's captivating story about her boyfriend's new car, and Julia shoots her a dark glance.

"So Emma was like, 'I can't be tied down, I need to *experience* things, I don't believe in monogamy', and I'm just sitting there, like, I can't believe I fooled myself into thinking I was in love. But, somehow, I can't imagine not having her in my life, and really that's the first time I've felt like that since —" Alex looks away and drinks, and that's when I realize there's still a lot I don't know about my best friend. She's not the sharing type — with feelings *and* with her girlfriends.

"But you know," she continues, "I can't give her what she wants. I mean, there's nothing wrong with open relationships," she casts me an apologetic glance, "but I'm just not meant for that. I tried several times and I'm physically incapable of accepting that the person I love sleeps with other people."

After dinner, we go to La Pharmacie and the place is packed with costumed people. We order a pitcher — Alex warned us that she needed to talk, but she also wanted to numb the pain, so we supply her with as much beer as we can.

As we order the second pitcher, it looks like the plan is working. Alex is now dancing with Lola Bunny from *Space Jam*. She looks like she's enjoying herself — I mean, who wouldn't?

As for me, a pretty girl with pink and blue pigtails and a baseball bat catches my eye. I reapply my green lipstick and make my way towards her.

"Harley Quinn and Poison Ivy. A match made in Gotham."

"I'm sorry, what?" she asks, glancing above my shoulder, obviously looking for someone.

"Our costumes."

"Oh, baby, there you are!" Harley grins at a guy with green hair and emo makeup.

"I see you're here with your origin story."

"What? That's my boyfriend."

Hashtag relationship goals, am I right? I shrug and go back to my friends. "Straight girls are harder to weed out in costume," I declare as I steal a sip from Georgie's beer.

"You might have more luck with Holtzmann from *Ghostbusters*," a voice behind me says.

"Hugo! Didn't you have a gig?" I turn around and hug him, although it's not an easy task, what with his Gengar costume hindering his movements.

"Cut it short. People don't go to music gigs on Halloween, turns out."

He hugs Mitch hello before pointing me in the direction of the (probably) queer Ghostbuster, with blonde hair and yellow-tinted glasses. As luck would have it, however, she's quickly joined — and kissed — by a tall black girl dressed as Patty from the same movie.

I turn back to Hugo, who does a sort of wiggle, which I think was intended to be a shrug underneath the ten pounds of costume. "I was right, though," he says. "Shots?"

He goes to the bar to order — people are jumping out of his way, scared of being mowed down by a seven foot tall purple ball.

"You know," Mitch says, fiddling with a threadbare friendship bracelet around her wrist, "I'll never get how you do it."

I shoot her a puzzled glance.

"Walking up to strangers out of the blue like this." She nods in the vague direction of Harley Quinn. "I mean, I have to rehearse my Subway order before going up to the counter, and I blank if I'm interrupted. Do you know how many times I've had weird sandwiches because someone talked to me while I waited in line and I got caught unprepared?"

She chuckles, so I get it's not a sore spot, it's mostly just annoying, but I know her anxiety doesn't go easy on her. I get it — I have anxiety too, just, not the same kind.

"Well, you know, I'm mostly doing it for the thrill of discovering new people. If things go badly, chances are, I'll never see them again, so it doesn't worry me. I don't know them, so what's the worst that could happen?" I shrug. "What *does* scare me, though, is disappointing or shocking the people I know. I have this irrational fear of losing the people I love. Why do you think I never came out to my family?"

Mitch nods. "Yeah, I guess that makes sense. I wish I could just tell my brain, *Chill out, you'll never see them again*, though. I'm just terrified of being that girl who took thirty seconds too long to order at Subway."

Hugo comes back with the shots and we drink to cries of "Fuck anxiety!"

Alex doesn't leave Lola Bunny's side all night. At the end of the night, they leave together.

"Bonnie, Bunny — who fucking cares?" she slurs at me before following the girl in a cab.

Probably not the healthiest decision, but the girl *is* dressed as one of the sexiest cartoon characters in history, so, really, I can't blame Alex.

NINE

Bright orange leaves crinkle under my feet as I walk down Saint-Denis Street at a brisk pace, checking my watch every few seconds. As soon as I look away, I completely forget what time it read. I want to make a good impression on my first real date with Jeff — I can only hope there will be many others.

I'm irrationally scared he won't like me. That it was just a bone-the-groupie thing. Which is ridiculous, because he was the one who called to ask me out. I'm also apprehensive because he refused to tell me where we're going. He said it was a surprise, and told me to meet him at the corner of Saint-Denis and Ontario.

Jeff is already there when I arrive. I look at my watch again. Am I late? I did take an awfully long time getting ready. I must have tried on fifteen different outfits. Too sexy. Too serious. Too casual. Too formal. Too many buttons to undo — if you know what I mean. I finally settled on my favourite green dress, which had been, of course, my first choice. I always get compliments when I wear it — people say it goes wonderfully with my red hair.

My watch tells me I'm right on time so I take a deep breath and admire Jeff. Hands stuffed deep in his pockets, he's leaning casually against a lamppost, which just goes to emphasize how tall and lanky he is — just my type of guy.

When he notices me crossing the street, he straightens up, rakes a hand through his hair and grins.

"You look stunning, love." He just stands still and keeps looking at me.

"Thanks! But the suspense is killing me, will you tell me where you're taking me?"

"As you wish." He grabs my extended hand and leads me up the crowded street to a bar.

I walk in and my jaw drops. I had no idea such a place existed. The room is covered in wall-to-wall shelves overflowing with board games. At every table, people are playing.

"This is amazing," I breathe out.

"I knew you'd like it."

I let out a relieved sigh. He isn't the kind of guy who takes you to dinner and a movie because it's the easiest way to pass the time before he can bed you. Jeff put thought into this — he's genuinely interested in having fun with me, fun of the non-sexual kind.

We sit at a corner table and he takes off his jacket, revealing that he, too, chose his outfit with care. Instead of the hoodie and ripped jeans I first saw him in, he's wearing a striped button-down with a skinny tie and dress shoes. Handsome as hell.

We order food and drinks and start playing Cards Against Humanity. I'm not sure horribly offensive jokes are the best way to make a good impression, but I think we're past that. We laugh until our sides ache. Jeff commits the mistake of taking a sip while I read a particularly raunchy card. Sangria comes out of his nose, which only makes me roar harder.

We decide to play a trivia game to give a break to his barely recovered respiratory tract and to his shirt, which is now sporting a faint pink stain. He takes a deep breath to calm down and the giggles recede at last. He looks at me with a fond, tender smile.

"I'm so happy I met you. I haven't had this much fun with a girl since — " Jeff trails off and looks away. His smile fades.

"Since?"

"Since Mia. My first love. We were together for almost two years. Really messed me up."

"I'm so sorry." I don't know what to do or say — I barely know him.

"Don't worry about it. I'm over her. In fact, I had just decided I was ready to meet someone else, and you came along."

To my relief, his sweet smile comes back. He pulls a card out of the box.

"Cinema. Who directed the 1981 movie *Chariots of Fire*?"

I'm taken aback at the sudden change of subject. I guess he, too, realized it was a heavy topic for a first date.

"Um… I've never seen it."

"Hugh Hudson," he reads off the back of the card, shrugging. "Great soundtrack, though."

We take turns asking questions and soon we're back to joking around and chatting freely, all thoughts of exes and broken hearts forgotten. Beer follows sangria and I lose track of time. When I look at my watch, it's already one thirty in the morning.

"Crap. I missed the last train."

"Guess you're gonna have to come home with me." He heaves an exaggerated sigh.

"Oh, I'm sure you're real disappointed."

"I am, but since I'm so generous, I'll gladly offer you shelter for the night."

"And a warm body to cuddle with?" I bat my eyelashes and flash him my brightest smile.

"Alright," he sighs again, "that too."

"Thanks!" I press a kiss to his cheek.

¤

We walk four blocks to Jeff's place. He fumbles for his keys and I can't stop laughing — and I can't remember why. Maybe the sangria was a bit stronger than we thought.

"Shh, you'll wake Justin up," he stage-whispers, and we crack up again.

It turns out Justin isn't even here — would Mitch have something to do with that? — so we can go straight to Jeff's room without having to make awkward small talk. You know, the kind when they're all *hey guys, had a good night?* but you know underneath it all they're just hoping you won't make too much noise.

Jeff's room is a typical band dude room, filled with more instruments than furniture. I can spot several guitars, a keyboard, speakers and an amp. One wall is covered in posters and postcards depicting Big Ben, double-decker buses and red phone booths. He wasn't kidding about his London obsession.

Tipsy and horny, I barely wait until he's fully inside the room to pull him closer by his belt loops. He's so gorgeous that I almost just want to make out with him for hours, but I also really, really need to fuck him. I somehow try to do both at once, so I pull his shirt above his head while trying to kiss him. Our arms get stuck in the shirt above his head and I miss his mouth, ending up licking his cheek. We start laughing again, arms stuck and all, and tumble on the bed.

I kneel above him and he grabs the hem of the shirt to disentangle me. His hands brush against my sides, and *oh*, the craving intensifies. I can tell he notices because he instantly follows my mood switch — sexier, less playful. He tosses the shirt across the room and I follow his lead, discarding my dress. He falls back to the bed, speechless.

"Like what you see?" I shimmy and my boobs wiggle.

Jeff nods and flips us around so he's on top and I'm face down on the bed. Taking his time, he starts trailing his hands across my back, down my spine, softly, slowly. He plays me like a guitar, raising shivers from deep within my skin. This must be one of the most erotic things I've ever experienced. His hands are soft, except for the callous tips of his bass-playing fingers. These rough spots scratch me just right, pulling quiet gasps from my throat.

He lies right on top of me, naked skin against naked skin. I can hardly breathe, but I love feeling him so close, closer than close. He buries his face in my hair, breathes in and out, tickles the nape of my neck. He shifts to kiss my cheek and suddenly I can feel his hardness through his jeans. I roll over and pin him under me. Our breaths come in hard and quick together — mouths open, panting. I can't wait anymore. I take his bottom lip between my teeth and pull, ever so softly. Our tongues meet, lazy but intense, and all I can think is *at last*.

¤

I wake up the next morning to a soft melody slowly seeping into my dreams, pulling me out one note at a time. Jeff is sitting next to me, strumming on an acoustic guitar.

"You also play guitar?"

"My dad taught me. It's not that different. I prefer the bass, though."

"Yeah?"

"It's just more raw, you know. More animal." He stares deep into my eyes as he explains. I might need a second round soon. "With guitar, it's melodious, it's all about the song, you know? While on the bass," he sets a beat on the lower notes, "it's all about rhythm. The skeleton of the song, on which everything else is grafted."

"I never thought of it like that. It's beautiful."

He smiles softly and goes back to the slow melody. I lay my head on his shoulder, breathing him in, his woody scent with just a touch of coffee. His music cradles me, engulfs me, until I drift back to sleep.

¤

I wake up again to a midday sun and the enticing smell of bacon. The bed is empty, so I slip into one of Jeff's T-shirts and follow my nose to the kitchen.

"Damn, you really are perfect," I say as I see him cooking a breakfast of eggs and bacon.

"I try." He winks and hands me a plate.

"Slept well?"

"Better than in months." He kisses the top of my head. "Would you sleep here every night?"

"What's in it for me?"

"Sex."

"Mmm, tempting," I tease, kissing a trail up to his neck.

"You look really pretty in my shirt."

"Yeah?"

"Yeah, but I know you're even prettier without it."

"I'm told so."

I pull him close and kiss him. The kiss is lazy and soft — just the right fit for a cozy morning. Jeff buries his face in the crook of my neck. His fine hair, tousled from the previous night's activities, tickles me, making me giggle.

"Ooh, we got a ticklish one, do we?"

He runs his nimble fingers down my sides, excruciatingly slowly. My back arches and I let out a shriek of laughter.

"This is perfect." Jeff smirks. "I absolutely adore tickling people."

"You — are — evil!" I manage to get out between fits of laughter.

"You love it." His smirk morphs into a hungry grin and the vibe switches at once from playful to sensual.

"So, do you have somewhere to be today, or...?" My voice is low and deep; my eyes are begging for a repeat of last night.

"I'm all yours."

After breakfast, we go back to bed for the whole day, only getting out to pay the pizza delivery guy. In between bouts of passionate lovemaking, Jeff plays a few songs, but the way he looks at me while his fingers dance on the strings soon makes me want to jump on him again — after setting the guitar safely out of harm's way, of course.

TEN

I push the door of Le Trèfle on my morning break the next Monday, eager for a cup of anything warm to fight the crisp October wind. Mitch fixes me a chai latte before taking off her apron and sitting at a table with me, taking advantage of the unusual lack of customers.

"So, I heard you and Jeff really hit it off?" She grins expectantly, a lewd eyebrow wiggle thrown in for good measure.

"Where did you hear that?" I cock an inquisitive eyebrow.

Mitch blushes and shrugs dismissively. "Justin texted me this morning."

"Your new boyfriend's a gossip?"

"He's not my boyfriend."

"Yet."

"I don't know if I want him to be…"

"What do you mean? I thought you liked him?"

"Weren't we talking about you hooking up with a gorgeous bassist, actually?"

"He's hilarious, great in bed, we got tons in common and we spent the whole day together." I spout quickly, eager to know more about her news. "Why don't you want Justin as a boyfriend?"

"Oh, look at the time! Break's over! See ya!" Mitch grabs the apron off the back of her chair and disappears in the backroom, even though the café is still devoid of customers.

I grab my to-go cup and shuffle back to Quarante-Cinq, despite my break not ending for another ten minutes.

¤

After a couple of busy weeks during which David had mostly night shoots and I worked during the day, we're in dire need of a date night. I get home before him, put on a pretty dress, and make one of his favourite meals — baked salmon.

He comes home looking gorgeous in his usual work clothes: plaid shirt, bowtie and Oxford shoes with nice jeans, perfect for a shoot.

"Smells good," he says between welcome home kisses. "Salmon?"

"Your favourite."

"Next week, it's my turn to spoil you."

"Deal."

We sit down at the dinner table with a nice bottle of white wine, and unwind.

"I finally convinced Mitch to stop changing subjects, and get this: she and Justin went back to her place the other night, and he passed the Gaspard test!"

"No way?"

Gaspard is Mitch's notoriously unfriendly cat; he likes *nobody*. I have yet to make physical contact with him, and I have known Mitch for two years.

"He spent the whole night in Justin's lap."

David lets out a long whistle.

"And when I say the whole night, I mean the whole night. They stayed up talking until eight in the morning."

David looks at me tenderly. "Remember when we used to stay up all night and talk?"

"Alas, we're an old couple that goes to bed at a reasonable hour."

"Maybe tonight we could... not do that?" He pulls me to my feet and grabs the bottle of wine. I follow him to our bedroom. We've got a lot of 'catching up' to do.

¤

In the two weeks following Alex's break-up, I barely hear from her at all. We usually text each other at least twice a day, so I know she's probably cooped up in her studio, painting abstract representations of Anger or Pain. Despite her many protests that "Of course I'm fine, *Mom,*" I pester her until she agrees to meet for sushi.

She walks in the tiny restaurant — one look suffices to confirm she is far from 'fine'.

She's dressed from head-to-toe in brand new clothes: a shiny, purple biker jacket and combat boots I've never seen before. In her hands are two bulging shopping bags. Alex only goes shopping when she's down. It's the only time she allows herself to "partake in the capitalist and patriarchal fashion industry." Even her hair is new: bright pink, as if the neon colour could distract from her distress.

A bright grin lights up her face when she sees me, but it doesn't quite reach her eyes.

I hug her, hard, and feel some tension in her shoulders lift. She quickly pulls away, however, and I can't see the expression on her face because she looks down as she takes off her jacket and scarf — also a new acquisition: a cheap replica of an Alexander McQueen skull scarf. We sit down and order, and then we can finally talk.

"I'm so glad we're doing this," I say with a warm smile. "I've missed you."

"I've been awfully busy — I picked up a few more shifts at the café. Business is booming with the end of semester approaching and the cold weather."

She's right, of course, but I know her; she clearly took on more shifts to avoid having to think or feel.

"Listen, honey, you know I'm here for you, right? If you need to talk, or you just want to have fun and forget about things, okay?"

She suddenly gets really serious.

"Yeah, babe. I know. I'm just — I don't really know how to deal with all of this. Relationships aren't my thing, so I don't have a lot of experience in break-ups. Like, is it supposed to hurt this much?"

Her voice cracks and she stuffs a kamikaze roll in her mouth, an excuse to stop talking.

"Yeah, honey. It means you cared about that relationship. Look, I can't promise it will get better instantly. These things take time. But I promise to be there for you every step of the way. To cheer you up, to listen, to cry with you, or to act like thirteen-year-olds."

Alex's eyes brim with tears, but she hurries to wipe them on her scarf when she thinks I'm not looking. "Thanks, babe."

We end up playing pool in a dingy bar, getting drunk enough that by the end of the night, she laughs and checks out girls with me, like her usual self.

ELEVEN

The following weeks are spent in a whirlwind of work and dates with Jeff. Things with him are so different than with anyone else I've hooked up with. He's not a booty call kind of guy; he genuinely puts time and effort into surprising me. Every time I think he can't possibly top the previous date, he comes in and sweeps me off my feet again: high tea at Cardinal Tea Room; a champagne bar where you can saber your own bottle; an impromptu weekend away to a Vermont bed-and-breakfast.

When Jeff drops me home after the weekend, I walk into an empty house without so much as a note hinting at David's whereabouts. I rack my brains, trying to recall any plans he told me he had this weekend, but come up with nothing. I decide to text him.

Amy Evans — Hey sweetie, I'm back home <3

David Paradis — Nice of you to check in.

Amy Evans — Where are you?

David Paradis — What, you get whisked away by some dude all weekend and I'm supposed to just wait here patiently?

What's with the attitude? David's never been the passive-aggressive type — that's why our open relationship works so well. I decide not to answer. Better to talk about this face-to-face.

David comes home two hours later without a word — not even a hello. He hangs his coat on a hook by the door, toes out of his shoes, goes to the kitchen to make a cup of tea, all while pointedly avoiding looking at me.

"David."

He fills the electric kettle and looks away.

"David, we have to talk about this."

"About what?" he suddenly snaps, his words like harsh darts, drastically opposite to his usual content, composed self. "About how you decided out of the blue to go gallivanting with some jerk you just met? You didn't think I could use a little heads up?"

"I didn't know!" My own voice gets louder and louder, until I'm basically shouting. "It was spontaneous! He surprised me with the news on Friday."

"So you jumped on the occasion, right? Anything is better than being stuck home with me?"

"What's that supposed to mean?" My hands are shaking. Heat is pooling in my ears and my jaw clenches shut.

David grabs his cup of tea and rushes past me to lock himself in our room.

"David!" I call after him. "Talk to me."

I'm greeted with nothing but silence.

"Come on, let me in. We'll talk this through."

David sniffs sarcastically.

"Please, I don't want to fight." Dejected, I sink to the floor, huddled against the wall.

I hear a rustle and a thump on the other side of the door, telling me David must have done the same.

Minutes pass without a word. Blood rushes through my ears. My throat closes up. I take a deep breath as tears roll quietly down my cheeks. I can't take this silence.

I knock faintly on the door — a quiet white flag, an olive branch.

"David," I whisper.

"I — I miss you." He speaks in barely a murmur. Somehow, the sound carries through the inches of wood isolating us. I am flooded by his sorrow.

I press my palm flat against the door, as if I could send some comfort through it. I hear a choked sob and the sound of the lock turning. The door opens by just an inch. I figure that means I'm welcome in the room. I get up and push the door slowly.

David is curled up at the foot of the bed, shoulders shaking slightly along with his silent sobs. The sight is heart wrenching — my eyes fill with tears. I sit down next to him, carefully, and put a tentative hand on his shoulder.

"I miss you too," I whisper.

Another hushed sob. He straightens up to look at me. "I know we tried so hard to make it work, and I hate myself for feeling like this because it goes against everything we agreed upon when we started this. But, then again, everything is changing. None of this fits our arrangement."

"What do you mean? If I've broken any rule — "

"You're in a relationship with Jeff."

The realization drops like a bomb in the room, driving a wall between us. I withdraw my hand from his shoulder like I've been burned. David turns away.

"It's increasingly hard to keep my jealousy in check," David continues, "when you're changing the rules without telling me." More sobs punctuate his sentences — each one wrings my heart a bit more.

My mouth hangs open, but words refuse to come out.

"At first, I let it go — I figured it was the thrill of meeting someone new, ya know? But it's been weeks. Every time you see him, you guys dive deeper and deeper into this relationship and I — " His voice cracks. "I feel like I'm losing you a bit more each day. We haven't had a dine-and-dish in weeks — the only thing I know about this relationship is your hurried texts saying where you're going."

"I — I don't know what to say." I wring a corner of the duvet cover in my hands, trying to wring out my feelings. "I never saw it coming. I didn't even realize it happened."

"You didn't?" David speaks in an incredulous tone.

"Well, of course, I was like 'Ooh, this is different, it's quite nice', but I never stopped to think about how I was breaking our rules."

David lets out a deep sigh. He's stopped crying, but still has his back to me. I wish I could see his face, get a read on it. Is he mad? Just disappointed?

"I fucked up," I say. "I'm so, so sorry."

I can't believe I messed up this bad. We usually talk about everything. It's the only way an open relationship — or any relationship — can survive. We've both been so busy with work, dates, anything that wasn't our couple, that I let this get out of control.

"When did we stop making 'us' a priority?" David asks, finally turning to face me.

His eyes are red; his face streaked with tears. His glasses hang askew off his nose — it makes him look adorable. I give a tiny smile and adjust them.

"I think I took you for granted."

David nods, a forlorn look in his silver eyes. I hold out my hands and he takes them.

"Where do we go from here?" he asks, his voice timid, but raw from crying — so different from the confident David I know.

"I guess we need to review our rules — what we keep, what we change. Whatever you're comfortable with. If I need to end it with Jeff, I will."

"I don't want that." David squeezes my hand — to comfort me or himself, I'm unsure. "He makes you happy, of that I'm certain."

"He really does." I smile wistfully.

"Well, then, the answer is simple, isn't it?"

I shrug, unwilling to hope for what I really want because I know it's hurting him. A square of late afternoon light frames his face as his smile reaches his eyes.

"This isn't just about sex — about booty calls — anymore." He nods as he speaks, a warm glint in his eyes suggesting he's actually happy with this turn of events. "We're allowed to date other people. On a regular basis, I mean."

"You sure you're okay with this? I don't want you to do this purely for my sake."

"I know, *chaton*. In fact, there's this girl, Véronique. I wanted to make a move, but I know she's interested in more than just a one-night stand. I think I'll ask her out now."

I cuddle in closer and shut my eyes, breathing him in. "I hope it'll work out."

"With Véronique?"

"Yeah. And with us."

"It has to. *Je t'aime.*"

TWELVE

Alex wasn't exaggerating when she texted me she was in serious need of a drunken girls' night. She gets to my place around eight with a bottle of wine and one of raspberry-flavoured vodka. I find two avocados in the back of the fridge, so we whip up a batch of guacamole.

"So, there's this new girl at the café," Alex tells me with wide, gossipy eyes. "She's gorgeous, with pink hair, and she does stand-up comedy."

Talking about a girl — a good sign of healing. She hasn't shown interest in anyone since Lola Bunny on Halloween. They slept together once, but that's about it. I'm so glad she seems ready to get back out there.

"You should come around one of these days, I'm sure you two would hit it off," she continues.

Maybe not, then.

Apparently she's at the 'get Amy laid and drink a lot in the process' stage of recovery. She's always been able to outdrink me easily, but this is ridiculous. I'm still working on my second glass of wine and already the bottle is empty.

"Know what we should do? Karaoke." Alex's words are not yet slurred — she's tougher than that — but I recognize her typical drunken enthusiasm.

"Sure." I set up my laptop and find a karaoke YouTube channel.

Meanwhile, Alex goes to the kitchen and comes back with the vodka and two shot glasses.

"Shots after all that wine? Honey, you're nuts."

"Hey, it's just the two of us, and I have no place to be tomorrow, so I don't mind the hangover. Come on, live a little!"

"I live a lot, I'll let you know. I just thought this was gonna be a lazy night at home."

She's already pouring as I explain my point. To my surprise, flavoured vodka is actually not that bad. We each knock back two shots before starting to sing. We choose cheesy songs from our childhood — Spice Girls, Britney Spears, that kind of thing — and we decide to make it a Girl Power Night, so we only choose songs by female artists. Every four or five songs, Alex calls "Shots!" and we do one more.

The lyrics get blurrier after each one, and I'm pretty sure we're wrong about our 'amazing talent', as Alex puts it. After a while, we're too drunk to even choose a song, so I switch off the laptop and we pass the bottle, glasses forgotten on the coffee table.

"You know what would be great?" Alex asks as she passes me the bottle. "If we fucked."

I choke on vodka and it almost comes out of my nose.

"Don't you want me?" she asks defiantly.

"Honey, I've wanted you ever since the first latte you served me at the café. I never thought you wanted me back."

"So you're in?"

"I don't think it's a good idea. You're still trying to get over Emma, and you probably only want this because you're drunk."

"No, babe, it's the perfect way to get over her! You see, it still hurts because I can remember what she looks like, the way she fucks, how she sounds. I need you to help me forget her."

My brain tells me this is a terrible idea. This could destroy our friendship. Still, I can't focus on anything other than the way her lips wrap around her words — the way she says *babe, fuck* or *I need you*.

"I don't know…"

"Yeah, you do …" She climbs on top of me, straddling my thighs. The way she stares at me, waiting for an answer, drives me crazy. Her hands run up and down my arms, and she bites her lower lip, trying to convince me.

"Swear to me this ain't gonna fuck up our friendship."

"Babe, of course. We're stronger than that, you know it."

I give the slightest nod and we both know this is me giving up, giving myself up to her.

She leans in, grinning, and I know we're both thinking the same thing: *Oh my god, we're actually doing this!* And then our lips meet and life is nothing short of amazing.

Alex drags her tongue stud across my lips, cold hard metal contrasting perfectly with her feverish, supple lips, and it's incredible to finally be doing that with someone I know so much. She moves a certain way or makes a certain sound and I recognize it, and some voice repeats *It's Alex* over and over in my head. It electrifies me. I fantasized about that tongue piercing for so long — I want it all over me.

Hard and soft, that's Alex. She digs her chipped black fingernails hard in my arms and bites my lip, but her thighs are soft under my hands — under her leather skirt — and she moans softly in my mouth.

She gets up and takes my hand, guides me to my bedroom. Usually David and I have this rule against bringing people back home to hook up, but this is Alex. I know he'll understand — he knows I've always wanted her and how much she needs to forget right now.

Alex lies down on the bed, pulling me on top of her. Her hands find their way under my shirt, smooth caresses across my back. One of my hands is buried in pink hair on one side of her head, the other is scratching at her scalp on the shaved side. Our mouths find each other again. The urgency makes everything messy; teeth, tongues and lips and that metal stud, all engaged in a mad dance, a frantic search for pleasure.

She unhooks my bra under my shirt, and I scramble to my knees because I need skin *right now*. She takes off my shirt and bra and sits up so I can take hers off too. Her left nipple shines with a glinting ring. I knew she had it pierced, but I'd never seen it before. The icy steel set into her scalding, silken skin enthrals me.

My mouth latches onto it. My lips curve around the ring, sucking the nipple in. I drag my teeth against the skin, playfully tugging at the nub. My tongue licks a trail down the curve of her breast, following the gentle swirls of the tattoo hidden under it, spreading on the valley of her rib.

"Babe, that tickles," she laughs, and pulls me up to kiss me.

My hand slips under her skirt, trails up her thigh and meets, unexpectedly, her soaked folds. No underwear.

My mind short-circuits.

THIRTEEN

I wake up the next morning in an empty bed. I yawn and stretch, figuring Alex went to the bathroom or something. I decide to get up and surprise her with breakfast. As I gather yesterday's clothes from the floor, I realize hers aren't here, and neither is her backpack. The apartment is empty, except for David snoring on the living room couch.

She left.

David wakes up and sees me standing there.

"How was it?" he asks, wiggling his eyebrows lewdly.

"She left."

"I'm sure she had someplace to be this morning." He uses his calm, level tone — the one he takes when he knows I'm about to spiral.

"No, she told me last night we could get drunk because she had no plans today."

"Well, text her before you panic." He scrambles off the couch and his back cracks.

"Oh, honey, I'm so sorry we made you sleep on the couch. And that I broke the not-at-home rule."

"Amy. This is Alex. Of course I understand."

"Thanks." I kiss him tenderly.

I take a deep breath and sit down. I urge myself not to panic until I hear from her. I take a few minutes to compose a light and breezy text message. I don't want her to think I'm freaking out.

I rewrite the text a few times and ask David to read it to make sure it's not too needy or panicky. When I finally press 'Send', it reads: Hey honey! Had a great time last night. Wish you stayed for breakfast.

David agrees that it's friendly and sweet, without being clingy, and that you can't tell I'm worried.

Each hour that passes without a reply from Alex increases the weight pressing down on my chest. My heart is in a vice grip; I can barely breathe.

I text Mitch, Cory and Georgie, but no one has heard from Alex. I refresh her Instagram account endlessly, but no new update appears, no Stories.

Around eight o'clock, I decided I've waited long enough. I try to call her. It goes straight to voicemail. Trying to steady my strangled voice, I leave a message, hoping I don't sound too worried.

I stay up as late as possible, fearing she might call while I'm asleep. When I finally go to bed around two in the morning, I lie awake, tossing and turning for several hours. David's body next to mine, however reassuring he tries to be, only reminds me of the bed's previous occupant.

¤

The crisp autumn morning sun shines on me through the kitchen window. Outside looks like a Christmas card — snow came early this year. I cradle my tea mug in my hands and can't bring myself to care about the stunning view. Christmas is coming fast and I might have to spend it without one of the most important people in my life.

It's been nearly one week. She still hasn't called or replied to my numerous text messages. She hasn't contacted anyone else in the gang. Mitch says she took one — or more — week off work. Of course, when I went to her place, no one answered.

Tears drop into my lukewarm tea. A dull, empty ache has taken permanent residence in my chest.

I can't believe I'm losing Alex because of a drunk fuck. And the worst is that I don't know her reasons. I can't ask her what's wrong — what I can do to fix things. The only thing I can give her is time, but it's incredibly hard to do when I don't know if this is fixable. Maybe she doesn't want to see me ever again. Maybe she just wanted to fuck me and now she got what she wanted and doesn't want anything to do with me anymore — she got me out of her system.

A voice inside my head — sounding strangely like David's — tells me that it's not true. We've been friends for too long for it to be reduced to that.

Which is why it hurts so much. Three years of friendship just thrown aside, broken, destroyed — and for what? A mistake? I have to talk to her before I lose my mind. With a sigh, I reach for my cellphone to text her, again.

This text obviously goes unanswered, like the others before it and those sent by Mitch, Georgie, or Cory.

I still click on Alex's name, however, when I send the Facebook invitation for our traditional Christmas party. I can't help but hope the Christmas spirit will get to her and she'll come back — even though she doesn't believe in that sort of thing.

I don't know how I'll get through this. Alex is as good as family in my heart; I can't bear the thought of spending Christmas without her. I have the feeling I'll get drunk and do something stupid, like hook up with the girlfriend of one of David's bros. Even that prospect sounds dull when I can't share the laughs with Alex.

The doorbell rings. I drag my body to the front door. I don't want to see anybody, but I feel obligated to answer, on the tiniest chance that it might be Alex.

On the other side of the door is Mitch. She offers a sad little smile and opens her arms wide.

"I just saw you sent the invitations. I figured it's probably rough for you?"

I throw myself in her arms and let the tears come.

"How do you know me so well?" I ask between sobs.

"I just hate to see people I love feel crappy." She guides me inside and closes the door behind us. "Come on, I'll make some tea."

I nod, wiping my tears on my sleeve. She fills the kettle and takes two mugs out of my cupboard.

"I've never been the best at saying the right thing, but can I offer you hugs and a sympathetic ear?"

"That's exactly what I need right now."

I tell her the whole story. Cory, Georgie and Mitch only know that Alex went AWOL, but they have no idea why. Mitch listens to me without a comment, judging glance, or surprised gasp. After I'm done, she hugs me tightly.

We cuddle under a blanket, cradling our warm mugs in our cold hands, watching old episodes of *Friends*. Once in a while, we pause the show to share memories of Alex. We laugh a little and cry a lot, in a way that's strangely reminiscent of a funeral. I guess it's fitting since I'm mourning a friendship.

"You know, sometimes I see something she'd love and I start to text her, but then I remember I can't. And it's like all the pain comes crashing back again."

"It's not easy to say goodbye to that kind of friendship, sweetie. I mean, you talked everyday, you saw each other constantly — this is as hard as a break-up." Mitch drapes an arm around my shoulders.

"I think the worst thing is that she won't talk to me. I don't even know why she left." I lean into Mitch, seeking solace in her presence.

"Knowing Alex, it probably has more to do with herself than with whatever you could have done."

"It still fucking hurts."

FOURTEEN

It seems like Montreal has decided to reflect my pain this year. Winter comes around on the last days of November, covering the city in a thick layer of frost and sludge — exactly how my heart feels.

I find myself craving Jeff's company. We go on a few more dates and I attend his gigs. It does wonders for my mood, getting my mind off things. He's the only person in my life that doesn't remind me of Alex; I can hang out with him without feeling like there's an Alex-shaped hole in the conversation. My other friends are amazing, but it's weird to hang out with them without her, and they always handle me with kid gloves, her name an obvious taboo.

Around the second week of December, Jeff asks me over to his place to hang out and have a drink. Justin is out, so we can stay in the living room. They've got this little Christmas tree all lit up and decorated, with gifts under it — or more like beside it, since it's so small. It's super adorable and, in my experience, not something you often see in an apartment where there's no girl.

I plop down on the couch and Jeff joins me with a bottle of white wine and two glasses. I'm a bit surprised because he's usually more of a beer kind of guy. He sits down next to me, slides an arm around my shoulders, and looks at me tenderly, kissing my cheek. After a sip of wine, he lets out a contented sigh.

"You know, I'm really glad you came here tonight. I missed you."

I laugh softly. "We went out on Sunday."

"I know, but I wish I could see you every day."

I kiss the tip of his nose. "You're fucking adorable, you know that?"

"I try." He flashes me his widest grin — it's a bit crooked, which only adds to his charm.

I cuddle closer to him and sip my wine in silence, happy to be here with him. The wine is good, Jeff's body is warm and the only light in the room comes from the Christmas tree. The only thing missing to this sweet holiday movie cliché is a fireplace and maybe some crooner singing "Have Yourself a Merry Little Christmas". I haven't felt this content in weeks. I wish I could spend the whole holidays here in Jeff's arms — where it's impossible for me to think about my broken heart.

Whenever my thoughts drift off to Alex, Jeff always notices I look sad. Even though I haven't told him what's wrong, he always tilts my chin up, kisses me softly and says: "Hey. Don't be sad. We're happy, right?"

And I have no choice but to agree with him, because the truth is, he really does make me happy.

Jeff gets up to fill my glass and I involuntarily whine at the loss of his body against mine. He chuckles and I stick my tongue out at him.

"Hurry back…"

He fills both glasses and walks over to the Christmas tree.

"I've got something for you." He picks up a small package wrapped in red with a gold ribbon on it.

"What? I've got nothing — "

"I don't mind." He kisses me and hands me the present. "Merry Christmas."

I tear off the paper, my mind reeling with thoughts of *what the fuck?* and *why?* and *are we at the gift stage yet?*, rifling through records at work I know he'd like, but through it all, I'm still bursting with excitement because I absolutely adore surprises.

I open the box to find a pair of the most gorgeous earrings, shaped like tiny copper feathers. I can tell they'd go perfectly with my red hair, but I look at him, puzzled.

"I — what — I can't accept — "

"I know we're not official yet, but I thought, ain't no better time than Christmas…"

"Jeff, there's a reason we can't be official, you know."

"What? But I thought we — why?"

He looks utterly confused, and I am too, because didn't we already go through this when we first met?

And that's when it hits me. I slap a hand against my mouth.

"Fuck. I didn't tell you, did I?"

FIFTEEN

"Tell me what?"

"Oh god. Oh god. Okay, there's something you need to know." It's all coming back to me in a rush of mistakes and bad decisions.

"Figured as much," he mumbles. His face is closed off. He scoots over to the other end of the couch, the earrings on the middle cushion like a wall.

"I've got a boyfriend."

Jeff's jaw drops.

"We're in an open relationship. Which means we can see other people on the side, but at the end of the day, I go home to him."

"I thought you loved me."

"I do!" It's true. I realize it as I say it. "But I'm in love with David. So I can't be your girlfriend. And I can't accept these." I push the earrings towards him. He eyes them angrily, as though it were all their fault.

"I really thought what we had was real."

"It is!" My eyes fill up with tears. I try to take his hand, but he jerks it away and folds his arms. "Everything I said to you, I meant it! It's just that usually I have this conversation before starting anything."

"So you lied to me."

"It all happened so fast — I had to leave with Mitch. I completely forgot! And then I figured I did tell you, because I always do!"

"Always? So there's been others like me?"

"There's been others, but not like you. Usually I stick to one-night stands. But with you, it's different. I really like you. I wanted — I want you in my life."

His face softens, but he looks away.

"I — I love you," his voice cracks, "but I don't think I can do this."

Tears roll down my cheeks. It's getting harder and harder to keep myself from sobbing hysterically. Jeff takes my hand.

"I'm not mad at you," he says softly. "I'm not saying I don't ever wanna see you again. But I need time to get used to this. Sharing you is not what I had in mind."

He wipes away my tears with his thumb and I manage to come up with a half-hearted smile.

"Have a happy Christmas," he says. "Let me get used to the idea, and keep these as a promise that one day I'll be back." He closes my hands over the earrings box.

Tears fill my eyes again, but this time, it's relief — relief that I didn't lose another best friend; relief that I didn't scare him away; relief that I can at last admit to myself that I'm in love with Jeff. I nod, unable to speak, and he hugs me close.

"I love you," he whispers in my ear.

I play it over and over in my head on my way home, tears falling freely down my face.

¤

As soon as Mitch hears my voice over the phone she knows something's wrong.

"I'm coming over."

When she enters the house and hugs me tight, I start crying like a baby again. I managed to stop sobbing yesterday before I came home to David. Now that love is part of the equation, I couldn't face him just yet. But now Mitch is here to listen to me, offer hugs and advice, no judgement. If she managed to listen to the tale of how I fucked my best friend and lost her in the process without judging, I know I can tell her anything.

She pours two glasses of wine and we plop down on the couch. I tell her the whole story.

"But the thing is," I finish, taking a sip of wine, "I think I fell in love with Jeff."

Mitch's eyes widen slightly. "What about David?"

My eyes fill up with tears. "That's the problem. When we opened the relationship, falling in love with someone else never even occurred to us. We were — we still are — in love. This was just meant to allow us to act on crushes, have a bit of fun."

"But you still love David, right?" she asks in a soothing voice.

"Of course I do! I just don't know how I'll be able to tell him. He's open-minded, but I have no idea how he'll react. What if he can't deal with it? I mean, I'd never choose Jeff over David, but if it comes to a point where I have to end things with Jeff… I'm scared I'd start to resent David." I wave my arms around in despair and the wine sloshes around in my glass. Mitch takes it gently from my hand.

"Sweetie. You and David are the greatest couple I know. Not everyone would be able to carry on with this sort of arrangement, but you guys make it work. You know why? Because you talk. You are completely open with each other."

I blow my nose in a tissue and nod, because of course, she's right.

"And that's why," she goes on calmly, "you're gonna tell him. He'll listen and you guys will talk. I can't promise you he'll be okay about it, but I do know you'll be able to discuss it. You'll feel better afterwards."

"You sure?"

"Of course, sweetie. It's you and David. Promise me you'll talk to him."

I promise, and she hands me a donut.

"Thanks, Mitch. For everything."

We put on *Love Actually* and we spend the whole time laughing, except at the end where we both cry uncontrollably. It's not the same, watching this movie without Alex; it's her favourite and we always used to watch it at Christmas. She and I used to crush on Hugh Grant's assistant, and she always had a feminist rant ready for Snape's midlife crisis and his cheating on Trelawney.

¤

David comes home around midnight. I just got out of the shower, where I had another good cry and gave myself a pep talk to face this discussion.

"Mmm, you smell good!" He buries his face in my neck and kisses me right above the clavicle — where he knows I'm ticklish.

"How was your date with Véronique?" I ask, because I've never been a fan of the whole *honey, we need to talk* thing — too dramatic.

"Good. We grabbed a bite and went to the movies. I doubt it'll last longer than a week or two."

"Aw, that's too bad, you were looking forward to this." I adjust my bathrobe around me and wrap my damp hair in a towel.

"Well, it didn't click." He shrugs.

"About that..." I take a deep breath and lead him to the living room couch. "Last night, Jeff gave me a Christmas present, earrings. Turns out, when we first met, I completely forgot to have The Talk with him. So he thought he and I were an item."

"Ouch," David remarks, scrunching his face. "Poor guy."

"Yeah, so I told him everything. And he said he loves me, but he had to break it off. He needs to get used to the idea. He said he'd come back one day."

"Amy, I'm so sorry — " He tries to hug me, but I keep him at a distance. If I don't say it now I never will.

"I fell in love with him."

"Uh." His arms fall to his sides. He stands up and walks around the living room, raking a hand through his hair, as if he didn't know what to do with himself.

"I — I don't know what it means. I still love you — I mean, obviously." I offer a tentative smile.

David is still speechless, and I can't read him — is he shocked, or mad, or something else? I close my eyes and brace myself for the worst.

"We, um, we didn't foresee this in our ground rules." His voice is calm, albeit shaky. He doesn't sound angry; I heave a relieved sigh and open my eyes.

"No, we didn't."

I wait for him to say something, but he doesn't. He still looks astonished, a bit distressed.

"So, what do you think?" I urge him. The uncertainty is killing me.

"You love him?"

"Yes."

"And he loves you?"

"Yes, but he needs to not be with me for a while."

"And you love me?"

"Forever. Never doubt it." I take David's hand between mine.

"He makes you happy?"

"Before I fucked it up, yes."

"As far as I'm concerned, this doesn't break any rules. If I remember correctly, as far as whatever you're doing outside of our couple makes you happy and doesn't interfere with us, you're free to do whatever you want. Or, should I say now, love whoever you love."

"Are you serious? You're okay with this?"

"I mean, I can't say I'm one hundred percent happy about it, you know? Like, there's a small part of me that's worried if you start giving your love elsewhere, there'll be less of it for me. Rationally, I know that's bullshit, and the rest of me that's able to feel compersion is really happy for you — I mean, more love in the world is always a good thing, but yeah…"

"I feel so guilty asking this of you — I mean, I feel as if lately I've been asking an awful lot of compromises from you. We keep changing the ground rules to accommodate my relationship — or whatever it is I had — with Jeff."

"A relationship isn't a static thing. It's meant to grow with the needs and desires of both people in it. And I can't say it only benefits you. In fact, maybe these new changes are gonna help me. I mean, I always have a hard time finding someone for more than a week, and I think it might be because I don't let myself *seek* anything more? Like I have trouble connecting with people on a superficial, sex-only level."

"Wow." I hold out a hand, needing to touch him, to reassure myself that this is happening — this isn't me daydreaming about this outcome over and over. But in all of my enactments of this scene in the shower, I never envisioned a scenario in which David was okay with this. I couldn't allow myself to hope.

David takes my hand in his — his warm, firm, real hand. He pulls me into his arms — still the place where I feel most at home.

"I just want us to be happy," he whispers against the top of my head.

"I think we are."

SIXTEEN

The doorbell rings and I hurry to answer it, cursing as I wobble like Bambi on my stilt-like heels.

"Merry Christmas!"

On my porch stands Hugo, arms laden with bread and cheese, a bottle of red tucked under his arm. I invite him in and rid him of all the food so he can take off his coat. I almost drop the wine — Hugo looks drop-dead gorgeous in a navy blue suit — no tie, the first button of his grey shirt carelessly undone.

"You clean up nicely," I remark casually, like I didn't have to pick my jaw up from the floor at his sight.

"My Ramones tee was in the wash." He shrugs and leans in for a peck on the cheek.

"Gibson, you beautiful bastard!"

"David! How's it going, man?" David and Hugo do that kind of one-armed hug dudes always do, with the mandatory two claps on the back.

I slip to the kitchen while my boys catch up about Dungeons and Dragons and how long it's been since their last campaign, and I set up Hugo's food on the buffet table.

The evening is amazing. It's pretty great to see all our friends dressed to the nines, gorgeous and happy to be together. An occasion to partake in excellent food and booze doesn't stink either.

The night seems to fly by at the speed of light. I eat a lot, drink a lot, catch up with friends I haven't seen in a while, meet new significant others. I run all night between the living room where people are dancing, and the kitchen where they are eating.

My new dress gets me a lot of compliments — it's a purple dressy affair I bought to cheer me up after the ordeal with Alex. It fails to make up for her absence, however.

Julia's punch is incredible — I might take one too many cup. When I get up to find David in the living room, I almost turn an ankle.

"Fuck! Okay, everyone has seen the shoes, now I can change into my flats." Mitch and Julia laugh.

I make my way to the bedroom, weaving through drunken guests in our long, narrow hallway. A relieved sigh escapes me as I sit down on my bed and take off my high heels. I massage my feet, trying to regain some feeling into my toes. I should have listened to Mitch when she said buying these shoes was a mistake.

"They say I give great foot rubs," a voice at the door says.

I look up to see a pretty, chubby brunette I don't know. We got introduced earlier, but I can't recall her name, nor who brought her. I must look puzzled, because she chuckles and introduces herself.

"I'm Chelsea." She kneels in front of me and takes one of my feet in her hands.

I chuckle nervously, a bit weirded out at this stranger offering random foot massages. When she starts rubbing, however, all awkwardness vanishes. Her hands are soft and warm; she's indeed gifted. She kneads a particularly sore spot with her thumb and I let out an involuntary moan.

Her eyes snap up and she smirks.

"You like that?"

"Good god," I exhale.

Chelsea nudges the door shut and goes to work on my other foot. I lean back on the bed and close my eyes, enjoying the incredible sensations.

Suddenly, her hands are gone. I'm about to open my eyes to see what's going on, but I feel a dip in the mattress and her lips are on mine. She kisses me softly — shy, but curious. I open my eyes and she smiles.

"I've never done anything with a girl," she confesses coyly.

"Want to?"

She shrugs and giggles. "Yeah."

I pull her on top of me and kiss her again. This time she's more adventurous; she deepens the kiss. I slide a hand under her top, letting my fingers dance on the small of her back. Her hips stutter between my thighs and she laughs again.

"That tickles."

As I grab the hem of her shirt, the doorbell rings.

I'm pulled out of the moment, and the memory comes crashing back.

"Shit. You're Felix's new girlfriend, aren't you?"

"I thought you knew."

"I met so many people tonight — I forgot."

I scramble off the bed and straighten my ruffled clothes. I slip into a pair of flats and head for the front door.

"Hey."

Alex Bell is standing on my doorstep.

SEVENTEEN

"Merry Christmas!"

I can't stop grinning. I know there are thousands of reasons she could be here, and she might still be angry, but at least she stopped ignoring me. I know I should be mad at her for what she put me through, all the heartache and worrying, but I just can't bring myself to be anything but overjoyed at the fact that she chose to come here.

That might be the best Christmas present I've ever got.

"Can you come outside?" She glances warily at the party going on inside.

"Sure." I gesture at David and he brings me my coat. He smiles at Alex, but says nothing.

I close the door behind me. Questions whirl around in my head and I struggle to keep my mouth shut. Knowing Alex, the wrong words could have a disastrous effect. She leans against the railing, silent. I can't help feeling jealous of her combat boots. My flats and short dress don't exactly offer me protection from the cold.

We stand silently in the snow for a while, staring at the neighbour's inflatable waving Santa. I'm about to lose patience because, damn it, I can't feel my toes. Alex pats her pockets until she finds a pack of cigarettes. She shields her lighter from the biting wind and lights up a smoke.

"You started again?" I ask as a reflex before I can catch myself.

"Yeah." She takes a long drag and looks away, blowing a cloud of smoke. "It's Christmas. And, at Christmas, you tell the truth."

I smile. She just quoted our favourite movie, *Love Actually*. Somehow, it almost makes up for everything else.

"So, the truth is, I love you."

"What?"

"I'm in love with you. Ever since we first met."

I don't know what to say. Out of all the possible outcomes of this situation, that was the one I never expected.

Her cigarette hangs between two fingers, forgotten, almost burning a hole through her glove, but somehow Alex doesn't seem to care. Her eyes are fixed on me, obviously waiting for an answer.

Which I can't give to her.

I'm rooted to the spot. My lips are sealed together. My brain shut down. I can't even look at her.

Alex came all this way to finally tell me the truth — the reason why we both suffered for weeks — and I can't bring myself to answer.

I owe it to her.

"What? Why?" This is dumb. As if you need a reason to fall in love with someone. "Why didn't you say anything?" I finish lamely.

She takes one last drag of her too-short cigarette butt, throws it in the snow and buries it with her feet. It's her turn to avoid my gaze.

"David." She shrugs.

"But — our arrangement — we could — "

"Babe." I relish the familiar pet name; I didn't realize I missed it so much. "You saw what happened with Emma. Open-rels aren't my thing."

"So why did we — "

"I was drunk and hurt. It was a mistake. That's why I dropped off the map for a while." She looks away and lights a second cigarette.

"I don't get it."

"I couldn't get a taste of you without wanting you all to myself. This whole hermit thing was just me trying to come to terms with the fact that I can't have you."

"You really hurt me." My mind is reeling. I voice the first thought that comes to mind.

"I hurt everyone. Including myself. Always do." She shrugs and looks at me. "I'm sorry. That's why I came here. To tell the truth and apologize."

"I'm glad you did." Her confession hurt, sure, but less than all those weeks kept in the dark.

I really should be angry with her, I fleetingly think. But, honestly, I missed her so much I'm willing to forget everything that happened, if it only means I'll get Alex back in my life.

She nods and smiles, lips curling around her cigarette — fuck, I missed her smile so much.

"Okay, my toes really need to be inside right now, and I think a beer would do you good. Come in?"

"Yeah, okay."

She takes off her beanie when she walks in, revealing maybe half a centimetre of buzzed off brown hair — her natural colour.

"You shaved your head!"

Alex shrugs. "Low maintenance. Lost my hairdresser, you know," she adds, shame and regret fleeting in her eye.

"I love it."

EIGHTEEN

Jeff Williams — Merry Christmas love <3

Jeff's text brings hope into my heart. I know it's only been a few days since he called it off, but I already miss him. I dreaded the long months without hearing from him again. I know this text isn't much — it doesn't mean he wants to see me or anything, but it shows that he's thinking of me, that there's no hard feelings. The use of the familiar pet name makes me all giddy and I can't help grinning as I pocket my phone.

Charlotte stares at me suspiciously. We're spending Christmas Eve at our parents', cradling piping hot mugs of mulled wine. Dad's side of the family is reunited in the furniture-crowded living room. My parents own an antique shop, and sometimes their house almost feels like the store's warehouse. With my grandparents, four aunts, three uncles, a handful of cousins with their significant others, and us, the place is cramped. No one else but Charlotte is looking at me, so I have no idea what I've done to deserve it.

"Can I talk to you for a sec?" she asks dryly, going upstairs to her room.

I follow her, shooting a clueless glance at David, who shrugs. Charlotte closes her bedroom door behind us and asks in an angry whisper:

"Are you cheating on David?"

"What? No!"

"Look, I don't wanna ruin Christmas, but Vanessa told me everything."

My heart sinks. How naïve of me to assume Vanessa would keep her end of the deal. Why am I not surprised?

I have no idea what happened to finally push her to do it — I mean, it's been months since I last saw her. I haven't even thought about her in weeks. Knowing her, she was probably just bored and thought she'd have one more laugh at my expense.

Charlotte looks at me, arms crossed, eyes filled with contempt. She's always looked up to me, and she loves David — we've been together most of her teenage years, so she grew up with him around.

"Honey, no! It's — it's complicated. It's a long story, and I don't think this is the place — "

"You don't trust me?"

"Of course I do! But it's Christmas. The whole family's waiting for us. Listen; meet me for lunch sometime this week, okay? I'll tell you the whole thing, I swear."

She still looks sceptical, but she nods.

"Just don't say anything to Mom and Dad, okay?"

"Sure."

I know I can trust her, even though she still looks mad at me. She manages to put on a smile before joining everyone in the living room. We're just in time for our traditional gift exchange. The type of exchange where you buy a gift fitting for anyone and then everyone steals each other's presents.

A gift appropriate for anyone: that's a feat. Grandpa Dustin, my middle-age aunts and my teenage cousin, Zack, sure do like all the same stuff. I usually just buy a bottle of wine and call it a day. My uncles, however, think it's hilarious to buy inappropriate gifts no one would possibly like.

Last year, I got a deck of playing cards, each depicting a different scantily clad lady. Not altogether a bad gift — it did spice up more than a few strip-poker games — but quite embarrassing to unwrap in front of your grandparents.

When my turn comes to pick a gift under the tree, I select the most inoffensive-looking gift: a book-sized box covered in smiling Santas. On Charlotte's turn, she steals my gift instead of picking a new one. She proceeds to do that at every single turn until everyone has a gift.

She might have agreed to give me the benefit of the doubt until she hears the whole story, but she is clearly trying to spite me.

When unwrapping time comes, I end up with a big, flat box wrapped in palm trees decorated like Christmas trees. Uncle Greg guffaws, looking at me expectantly. I open the box to find one of these ugly Christmas sweaters, depicting Santa taking a shit.

Classy.

"Go on, try it on," Greg says, backed by my other uncles who obviously think this is the funniest thing ever, while their wives and sisters look appropriately scandalized.

"Maybe later, after more wine," I answer, wiggling my mug to show it's empty — a good excuse to escape to the kitchen. I'll probably give the sweater to Mitch; it'll make a nice basket-liner for Gaspard.

When I come back with a full mug of wine, Charlotte is unwrapping her gift. She ends up with a nice gift basket of honey-scented soaps and lotions. A gift she stole from me, of course. David is quite happy with his shaker and shot glasses set. Figures that I'd be the only one stuck with a shitty gift while everyone else got nice, useful stuff from my aunts. Zack, the only one who's still underage, ends up with my gift, the bottle of wine. He's overjoyed, until his mom, Aunt Joyce, forces him to trade with her for Travel Scrabble.

My uncles' inappropriate — and often straight-up racist — banter about politics exhausts me. I have to physically restrain myself from piping up to set the record straight. Desperate to escape the conversation, I end up in the kitchen again, trying on the vile sweater to make my cousins laugh. I can still hear my uncles, though — they have no concept of indoor voices, especially when wine is involved. Echoes of "Stealing our jobs!" manage to cut their way through my cousins' laughter, so I grab a bottle of water and step outside with Mom and the other smokers for a breath of fresh air.

I guess calling it smoking is generous. For every drag Mom inhales, she has to take a five-minute break to cough. Soon my aunts and Grandpa have finished their cigarettes, leaving Mom and I alone outside. Her cigarette burns forgotten in her hand while she hacks a lung on the back porch.

"I hate seeing you like this," I say softly, my eyes fixed on the rainbows the Christmas lights paint on the carpet of snow.

"Don't say it, Amy. I'll stop when I'm ready."

"I don't wanna lose you." My voice breaks as I say it.

"Don't be so dramatic, Grandpa has smoked all his life and he's still with us, isn't he?"

I shrug. We have this conversation at least twice a year. Her coughing fits have been getting worse lately, though.

Mom brings up her cigarette to her lips to find that it burned to nothing more than a butt. She shrugs and buries it in the snow-covered ashtray.

At midnight, David brings me to my old bedroom — which is filled to burst with antique furniture and knickknacks now — where he hands me a present.

"Merry Christmas, *chaton*."

In it, I find an enlargement of my favourite picture of the two of us, sitting on the steps of the Epidaurus Theatre in Greece.

"Oh, this is perfect! Thank you, kitten." I kiss him tenderly, wishing we were alone together. "What do you say we stay home on New Year's Eve? No parties, no drama, just the two of us."

David cuddles in closer. "I'd love that. I miss you."

"I know I haven't been the best girlfriend lately. I struggled with what happened with Alex and with Jeff. But now I want to focus on what's important: us."

NINETEEN

Hands stuffed deep in my pockets, I drag my feet towards Charlotte's favourite Vietnamese restaurant, even though my raw cheeks beg me to walk faster and save them from the assaults of the icy Montreal wind. I dread Charlotte's disapproving glare. I keep imagining her crestfallen face, hurt that I'm not the perfect sister she always idolized.

I finally get to the restaurant and take a stinging breath of air. There's no turning back now. Might as well get in, order, and try to clear things up — at least a little bit.

Charlotte is sitting at a table in the back, sipping a glass of water. She glances in my direction as I enter, but her expression is unreadable. I can't tell if she's happy to see me, furious, or just curious.

I hang my coat on the back of my chair and the waitress comes before we can start talking. I don't even need to look at the menu before ordering my usual: pho bo. Charlotte orders the same thing. I smile at her — we still have so much in common, just like when we were kids.

She doesn't smile back. Her cocked eyebrow tells me she's waiting for an explanation. I take a deep breath and a sip of water, trying to gather my thoughts. My hands are shaking. I haven't been this rattled in a long time. People think I'm confident and self-assured, but that's only because I've learned to compartmentalize my entire life.

My family life and my love life — outside of David — were never meant to collide.

It feels as if my whole world is collapsing around me. What can I do? Damage control.

"Please don't hate me."

"I don't. I just think it's disgusting what you're doing to David." She huffs, not even looking at me.

"Oh, honey… Okay, listen. I'm not cheating on David, I swear. We have an arrangement — it's done in complete honesty."

"You guys are in an open relationship?" she suggests. I can't tell if she is accepting, amused, or appalled.

"Yes, exactly." My voice shakes in fear of her reaction.

"So what are you, like, allowed to do?"

"Pretty much anything as long as we're honest with each other and we don't neglect our main relationship. And, well, I suppose you guessed it, with what happened with Vanessa, but, um, I'm bisexual."

Charlotte nods, and her face softens. I can tell she believes me and isn't totally shocked by the idea. She's probably also relieved that David and I still love each other.

"But your arrangement's only for, like, one-night-stands, right?" she finally asks.

"Well, we also go on dates, you know? And recently, um, I realized it could lead further."

Before I know it, I'm telling her the whole story about Jeff and how I think I'm in love with two guys at the same time. Charlotte listens without judgment. I'm suddenly reminded of late nights when we were kids, sharing secrets and talking about our crushes in hushed tones so Mom and Dad wouldn't hear us.

Somehow, this all changed when I moved out. I guess I started seeing her as a child whereas I was an adult living on my own — so I moved her to the 'family' part of my life, instead of the 'confidante' part. That being said, I can't allow these compartments to crumble any further.

"I don't think it needs saying, but you won't tell Mom and Dad, right?"

Charlotte puts her hand on mine. "Of course I won't! I'm so glad you decided to confide in me. It means a lot. For a while, I thought you stopped trusting me."

"Oh, honey, it was never a matter of trust. It's just — I felt like all of this was so *adult*, I mean at first, it *was* just about sex — like, dude, I still feel awkward seeing you drink, I didn't want to tell you about my sex life!"

Charlotte laughs.

"I guess we should thank Vanessa for forcing us to talk about this."

"I wouldn't go *that* far."

TWENTY

"Hi, it's Alex."

The voice on the phone is unmistakeable — back then she used to call and start chatting away, greetings unnecessary. The new formality sends a wistful pang through my chest. I'm glad she called me, though — I'm just thankful she's back in my life, however different our relationship might be.

"Hey, how are you?" I try to inject as much cheerfulness as I can in my tone, so she knows how happy I am that she came back.

"Good. Are you going to Julia's New Year's party tonight?"

"Nah, David and I are staying in — we need some alone time."

The silence on the line might be half a second long, but it's charged with meaning. Alex probably notices too; she clears her throat and hurries to answer.

"Oh, right. Well, I won't go, then. Some of the guys at the café are throwing a party. I told them no because I — I'd just rather hang with you."

For a second, I half-consider convincing David to come to Julia's party. It physically hurts me to tell Alex no. I'm terrified she's going to disappear again.

But I can't. As much as it pains me to decline, I made a promise to David — I have to stop putting everything and everyone before our relationship.

"I know Cory and Georgie said they'd go to Julia's. Mitch, too, I think."

"Yeah, but you know I can't bear Julia without you."

We chuckle, and, for an instant, our old camaraderie comes back.

I want to cling to it and never let go. Anything to go back to the way things used to be. Anything to get my best friend back.

"Um. Well, happy New Year, then." Alex's voice is soft and raw, the way it gets whenever she feels vulnerable.

The sound of it tugs at my heartstrings. I feel like I've ruined everything again. I close my eyes and hope with all I've got things will get better — go back to the way they were.

"Happy New Year, honey."

¤

Midnight rings and somewhere, far away, a ball drops. I pause the movie and turn to face David. He cradles my face between his hands. He stares at me with so much love in his eyes, discovering me all over again. That's what tonight is all about: getting back together. We eat a nice, long dinner, talking for hours around the fondue pot about nothing and everything. We make resolutions for the New Year. David wants to undertake a new photography project.

"I'm sick of weddings and graduations, you know? I want to make art! I'm thinking of buying underwater gear for a special series."

"Ooh, I love underwater photography — it always looks so magical."

"I want to make a series of diverse mermaids. Like, mermaids of different genders, ethnicities, body types, that kind of thing." David shrugs and pours himself some more wine, as though it was no big deal.

"This is amazing! It's everything I never knew I wanted, seriously."

David chuckles. "I know this girl from school, she's a costume designer and she already has a few mermaid tails — enough to start the series. I'll have to find someone else for the rest, though."

"I'm sure Charlotte would love to help you! She's only been in fashion design for a semester, but you know how good a seamstress she is."

David nods pensively, a smile slowly growing across his face.

"Will you be my first mermaid?"

"Are you serious?"

"I can just see this gorgeous red mane floating in the current..." David trails off, burying a hand through my hair. The look in his eyes says 'I don't know if I want to take your picture or just take you.'

After dinner, we take a bath together, enjoying each other's presence, remembering all the reasons we fell in love. Bundled in our warmest pyjamas, we settle under a blanket to watch Christmas movies.

When I kiss David at midnight, he feels like home. I can almost hear my heart sigh in bliss. I pull him closer. His body fits perfectly against mine; I lose myself in this perfect embrace, this reminder that we are meant for each other.

Will Ferrell and Zooey Deschanel are frozen mid-skate on the television screen, completely forgotten as David picks me up and carries me to our bedroom to ring in the New Year perfectly.

As David climaxes, he reminds me how much he loves me, over and over. I make a silent promise to myself that I'll never let things fall so low between us again. I'll always make time for us.

TWENTY-ONE

"So… I met a guy at Quarante-Cinq's Christmas party!"

"By 'met' do you mean 'fucked'?" Cory asks me.

"Ooh, this is gonna be good! Jen, I'm taking my break!" Mitch calls to her coworker. She takes off her apron and sits with us. "Okay, I'm ready. Spill."

"Well, his name is Benoit and he's a band manager who comes in all the time with new records. I never saw him before because he usually comes by at night, but we've flirted a lot over the phone. Jude said he's asked a lot about me."

"They did?" Georgie asks, surprised. Jude barely ever gossips, so this is, indeed, surprising of them.

I pause to take a sip, and build the suspense, revelling in my friends' eager expressions.

"And?" Cory breaks the silence.

"He's gorgeous, with this urban lumberjack thing going on — man-bun, beard, plaid shirt."

I take another sip, my friends hanging onto my every word. "Oh, and he's amazing in bed," I add, almost as an afterthought.

"I knew it!" Mitch exclaims. "You had that look on your face you get when you hook up with someone new."

"What look?"

"I don't know, you get this kind of — glow?" She looks at Georgie, who nods in approval. "Like you just made an amazing discovery or something."

I'm pretty sure at this point I'm beet-red. I take a sip of tea, fiddling with the teabag string to avoid answering.

"Don't be ashamed, girl," Cory says, "it's adorable."

Georgie furrows his brow. "Didn't David come with you to the party? Did you just ditch him?"

"He left early — you know how he is with parties, he mostly came for the free food."

"True. He and Jude demolished the buffet."

"So, will you see Benoit again?" Mitch asks.

"Try and stop me."

¤

I don't have to wait very long for my phone to light up with his name — Benoit Fortin. He asks me on a date: dinner and a comedy show. Points for originality!

On Friday, I put on my cutest green dress and hurry up to meet him at the subway station near the Thai restaurant he suggested. Benoit beams when he sees me, as though I'm the prettiest sight his eyes had ever seen — even all bundled up against the January weather, with my Ravenclaw scarf and matching earmuffs.

He takes my hand — or actually, he awkwardly holds my big mitten in his big mitten — and we get out in the blizzard, weaving between tall snow banks to reach the restaurant.

"You know what I don't get?" Benoit asks, playing with the corner of his paper placemat once we're seated in a booth. "Why they don't give you crayons in every restaurant. What, just because I have to do my taxes now, means that suddenly I can't draw a superhero while waiting for my food? Ageism."

Benoit says this with a straight face; only a faint glimmer in his eye hints that he's kidding. I crack up. His eyes light up when he realizes we share a similar sense of humour — along with a common love of Thai food.

After dinner, I go to the bathroom, only to discover a few red spots in my underwear. My period came two days early.

Fuck. I was really looking forward to have sex with Ben again tonight. I'm not much of a fan of period sex — especially with someone new. That's why I usually schedule dates around it. It sucks for tonight, but at the rate this date is going, there probably will be a third one, so I've got that to look forward to. I rummage through my purse and sigh in relief when I find a tampon.

Benoit has already paid when I join him. I thank him and insist I'll buy a round of beers at the bar.

The show is great — it's one of these showcase things with several comedians, and most of them are hilarious. I notice Benoit and I laugh at the same jokes. A good sign, if this is to lead to a third date.

Afterwards, Benoit asks me back to his place.

"I had a great night, and I'd love to — in fact, there are *some* things we could do, but — I just got my period. Two days early." I cringe to let him know how much this pisses me off.

Benoit also cringes, although in obvious disgust. "Um, why are you telling me this?"

"So you know we can't — "

"I mean, that's just disgusting! You couldn't make up an excuse?"

"Seriously? You're an adult and you can't hear about menstruations?"

"Don't say that! People are staring!"

People are filing out of the bar, but no one is paying any attention to us.

I raise my voice, delighting in the clear distress in his eyes. "Sure, cause these total strangers couldn't possibly handle hearing about my uterus doing its job! Oh, wait, no, that's just you."

Benoit looks frantically around, his panic increasing by the second. "Will you stop it?" he hisses through his teeth.

"Oh, honey." I look at Benoit with mock empathy. "If you're too immature to hear about my vagina when it bleeds, you're too immature to put your dick in it."

¤

"This is why I don't hook up with people from work. It always ends badly and then you're stuck seeing them every day," Cory says, with a look that says *I told you so*, leaning lazily against Le Trèfle's counter while Mitch pours his coffee.

"You don't hook up with colleagues," I point out, "because you're in a committed, monogamous relationship. And don't give me that look. You were the first one to jump at the news that I met someone."

"And besides," Mitch pipes up from behind the counter, handing Cory his coffee, "it's not as if she'll see him every day; he never comes by during her shifts."

"On the bright side, I got my one bad call of the year out of the way in January, so the rest of the year will be amazing!"

"Hear, hear!" Mitch raises her coffee cup.

TWENTY-TWO

A few weeks later, I get off work around eight — business is slow, so Georgie said he'd be okay to close by himself. I decide to wait for David at a café near the dance studio where he's shooting.

Upon entering, I immediately notice the very cute barista wiping the counter wearily. He looks up when he hears the door closing behind me. The café is empty — eight-thirty on a windy February Wednesday; he must be as busy as we were back at Quarante-Cinq.

"*Bonjour* — Hi!" he greets me.

"Hey, can I get a tall Earl Grey, please?"

"To go?" he asks, his hand hovering wishfully near the ceramic mugs.

Why not? He's super cute, with his almost white bleached hair, cropped on the sides, but messy on top — striking against his black uniform apron. We're both bored and David won't be done for like an hour.

I flash him my brightest smile — the one that says 'I want to get to know you' — and perch myself on the nearest stool. "For here."

His bored frown turns into a smile and we end up chatting away for the better part of an hour. Turns out he went to art school with Alex and he's working on a series of sculptures.

My phone chimes up with a text from David saying he's almost done. I start gathering my stuff and drain the last of my tea.

"Your boyfriend?" he asks, trying too hard to be casual.

I nod and his smile falters. He grabs a nearby broom and starts to turn away, but I reach across the counter to put a hand on his shoulder. He turns to face me. I lean in close and stare into his eyes.

"I'm in an open relationship."

His eyes widen as it dawns on him. "I'm off at ten."

"Well, I have to meet him, but here's my number."

I reach for the pen sticking out of his apron pocket, scribble my number on a napkin, and walk away. I'm not even two steps out the door when it hits me. I hurry back inside.

"I don't even know your name!"

"Vince." He beams at me.

"Amy."

"I'll call you, Amy."

¤

Vince and I text back and forth for a week before he invites me to the vernissage of his friend Lola's exhibition. I don't know much about art, but from what I've learned with Alex and David, I'm able to follow Vince's conversations with his fellow artists and critics.

After three hours of Vince theorizing and networking, and me eating more hors-d'oeuvres than I can count to avoid making an ass of myself by bullshitting about stuff I don't know, Vince finally suggests we leave. We have a glass or two at a nearby wine bar before he invites me back to his place. The thought of connecting with him on a physical level after all these discussions about abstract art is so welcome, I almost shout, 'oh, thank god!' out loud.

I agree, maybe a bit too enthusiastically, but the bright smile he offers in response makes it all worth it. I trail a hand through his tousled hair and it really is as soft as it looks. I pull him towards me and give him the gentlest kiss, calculated to leave him wanting more. A glint lights up in his eye, telling me it worked like a charm.

His place is a fifth-story walk-up studio. One huge room stuffed wall-to-wall with sculpting supplies and half-finished pieces. A bed occupies the corner closest to a door I assume must lead to the bathroom.

"Beer?" Vince asks, moving an easel blocking access to the fridge.

"Please."

We sit down on his bed — literally the only surface not housing some kind of work-in-progress. We sip our beer and he tells me the story behind some of the pieces displayed around us.

He looks so passionate about his art, I can't help being interested, even if I've heard enough about abstract art tonight to last me a decade. He talks animatedly about a wood and steel structure perched on a cinder block next to the bed. He explains his process, getting so excited about it he completely forgets he's holding a beer. He gestures haphazardly, painting me a mental picture of him trying to get the cinder block up the five flights of stairs, when his beer sloshes in the bottle and most of it ends up on my shirt.

"Oh, shit!" he exclaims, looking around for a towel and a place to put his beer down.

He finally hands me a paint-splattered rag and sets his beer precariously on an easel, among various bottles of paint and other chemicals. I put mine on the floor next to the bed.

"I'm so sorry," he says as I pat my shirt dry with the cleanest corner of the rag.

"You know what? It doesn't matter." I give him a seductive smile and start unbuttoning my top. I shrug it off and hang it on yet another easel — maybe it'll have time to dry off while we're otherwise occupied.

I turn to face Vince and slowly stalk towards him, hoping I don't smell too much like a bar mat. As I approach him, I undo the zipper of my skirt and shimmy out of it, drawing it out until Vince can't take it anymore. He stands up and pulls me to him. I push him to a seating position and straddle him, feeling very much like a lap dancer in my underwear and high heels.

The thought sends a jolt of excitement along my spine. I press myself closer against Vince. His grey eyes are clouded with arousal. He cradles his hands in the arch of my back, raising goose bumps down my sides.

A low growl rumbles down Vince's throat. He captures my lips between his, shallow breaths mixing together in harmony. The rest of our clothing discarded in a hurry, we lay entwined on the bed, hastily trying to touch, to see, to taste everything at once.

"I need you," I moan desperately into his mouth.

Vince pulls away to rummage in his bedside table. I nestle against his back, the lack of touch excruciating. I pepper kisses up and down his spine, while he tears open a condom wrapper. I trail my fingers across his pale expanses of skin, but I can feel he's distant. He grumbles under his voice and it seems like he's fiddling with something. Kneeling behind him, I peek over his shoulder.

"Need some help?"

Vince defensively folds over himself, but I can see what the problem is. He's struggling to put the condom on because his dick is limp. I snake a hand around his waist to take care of it.

After a few minutes, the situation is still, to put it plainly, flat. Vince pushes my hand away and starts in on himself, in frenzied, violent strokes. His shoulders are squared, closed off. Arousal is absent from his face, replaced by an angry determination.

"Maybe I could — "

"Oh, shut up!" Vince pushes me away and I fall to the mattress.

Without a word, I gather my clothes and get dressed. I pull on my pumps and retrieve my purse.

"What are you doing?" Vince demands, still pulling hard at his limp dick.

The only answer he gets is the slam of the door.

¤

"Two bad calls in a year? Or worse, a month? What the hell?"

"This might not mean anything, *chaton*," David tries to reassure me.

"I might be losing my superpower," I sigh, hamming up the dramatics.

"Well, you still have your other superpower," he says.

"Which is?"

"Making me happy," he answers with a smug grin.

"Oh my *god*, you're so corny, gross."

He feeds me a bite of risotto while my mouth is ajar in what could be either awe or incredulity at his dorkiness.

"So anyway, enough about my lame-ass hook-ups, what's up with you?"

A smile creeps up on David's face and he tries to hide it by being engrossed with the wine bottle on the table.

"I was right about the new boundaries helping me. I — I made a connexion with someone. They're amazing and we're having a lot of fun."

"They?" David has only ever been with girls before. He doesn't identify as straight because he says the potential for attraction to multiple genders is very much present, but it hadn't happened yet.

The wine bottle seems increasingly interesting and a blush creeps up on David's cheeks. I rest a hand over his on the table.

"Hey. You can tell me, kitten. I swear I won't judge you."

David finally meets my eye and he looks thrilled, but scared, like you do when you have a really nice secret and you're afraid letting it out might ruin it.

"It's — you know them."

My eyebrows knit together as I'm racking my brain. Is he using *they* pronouns because he's scared of admitting it's a guy, or is he actually talking about someone with this set of pronouns?

All of a sudden, a memory comes back — something I had never paid attention to at the time.

Quarante-Cinq's holiday party — me letting lose on the dance floor with Georgie and Cory, making eyes at Benoit. In a corner, very much interested in *not dancing*, David and Jude in an animated conversation. It seemed unimportant at the time — I was just happy David wasn't alone and brooding, like he is at most parties.

"Jude?" I ask in a small voice, unsure what my emotions are doing at the moment, but trying my hardest not to rain on David's parade.

David nods, not quite able to hide the smile creeping up on his face.

"At the holiday party?" I ask.

"Well, I always felt some kind of connexion with them — we always bonded over not liking parties, and our shared interest in photography — but I never allowed myself to explore it. I felt like this connexion deserved so much more than a hook-up. So, now that you and I expanded our boundaries, I decided to give it a try."

I nod to urge him to keep talking, speechless.

"We... went on a few — I guess you could call them dates? We go to interesting places with our cameras and photograph each other at the same time — some sort of reverse point of view thing, you know? And, well — we made out a few times."

My eyes widen and my voice comes out all strangled. "A few times?"

David looks down at his plate, pushing his last few asparagus bits around on his plate, avoiding my eye.

"I know — I should have told you sooner, but." He sighs and looks up at me. "There's no good reason to break our rules, I know. I got carried away — I wanted to see where this led in case it ended up being a fluke. I was scared you'd get jealous, since they're your coworker and — ya know, I usually hook up with people you don't know."

Damn, he knows me well.

I *am* jealous.

It's so much harder to be level-headed and accepting about this when I know the person — when I can picture them together. If I'm honest with myself, I'm also a bit pissed at him for not telling me about it for — what, a month since the party? — and breaking our arrangement.

I realize I've broken the rules several times myself, and thus have no right to be pissed about it, but it's no use to try and be rational about this — my emotions are shitty fuckers and wrangling them is a full-time job.

I take a deep breath, trying to school my features in an agreeable, pleased-for-him expression. I can't say anything about my jealousy or any of these bad feelings creeping up. The thing is, David has made so many compromises, so many sacrifices for this relationship — changing the rules on my every whim — I can't be anything but a hundred percent supportive of this.

My heartbeat quickens and my hands start sweating as thoughts whirl through my head like a hurricane. What would David and Jude think of me if I said I'm not happy with this? They'd probably both think I'm a selfish, possessive bitch, and David would leave me for them. And Jude would probably leave Quarante-Cinq because they hate me.

So I plaster a smile on my face, wipe my hands on my jeans, and look up at David. "Hey, it's okay. I'm happy for you."

A blatant lie.

David's eyes light up. "Yeah? Even though I broke the rules?"

"I've broken them plenty of times myself," I say with a mirthless chuckle.

Of course, he sees right through me — and has the gall to look compassionate and understanding, because obviously *he's* the good person in this relationship. God, it's so hard to stay mad at someone who's so much nicer and more rational than I am.

He lays a hand on mine on the table, eyes all soft and sweet, searching for the glimmer of truth in my eyes. "You're anxiety-spiralling right now, aren't you?"

I give the tiniest nod.

"Hey, you don't have to pretend — it's me. It's okay if it's bothering you, we'll talk through it."

I let out a long sigh and hide my face in my hands. "Why can't you just let me save face and be a terrible person all by myself?"

"Amy. You're not a terrible person. You're amazing."

I scoff. "Would an amazing person be jealous that you found someone you're really enjoying?"

"Amy, you're human. Jealousy is a human emotion. We're not trying to eradicate it — I get jealous too, sometimes — we just want to communicate so it doesn't control us."

"I just — did you know I've never experienced compersion? They say it's amazing and it makes all of it so much easier, but — what if I can't do it? What if I'm just stuck between kinda jealous and kinda okay with it?"

"Well, you never got many occasions to experience it, did you? I mostly had hook-ups, it's not like I formed fulfilling connexions that were making me really happy. Not like Jude."

I crack a tiny smile. He beams when he says their name, and, okay, that's nice.

"You guys are having fun?" I ask, because I can't get un-jealous if I'm not exposed to it.

He lets out a breathy chuckle. "Yeah. So much. I mean — we haven't had sex yet, but — um — we sexted a lot? I wanted to talk to you first before taking the leap."

"Oh." This is new — not only David waiting to hook up with someone, but most importantly, I had never thought of Jude in a sexual context before? I mean, they're just a coworker — this is a bit weird.

"How do you feel?" David asks. "I really wanna know, be honest with me."

"Mostly weird? I — you look so happy, I really can't be mad about that. But, I mean — it's Jude."

"Yeah, I get that. I felt the same when you started hooking up with Hugo. I know he was your friend first, but, I mean, I play D&D with the guy, I didn't really wanna think of him screwing you."

"Yeah, I guess that's true. What did you do to get over it?"

"I stopped thinking about it in terms of him screwing you and more in terms of my girlfriend is having a lot of fun with a good friend, and they're making each other happy."

"That makes sense. I mean, Jude is super cool so I can imagine you'd have fun with them…"

David nods, still beaming. "Wanna see the pics we took?"

"David!" I exclaim, mock-scandalized.

"Not *that* kind of pics, you heathen. The series we started."

"Sure!"

David pulls up a folder on his phone. "Jude sent theirs last night."

I swipe through a bunch of pictures, all of David with his camera, in different settings: a park, a bridge, a graffitied alley. On the first ones, he's in deep concentration, looking through the viewfinder of his camera to take a picture of Jude while they photograph him. As I swipe through, I can see a change in David. With every picture, he looks a bit happier, more carefree. By the end, he's not even looking through his camera anymore. He's captured mid-laugh, relaxed, a look of fondness and trust on his face.

He looks so happy, so right where he's supposed to be, my heart gives a squeeze.

But not a jealous one.

I realize I'm beaming.

I look up at David. "Dude, I think I'm compersing so hard right now."

"You are?" He grins in disbelief.

I point at the phone. "Look at you, so happy!"

He nods, a look in his eye like he's reminiscing. "Yeah, that was a fun day."

I take his hand. "Okay, you need to go see Jude right now. You're so smitten."

He kisses my knuckles. "Tomorrow. Tonight, I'm just yours."

TWENTY-THREE

Bundled up against the violent February blizzard, I walk as slowly as I can without actually freezing to death. I'm dreading going into work — my first shift with Jude since David and I had our big talk. I can't help thinking it'll be awkward as hell, no matter how much compersion I felt over the weekend. I walk into Quarante-Cinq to find Jude surrounded by mountains of cardboard boxes.

"Oh, thank god you're here. All the deliveries scheduled for tomorrow arrived this morning — they all wanted to beat the storm. I never thought 'death by CD avalanche' would be how I'd go, but I guess this is it."

Jude has always had a flair for the dramatic.

"At least the storm scared off customers so we won't be bothered."

And at least we'll be too busy for things to get awkward.

I come back after punching in, box cutter in hand, and start in on the closest box without a glance at the label. A pair of striking, familiar blue eyes stares at me from the sleeve of the album I pull from the box.

I almost drop the whole carton.

The J-Walkers have launched their first LP. And it's now in my hands.

I'm frozen in place, unable to set down the record or even look away from Jeff's gorgeous smile.

Seeing his face again, while I'm still waiting to hear from him, is excruciating. Thousands of cracks tear at my heart, knowing he might never contact me again. Maybe he just decided he wants nothing to do with me.

Before I know it, tears are rolling down my face. Unable to stop it, I begin sobbing loudly.

"Sweetie, what's the matter?" Jude emerges from behind a pile of crates and opens their arms wide.

I let them wrap me in a warm hug, my hands still clutching the album.

"It's just — an ex," I manage to get out between hiccupy sobs. They rub my back soothingly.

"Shh, let it out."

"I — I just wasn't ready to see his face today. I didn't know his album was out."

I take a deep breath and they hand me a tissue. "I'll be okay. I just — can you take care of this box?"

"Sure thing," they say with a compassionate smile, trading me the box of records for the box of tissues.

"Hey, Jude? Thanks. I'm — I'm glad you're with David. I thought things would be weird here, but…"

"Amy you were my friend and coworker first. You know I would back the hell away rather than doing anything that would make things awkward between us."

"God, you're incredible. I'm gonna have to tell David he did a great job choosing you," I say, wiping my tears dry.

"I mean, same."

I look at the album still clutched tight in my hands. Before I change my mind, I slap a twenty on the counter and ask Jude to ring it up.

I probably won't have the strength to listen to it, but I can't not buy it.

TWENTY-FOUR

Two weeks later, Georgie throws Cory a big bash for his twenty-fifth birthday. Their small apartment overflows with their friends and Cory's coworkers and classmates.

David and I manage to weave our way through the partygoers to hug the birthday boy. I find him with Mitch and Hugo, mixing drinks in the kitchen.

"Amy!" Hugo exclaims. He raises the shaker at me. "Sex on the Beach?"

"Or wherever, you know me." I wink and Mitch groans.

Hugo pours the drinks and we toast to Cory.

"Now, if you don't mind," Hugo says, pulling David by his sleeve, "I'm gonna steal your boyfriend. The rest of our D&D party is here and we have to talk about the next campaign. Georgie, man, you in?" He calls over his shoulder and Georgie nods.

"Can I come with? I wanna make a character!" Mitch shoots me an apologetic glance and follows the boys to Georgie's office.

I turn to Cory and raise my plastic cup. "To D&D widows!"

He laughs and drinks with me. Soon a group of his work friends join us with a bottle of birthday cake-flavoured vodka. Half of them sing "Happy Birthday", while the others chant "Shots! Shots! Shots!"

I retreat to the living room — the last time flavoured vodka was involved, I ended up sleeping with Alex and screwing up our friendship. Which reminds me that I haven't seen her again since Christmas. Everyone's been busy so we haven't done anything with all the gang. I thought it'd be too awkward to be alone with her, so I didn't ask, and neither did she. Our only interactions are likes and comments on Instagram. I thought she'd be here tonight, but she had to work.

"Penny for your thoughts?"

I snap back out of my mind to find a short brunette standing right in front of me.

"Sorry, I was just..." I trail off and shrug.

"In a galaxy far, far away?"

"Something like that." I chuckle. "Amy." I raise my cup.

"Katie." She taps her bottle of beer against my drink.

After the obligatory 'get to know you' small talk — she goes to school with Cory and they met in a biology class, works in a toy store, lives on the South Shore — she leans in and asks point blank:

"So, you're bisexual, right?"

I sputter and Sex on the Beach almost comes out of my nose. I'm confident and open about my sexuality — well, outside my family — but it's quite unexpected when a stranger straight up asks this within ten minutes of meeting me.

"Yeah, how did you — "

"Oh, I didn't guess — Cory told me I should talk to you when I came to him with… questions? About myself."

"Oh! Right. Sure, I'd love to help you out."

Katie rests a hand on my forearm, and for a split second I can feel my skin goose bumping under her touch — there might be something here.

"A party might not be the best place to discuss this," I point out. "Do you maybe want to go for a drink this week?"

"I'd love to!" She grins and presses a soft kiss to my cheek, right at the corner of my mouth — a bold move for a girl who's supposedly just 'questioning', I can't help but notice.

David is helping me into my winter coat when the front door opens and I find myself face- to-face with none other than Alex Bell.

"Hey," she says, in a tone that's half-glad and half-taken aback. "You're leaving?"

I can't tell whether she's sad or relieved.

"Yeah, David has an early shoot in the morning."

"Bummer."

I used to be able to read straight through her thickest façades, and now? I have no idea whatsoever how she's feeling. I don't want to show how much that affects me. I want our friendship to go back to the way it was, so I stick a smile on my face.

"Hey, there'll be plenty of occasions to see each other, right?" I open my arms and we share a split-second cursory greeting hug. Refusing to dwell on how awkward this is, I plaster on another grin and say goodbye to everyone.

I can't help but notice David being uncharacteristically cold towards Alex. He has trouble trusting anyone who has hurt me. I feel both a surge of affection towards him and a wave of melancholia that this is the state of my friendship with Alex. Trying to hang on to someone who has hurt me, who is barely more than a stranger to me now, without being able to let go. I refuse to lose this friendship once more.

¤

On Thursday, I meet Katie for drinks at La Brunante. I can't help noticing how good she looks — that silky black dress is definitely too dressed up for casual drinks that are not a date — or is that just wishful thinking?

Calm down, girl. You are here to answer her questions about sexual orientation. You're supposed to be Queer Yoda! Yoda didn't train Luke by trying to get into his pants.

Ew. Now that image is stuck in my head.

We have a few beers and chat a bit, before I finally decide to breach the subject.

"So, you said you had questions?"

"Well, not questions so much as a general curiosity, you know? Nothing that won't be answered tonight." She winks and drags a fingertip up and down my arm.

Alright, so that wasn't just wishful thinking on my part, then. I give her an encouraging smile.

"Tom is so excited about tonight," she continues. "It's his birthday gift, you know?"

My smile falters. "What is?"

"Well, you," she answers matter-of-factly. "The three of us."

"I'm sorry?"

"A threesome," she stage-whispers, looking around to make sure no one heard.

"You think I'm gonna have a threesome with you and your boyfriend?" I shake her finger off my arm.

"Isn't that why we're here?"

"I never even met him."

"But you're bisexual!"

I let out a long, exhausted sigh. Not this again.

"One," I start, counting on my fingers, "bi people are not automatically up for threesomes. Two, we don't sleep with anyone indiscriminately. We do have standards. Three, I like to meet someone at least once before agreeing to sleep with them. Goodnight."

I grab my coat and leave. Katie doesn't need a Queer Yoda. She needs a whole Jedi Council of Common Sense.

¤

"Seriously, dude?"

Cory raises his palms up defensively. "Amy, I'm so sorry! The truth is, I really don't know Katie that well. When she said she had questions about orientation, I just told her to talk to you at the party. I had no idea she'd go all creepy unicorn-hunter on you."

I sigh and take a long sip of tea. "S'alright. I just don't know how I didn't see it coming. This is my third bad call of the year, guys, and it's only February!"

"Wow, your radar's way off this year, huh?" Mitch notes, wiping the counter around the register.

"I just wish I'd stop meeting immature jerks."

"Here's to meeting mature non-jerks!" Cory raises his coffee cup.

TWENTY-FIVE

"Good morning!"

An unexpected, familiar voice greets me as I enter the café. I look up to see Alex beaming at me behind the counter.

"Hey! What are you doing here this early? "

"I switched shifts with Mitch — she's covering for me tonight."

"Oh. Do you have a — a date, or something?"

Alex's smile falters. "No, um — I just wanted to see you. You know, we couldn't talk properly at the party."

At that very moment, the door opens and in comes a gaggle of loud students. Alex glances at me, eyebrows raised in apology. She and her coworker get working, and soon the students file out of the shop, lattes in hand.

Alex sighs. "Maybe this isn't the right place to talk either."

We share a chuckle and it feels good — almost as if nothing had changed.

"So, did you want something?" Alex asks.

"Uh?"

"Coffee?"

For a moment there, I completely forgot I was on my morning coffee run. Seeing Alex was completely unexpected.

"Oh, right. A tall London Fog to go, please. Oh, and a double espresso for Jude."

"Oh, I haven't seen them in ages! I should come by the store sometime."

"Yeah, that would be great!" I sound so fake. She was my best friend and I don't even know how to talk to her anymore.

"So, what have you been up to?" she asks as she starts on the drinks.

"Not much. Mostly work."

Jeff. Hugo. Benoit and the others, I recall with a shudder.

My heart tightens. I can't talk about them to Alex. Not now, anyway. It would be like pouring salt on a wound. Like saying *Hey, remember how we can't be together? Here are all the people that have no problem fucking me, even though I have a boyfriend!*

"Cool," Alex says, as if we were mere acquaintances. Strangers who make small talk about work because they have nothing in common.

The thought breaks me. I can barely bring myself to look at her when she hands me my to-go cups. Another group of students comes in, saving me from having to find something else to say.

"I'm gonna be late for work," I call above the students' heads, leaving a ten dollar bill on the counter.

I walk out, tears filling my eyes. I was glad, relieved, when she came back, but now I wonder if our friendship is ever going to

be the same again. I can't bring it up to her, though — I couldn't
bear to see her leave again.

¤

I learned how to polish precious wood before I learned
how to count.

I know what that sounds like — it's actually because
Charlotte and I spent our childhood helping my parents around
the antiques shop. A lot of that time was spent dusting and, well,
polishing wood.

To this day, the smell of furniture polish and mahogany
still feels like home, just as much as Mom's fabric softener or
Dad's minestrone soup.

I'm spending the afternoon of my twenty-fifth birthday
helping Dad around the shop, and it doesn't even feel like work.
He's showing me how to repair an antique Tiffany lamp and
cracking jokes, and it feels like old times.

"You know, I wanted to name you Tiffany, but Geneviève
wouldn't have it."

"I'm not naming my kid after an 80's popstar, honey."
Mom rolls her eyes as she walks in from the front of the shop.

"It's not a popstar, it's a famous lamp — because our baby
will shine bright over the world."

"I can't believe it's twenty-five years later and we're still
having this discussion."

"It feels like only yesterday." Dad sets his screwdriver
down and takes Mom's hand to kiss it.

The copper bell hung above the front door rings and a few seconds later, Charlotte walks in the storeroom. "Ugh. Are Mom and Dad being disgustingly in love again?"

"You betcha," Dad says. "Divorcing is too much paperwork so we just decided to stay in love instead." He chuckles at his own joke, like he hasn't been telling it for the past twenty years.

Charlotte and Mom look at each other like at the camera in *The Office* — they refuse to show it, but I know they love Dad's jokes.

"So anyway," Charlotte says, putting on her cajoling face Dad has never been able to resist. "Can I have the big walnut dresser for when I move out?" She nods towards the front of the store.

"It's — pretty expensive, honey," Mom says.

"Pleeeease? It would be my housewarming gift?"

"Well, we *have* had it for a long time and nobody wants to buy it… I'll see what I can do, Char-ming." I know when Dad uses her childhood nickname that means he's sold.

"Well, *I'm* not helping you move this behemoth up to the third floor."

Char sticks her tongue out at me. Very mature.

The more I hang out with her as an adult, the more I notice just how much she's changed and grown up — she's constantly surprising me — but there are still moments like this where she goes back to being my immature baby sister who can drive me up the wall.

Comforting, in a way.

¤

"Happy birthday, *chaton*."

David beams at me over his menu. I feel so lucky — a gorgeous caring boyfriend, sake, and my favourite sushi restaurant. I couldn't ask for anything more. Well, there *is* one little thing…

Between two bites of sashimi, I put on my most endearing puppy face. "Sure you don't wanna go out with us tomorrow night? Everybody'll be there!"

"Amy, you know I hate clubs. Too loud, too crowded, drinks cost fifteen bucks… Nah, you go and have fun."

I pout for good measure, even though we both know it's no use — in all the years I've known him, I think he went clubbing twice.

"Fine," I say with an exaggerated sigh, "but I'm gonna miss you."

"You won't have time to miss me, *chaton*, — you'll be neck deep in drag queens on the dance floor."

"…fair enough."

¤

"What do you think I should wear tonight?"

"Um, I don't know?" Mitch hesitates on the phone. "Your new striped dress?"

"It's way too sexy!" I comb through my closet, hoping the perfect outfit will somehow jump out at me.

"Don't you usually dress kinda sexy when we go out?"

"Yeah, but Alex is gonna be there!"

"So?"

"I don't wanna tease her, you know, since she's got feelings for me? And I don't want to look like I'm there to flirt with other people either. Since the subject of hook-ups is still… delicate around her."

"Yeah, you're right. Maybe like a nice top and tight jeans? Cute, but not too revealing?"

"Yeah, maybe."

We go back and forth, trying to decide on an outfit. I rifle through my jewellery box, looking for accessories to go with my top, when I fish out something I haven't seen in months. My breath catches in my throat.

"Mitch? I have to go — see you later."

A rush of emotions washes over me, forcing me to sit down on my bed. I unclench my fist to take a closer look. Two tiny copper feathers.

Jeff's earrings.

They were hidden at the bottom of my jewellery box ever since he gave them to me. Looking at them hurt too much. They were nothing but a reminder of how bad I fucked up.

I still think of him. It still hurts. But as I lost hope he'd ever come back in my life, I forgot about the earrings.

Should I wear them tonight?

I hold one against my ear in front of the mirror, to see how they look. I shake my head, eyes filling with tears. I put them back in the box, as a promise and one last shred of hope.

He will come back, and I will get the chance to wear them.

Friday night, La Pharmacie. We used to do this all the time: Alex, Mitch, Cory, Georgie, Julia and I. We spent so many nights in our favourite bar, drinking, chatting, dancing, and watching the drag queens' show. That was before Alex disappeared. The rest of us tried going out again, but her absence was like a hole we couldn't fill, no matter how many drinks we ordered, how many drag queens we saw.

She's back now, but everything's changed. I miss our old friendship — the way it was so affectionate, almost intimate. There are so many fences between us now — unspoken obstacles to going back. I'm hoping tonight might change that. It's my birthday and I think the familiar setting might help us step back into the good old days. The only one missing is Julia. We've barely seen her recently, and, when we do, she always finds an excuse to go back to Jason as soon as possible. I didn't think she'd miss my birthday, though. She and I have been to every single one of our birthdays since we were seven, I recall with a disappointed sigh.

Alex calls a round of shots — apologetic or celebratory, I don't know, but the gesture is nice. She invites the shot girl in drag to drink one with us and they all sing "Happy birthday" to me as I turn beet red.

"Guys, I have the best news," Mitch announces. "My parents are going back to the Philippines to see Mom's family this summer. They won't use their cabin in Gaspésie this year, so I'm free to use it as I want!"

"Roadtrip!" Cory calls, raising his glass.

We all raise our glasses, cheering.

Mitch gives us some details and we agree to plan further when we're not actively getting drunk.

A hand squeezes my shoulder and I turn around to find Hugo beaming at me.

"Happy birthday!"

"Thanks!" I pull him into a hug. "What are you doing here?"

"Mitch invited me! Couldn't miss it!"

"Mitch! I had no idea! Any other surprises?"

She shrugs, an elusive smile on her face. "Just one more. You'll see."

"So," Cory says, "what's up?" He's got his gossip-hungry face on.

Alex and I look at each other as we realize this is the point of the night where we would usually dish on who slept with whom.

Don't look at Hugo, don't look! my brain screams.

Everyone at the table falls silent. The awkwardness is palpable. Out of the corner of my eye, I notice Hugo standing up.

"Beer, anyone?" He looks inquisitively at everyone around the table. "A pitcher? Good."

I let out a relieved breath.

Cory clears his throat and leans in conspiratorially.

"Guys. I slept with… Georgie!" he stage-whispers.

We all gasp at the fake gossip.

"How was it?" Mitch presses.

"Way better than with my boyfriend." He winks at Georgie, who slides an arm around his shoulders.

"You're an idiot."

"Yeah, but I'm your idiot."

"Alright, let's dance!" Alex jumps off her seat.

Loving couples probably aren't her favourite thing to watch right now. I follow her on the dance floor, not out of a big desire to dance, but mostly to give our friendship a chance. I figure I should stick with her, lest she treats us to another of her disappearing acts. I force myself to smile. I shouldn't think like that — I should just be happy she's here. Now isn't the time to be angry.

Luckily, it's way easier to reconnect while dancing than when trying to talk. We don't have to find the right words to say, we can just dance our hearts out like we used to.

A familiar beat comes on and our eyes meet. "I Don't Do Boys". We used to *love* this song and play it on loop while throwing impromptu dance parties in her bedroom. We throw our arms in the air and let out a whoop. She takes my hand and makes me twirl. I feel a rush of affection for her. I can't believe I almost lost her.

Alex notices me getting misty-eyed and pulls me into a hug. "Hey. I know I can never erase what I did, but I'm sorry. I truly am. Don't cry, babe."

The familiar pet name pulls a sob out of me. I missed it so much.

"Look, it's like we're slow dancing." She's right; the song is fast-paced, but we're swaying in the middle of the dance floor, locked in a tender embrace. I let out a chuckle and wipe away my tears.

"Sorry. I guess I'm a bit drunk."

"Don't worry about it. It's your party and you'll cry if you want to."

"Thanks." I take her hand and make her twirl. The smile on her face is contagious and soon we're kidding around in the middle of the bar like we used to. Our friends join us when they finish their drinks and we party like in the good old days.

Suddenly, Mitch starts beaming and I hear a familiar voice shouting "Wooh! That's my jam!"

I barely have time to turn around before Charlotte slams into me for a hug.

"Surprise! Happy birthday, sis!"

"Oh my god, hi! I'm so glad you came!"

As the night wears on, I notice Charlotte dancing closer and closer to Hugo. When Mitch introduced them, Char had that look on her face that screams 'smitten' — the same one she had back in high school, just before some guy broke her heart for the first time.

Hugo, ever the laid-back guy who likes everyone, indulges her by dancing with her — but I notice he stops her when she tries to grind with him. At the end of the night, they share a cab — she's spending the night at a friend's place so she doesn't have to pay the cab all the way to our parents' in the suburbs.

Mitch, who lives three blocks away from Hugo, manages to cram herself in their cab. She sends me a text the next day:

Michelle Murray — Hugo & Char went home separately, but there was definite tension between them.

Huh.

¤

My friends and I spend the next month in a frenzy of texts, trying to find two weeks when the five of us are all available to go on holiday. The hardest thing is to manage to get Georgie and I off work at the same time, since we work together and the shop is quite understaffed right now, but, with promises of overtime when we come back, we make it work.

"Would it be okay if I went away for two weeks without you this summer?" I ask David when a few of the details are settled.

"How come?"

"Mitch has got her parents' cabin for the summer, so we're talking of going for two weeks in June, but it would be a no-boyfriend kind of deal."

"Oh, absolutely," David says to my surprise. I felt kind of guilty leaving him alone in Montreal — we usually travel together. "Actually, June is gonna be a big month for me — I have like six weddings booked, and my mermaid project is really coming together. Oh, and Jason wanted to throw a D&D weekend soon, so it's good that the house will be empty."

"Oh, I'm so glad! I felt bad leaving you here alone."

"Don't think I won't miss you, though. Jason is not much of a cuddler."

TWENTY-SIX

Somehow, Cory's wish from last month got granted. Well, the mature part, anyway — jury's still out to determine if that one's a jerk.

I meet Marc, a 38-year-old lawyer, two weeks later, at a bar. He asks me out for drinks and I gladly accept. His age and classic good looks are the main reasons. He looks smooth as a fifties crooner — he's got some Dean Martin perfect hair and flawless smile thing going on, and a sort of raw magnetism I can't help falling for. Since he's older, I'm hoping he'll be more mature than Benoit, Vince or Katie. At the very least, if he's a jerk, I'll get a free drink and a good story out of it.

We meet in a high-class place — the kind of place called *lounge* instead of *bar*, where drinks cost more than most of my meals. I let him pay, partly because he looks like the kind of man that would argue, if I tried otherwise, and partly because if he chose the place, he can clearly afford it — whereas I can't.

Marc orders scotch older than me, in a smooth, warm voice that makes me feel tingly as if I'd already drank two of them. He sits close to me, turning his back to the rest of the room, like nothing else matters. He speaks in a low voice, so I have to lean in to hear what he says. He looks straight into my eyes; a velvety, soul-searching look that melts me into a puddle.

I know all his techniques — hell, I've used them all sometime. But flirting isn't like magic shows: you can know all the secrets, all the tips, and it still has an effect on you. That's because you know that, if someone is going to all these lengths, it means they want you.

And that is one of the biggest turn-ons there is.

I play along with all his tricks; I giggle when I'm meant to, let him put his hand ever-so-softly on my thigh, and kiss him just as softly on the cheek when I get up to go to the bathroom.

There's just one thing left to do.

"Marc, I have something to tell you."

He cocks an eyebrow up, interested.

"I'm in an open-relationship. I have a boyfriend, but we're allowed to… explore elsewhere, if you know what I mean."

"That's perfectly fine with me." Marc smiles and runs a hand along my bare arm. "Now what would you say if I asked you to come home with me?"

I smile coyly and toss my hair back. "I'd say I'd love to."

I feel no real connection with Marc. His conversation is vapid at best, but the way he carries himself and looks at me makes me hope for one great night. Sometimes, you just need a good fuck, with no emotional ties whatsoever.

Marc and I ride a cab to his bachelor pad downtown. His phone rings as we get out of the taxi. He takes one look at the screen and pockets it with an exasperated grunt.

"The wife. Why can't she understand a guy needs time for himself? God, she's clingy!"

"You're married?!" I hold the car door open and signal the driver to wait.

"Well, yeah." Marc shrugs it off. Under the glow of the streetlights, I can clearly see a tan line on his ring finger, which I hadn't noticed in the dimly lit lounge.

"Does she know you're with me?"

He laughs, not even looking at me as he tries to unlock his front door. "Sure, I'm just gonna tell her I'm cheating on her."

He manages to unlock the door and holds it open, flashing his patented movie star grin, waiting for me to come inside.

"Yeah, that's not happening anymore."

"What the fuck?" His smooth demeanour is gone. Right now, he just looks like the kind of guy who screams at waitresses in restaurants and sends his plate back thrice. "You mean you just came here to tease me?"

"I mean I won't help you cheat on your wife."

I climb back in the cab.

"You're such a hypocritical bitch. You told me you've got a boyfriend!"

"There's a difference between cheating and open relationships."

"Whatever, slut," is the last thing I hear before the door slams and we speed away from that disgusting individual.

I pull out my phone and instinctively type a text to Alex — she's always been my go-to person when I need to vent about how men are pigs.

I stop myself. My relationship with Alex is still fragile, if not inexistent. I can't tell her about my hook-ups yet. With a wistful sigh, I press Hugo's name instead. I quickly type I need a drink and hope he's not busy.

His answer comes a few minutes later: My set just ended. Wanna come over?

I give his address to the driver and get there before Hugo. I sit down on his front steps and text David to let him know where I'll be. Hugo gets here a few minutes later, case of beer in hand.

"I didn't know if you really needed a drink or if it was just an excuse for a booty call, so I stopped by the store." He chuckles and hugs me with the arm not holding the beer.

"A bit of both, actually." I hug him back.

His face falls; he's worried about me. I made the right choice in coming to see him. He'll talk me through my three months of bad calls, with the necessary distance David and I don't have. David and I share this stuff with no judgment, so he can't really make fun of these dudes, which is what I need right now. Hugo will then expertly rid me of my sexual frustration. He lets me in, takes two cans out of the case and sticks the rest in the fridge. He hands me one and joins me on the couch.

When I get to the part where Benoit freaked out about my period, Hugo lets out an unimpressed chuckle.

"What is he, twelve?"

"More like twenty-three."

"So you dumped his ass?"

"Of course." He clinks his can against mine.

I continue my story with Vince and Katie. Hugo is appropriately offended on my behalf.

"Which brings us to tonight, and my date with this guy Marc."

"Sounds like a douche."

"He is. But I didn't know that at the time. So this guy is older — "

"How old?"

"Thirty-eight. Smooth as fuck, charming, sexy, he brings me to this scotch lounge."

"Fancy," Hugo says, with a pointed look at his can of PBR.

"Yeah, he's a lawyer. So I'm totally charmed, right, and I explain to him that I have a boyfriend, and he's okay with it. But then we get to his place, and he gets a call from his *wife*!"

"Open relationship?"

"Cheater."

"Why am I not surprised?"

"I'm telling you, my radar is messed up lately."

"Well, you know," he nods wisely and takes a sip of beer, "you've gone through a lot of changes, relationship-wise, in the last six months."

I take a long drink from my can and reflect.

Jeff. Alex. Everything started right there. I bite my lip, deep in thought. "Makes sense. Like, everything got unbalanced when Jeff came along. When things weren't just about sex."

"Maybe, unconsciously, you started seeking something different, or you're sending out a different vibe."

"Maybe I'm so desperate for a distraction, I just ignore warning signs."

"You just need a good lay from someone you can trust." Hugo wiggles his eyebrows lewdly.

I swat him playfully. He catches my hand and peppers kisses on it, making his way up my arm, leaning closer and closer to me.

"You're probably right," I whisper, a second before his lips breathlessly press against mine.

TWENTY-SEVEN

Jeff Williams — I miss you…

Jeff's text floors me.

I stare at the screen for a good five minutes, thoughts running wild.

I don't know what to say. I miss him so much it fucking hurts. I've spent the last six months thinking about him. I'm deeply in love with him. I ache to be with him.

But.

I don't know what he wants. Is he ready to accept I have a boyfriend, even though I am wildly in love with him? Why is he texting me?

Because he loves you, stupid! says a voice in my head, but I can't allow myself to hope again.

With a sigh, I finally reply a non-committal, miss you too. I don't want to suggest meeting up, in case he's scared I'm moving too fast — even though it *has* been six months. I'll wait to see what he wants first.

Jeff Williams — Can we go somewhere and talk?

My heart soars. I text him back to accept, rewording the message twelve times before I finally deem it acceptable. We make plans to meet for coffee on Saturday. This means I only have two days to prepare. I need an expert.

Cory answers at the first ring.

"I need fashion advice," I say, in lieu of greetings.

"A date?" I can hear the excitement rising in his voice and I can tell he's already planning outfits in his head.

"Well, that's the thing. I don't know."

"Sweetheart, how can you not know?"

"It's Jeff."

"Oh."

"I mean, he did say he missed me, but he never said the word 'date'. He used the word 'talking'. And last time I saw him I broke his heart."

"It's not a date." Cory's voice is firm, certain.

"How can you possibly know this? I mean — "

"Oh, honey, oh, my sweet summer child, stop. He's a straight guy. There's no subtext. No hidden message. Don't worry your pretty little head about it. If he wanted a date, he'd have said so. He said he wanted to talk? It's a talk."

"Really? But — "

"No buts! What you *need* is an outfit that will convince him it's a date, even if he didn't know it at first. It's gotta remind him how much he loves you in a way he can't ignore."

I laugh and mentally browse through my closet. I hear another voice shouting at Cory in the background.

"What? — Oh, Georgie says you should wear your green dress, the one with the sweetheart neckline."

"Are you sure? The purple — "

"Sweetie, green is your colour. You look flawless in it."

"Alright, thanks!"

I hang up, a stupid grin spread on my face. I don't want to get my hopes up, but I can't help it. Jeff didn't *have* to say he missed me. That must mean he wants this to go somewhere, right?

I open my jewellery box reverently — almost holding my breath. I dig out the tiny copper feathers.

"Thank you."

¤

Before I leave for my not-yet-a-date with Jeff, I dig through the back of my closet until I find a Quarante-Cinq plastic bag. In it, still wrapped in cellophane, is the J-Walkers album. I play it while I get dressed, revelling in Jeff's voice.

I look exactly how Cory and I planned — and I'm wearing the earrings. I feel gorgeous. One look at me should suffice to make Jeff regret every second we spent apart.

But what if it doesn't?

What if he wants to meet up to tell me it won't work? Maybe he's just a decent person who doesn't want to do this by text message or leave me hanging?

As soon as I walk in the café, my doubts vanish. Instead of his usual hoodie, he's wearing a light blue shirt with the sleeves rolled up, and a necktie. He looks just like he did on our first date. A good sign, I hope?

He spots me and beams, and I manage not to faint. God, I missed that smile. I have been so busy trying to impress him that I completely forgot the effect *he* has on me. Of course I remembered the love I feel for him, but I somehow forgot how his grin makes my heart beat a samba; how the mere touch of his fingertips on my arm takes my breath away; how the way he calls me 'love' — and fucking means it — turns my legs to jelly. Not to mention the exquisite way his ass fills his skinny jeans.

All of this comes back to me, crashing like a wave, the moment his lips touch my cheek. I tighten my grip over his biceps ever so slightly — if I don't I'm pretty sure I'll melt or drown or implode.

I get a tall, black coffee at the counter — far from my usual order, but I need something to ground me and clear my head, if I'm to go through this with my life, my dignity, and my heart all intact. I join Jeff on a couch near the window. We take a few nervous, silent sips, looking outside at two dogs sniffing each other's butts.

How do you break six months' silence? What are you supposed to say in such a situation? *Hey, how've you been, sorry I fucked up your life?*

Clutching my ceramic cup like a buoy, I turn to Jeff and open my mouth to speak, even though I still don't know what I'm about to say.

"You're wearing the earrings!" Jeff grins and pushes a strand of hair behind my ear to get a better look. "They suit you."

"Thanks. It's my first time wearing them. I — I was waiting for you to come back." I glance at him, and a look of sadness fogs his eyes.

He clears his throat and rakes a hand through his hair, giving it its usual messy look. "Yeah ... You must be wondering what took me so long ..."

"Not really... I mean this isn't something you can decide in a hurry. You had to think long and hard about it. I have to admit, though, there were a few times when I thought you'd just never come back."

"To be honest, me too." Jeff stares deep into his coffee cup. "I spent the last six months nursing a broken heart and asking myself a million questions. I did a lot of research on open relationships, and many times I told myself I wasn't strong enough for this. That I should just walk away and spare us both more pain. But every time I tried to imagine never seeing you again, it was like torture — I knew it was a mistake."

Jeff looks away, silent for several, hard-pounding heartbeats.

I don't want to rush him, but my heart is about to jump out of my chest and straight into my coffee if I don't do something.

"So… what are you saying?" I ask tentatively.

He lets out a long, deep breath. "I never thought I could ever be in an open relationship, you know?" He shrugs. "But, I mean, I've read about it, and you seem happy in it. I guess what I'm trying to say is that I miss you and love you too much to let my fears stand in the way. I want to give us a try."

Our eyes meet, and through all the questions and issues still unresolved, one thing is obvious: we're both overjoyed by this decision. Jeff reaches a hesitant hand across the couch to hold mine. For a few minutes, we drink in silence, enjoying being finally together, before all the *talking* has to happen.

As the sun starts to set, turning Jeff's hair into a crown of solid gold, I have to physically stop my fingers from reaching to thread through it. If we want to get past handholding though, there are still a few things to address.

"So, this is new for me too," I say, breaking the ice.

His features knot in a puzzled look.

"I mean, before you, I stuck to one-night stands, booty calls, you know? It was never like this." I gesture at the two of us. "Love was never part of the equation."

Jeff smiles softly at the word 'love'. I know just how he feels — I want to say the word over and over. Revel in it.

"Of course, I had to talk about this with David."

Jeff frowns at the name, but at this stage I guess it's to be expected.

"We changed our ground rules," I explain. "He and I are now both allowed to date people on a regular basis, and even to pursue other romantic relationships outside our main one. What this means is that I'm free to call you my boyfriend, if that's okay with you."

"It's more than okay." Jeff tilts my chin towards him and plants a gentle, eager kiss on my lips. "Kinda wish we could get these six months back, though," he whispers, his forehead pressed against mine.

I nod and kiss him again.

"We'll have to make up for it by spending all our time together," Jeff says with a wink.

"Damn." I groan. "I just remembered I'm leaving for Gaspésie in a week."

"Bring me?" He looks at me with puppy eyes and I want to put him in my suitcase immediately.

"Can't. It's a no boyfriend kind of thing."

"Oh well." He shrugs, a sad smile on his face. "Let's make the most of this week, then."

"Better start now," I suggest, eyeing the door.

Thankfully Justin isn't home when we get to Jeff's place. That saves us the whole awkward situation of 'long time, no see,' which we all know actually means, 'long-time since you boned my brother.'

The familiarity of Jeff's room brings tears to my eyes. He still has musical instruments covering every inch of his room, and, on the walls, hang posters of London and of his favourite indie bands — some of which he made me discover. I listened almost exclusively to these bands when Jeff and I were apart; it made me feel closer to him.

Most importantly, his room smells like him — like Head & Shoulders shampoo and coffee and guitar wood. The smell alone gets to me and I suddenly pull Jeff closer, overwhelmed by an urge to just hold him and keep him in my arms forever.

"I missed you so much," I sigh, my face pressed hard against his chest in an attempt to take him all in.

Jeff chuckles and buries his hands in my hair. He takes a deep breath, doing the same: committing my scent to memory because it's been too damn long.

"I think you should know I'm never letting go." I smile up at him.

"I have exactly zero problem with that." He grins as he pulls me down on his mattress next to him.

He cups my cheek and looks deep, deep into my eyes, sighing in relief. His lips press against mine softly — I'd forgotten how each of his kisses is different, how every single one of them has a distinct personality. This one is tentative, almost shy, as if he wanted to test how much things had changed between us.

I close my eyes and deepen the kiss, letting myself go limp in his arms. He pulls me on top of him and unzips my dress, watching as I pull it over my head. His hands trail down my sides and I shiver as the cool air hits my naked skin. He splays his palms on the small of my back. His warm flesh almost burns in contrast to the cold.

He unhooks my bra and slides it down my arms, a tender smile gracing his features. I pull at his tie knot until it unravels in my hands, the silk falling softly on my thighs. I unbutton his shirt, savouring the way his muscles move under my hands. He sits up to let me push the shirt off his shoulders, and lets out a deep breath; his hands squeeze my hips and he buries his face in my neck.

"Fuck. You are so beautiful," he exhales and his breath tickles me, right at the spot where my earlobe meets my neck.

I'm straddling him and I squeeze his waist between my thighs. My hands wander all over him. I need him closer, to make up for all these months when he was so far away. I caress and grab, trying to drink him in — to quench my thirst of him. It's not enough — it'll never be enough — so I slip a hand between us and undo his belt.

Jeff smirks at me in the same way that has always made me melt, from the first time he laid eyes on me — the one that says, 'I know just how much you want me.' He helps me unzip his pants and kicks them across the room, along with his socks. We hear a loud thump as it hits the floor.

"Shit, my phone!" He cringes. "Ah, to hell with it." He grins and flips me over to be on top.

He traces every single curve of my body with his fingertips, staring straight into my soul in the most entrancing way. His touch is intoxicating, addictive. I have absolutely no idea how I managed to go that long without it. All I know is I could never do it again. My breath comes out shakily. I tremble under his touch — especially when he draws patterns inside my thighs, right at the edge of my underwear.

My entire body wakes up from a deep slumber, as if it had been waiting for him to come back. Jeff's breath is warm on my bare skin — I need more.

He bows down to press a kiss on my mound, right above where it becomes really interesting. My hips buck up of their own will, an unsubtle attempt at catching his attention.

Jeff chuckles. "Eager, much?"

"It's been so long."

"I know, love," he whispers.

I almost purr at the familiar pet name. I relish it, relieved to see that it's real. It wasn't just some crush built up in my head all these months.

It's love.

¤

"Do you really need *six* frozen pizzas?"

"*Chaton*, I'm playing D&D with four grown men for two days straight. In fact, maybe I should grab a few more."

"Oh, for god's sakes," I sigh as David dumps three more pizzas in our already overflowing cart.

He grins at me. "I'm gonna miss you so much."

"No, you're not. You're gonna be busy chopping off goblin's heads with my booty call."

David splays a hand across his chest, mock scandalized. "I'm gonna miss you during pizza breaks!"

"And at least you get to see Jude. I'm gonna be missing you *and* Jeff."

He scoffs. "Please. I give you two days before you meet a cute *gaspésienne*."

"What are you talking about? I don't meet people everywhere I go!"

"Sure, honey."

TWENTY-EIGHT

Two days before I leave for Gaspésie, I decide to surprise Jeff. I hear from Mitch that the J-Walkers are playing at La Brunante, so I arrange to get there a bit late — when they're already on stage — and hide in the crowd. During the last song of their set, I push my way through the crowd until I'm in Jeff's line of sight.

His eyes widen and a grin illuminates his features. He has trouble getting through the rest of the song, hitting a few wrong notes and bumping into Justin. He barely stays to thank the audience with the rest of the band. As soon as the last note of the song fades out, he jumps off the stage, his bass still slung over his back.

"Amy!" He pulls me close and takes a deep breath, as if trying to absorb my very presence. "What are you doing here? I didn't think I'd see you before you'd come back from Gaspésie!"

"I wanted to surprise you. Spend one last night together before I leave."

Jeff cradles my face between his palms and kisses me deeply.

"I'm so glad you did. I'm gonna miss you so much." He exhales and presses his forehead against mine, nearly hitting a nearby girl over the head with the bass still suspended to his shoulder.

"Oops." He apologizes to her and turns back to me. "I have to help the others pack the van, then I'm all yours." He kisses me one last time and climbs back on stage.

I wait for him at the bar, nursing a beer. Only a few minutes pass before he comes back, a spring in his step and the same blinding grin on his face.

"The guys thought I was being a pain because I couldn't stop talking about you. I almost dropped Jo's keyboards, so they told me to go — they'll pack without me."

"You are the cutest." I rake a hand through his fluffy blond hair. "So, what do you want to do?"

"Anything, as long as we're together," he mumbles, burying his face in the crook of my neck.

We end up going on a long walk, caring more about holding hands than about where our feet lead us. The early June breeze is still warm, the streets buzzing around us despite the late hour, everyone enjoying the first real summer nights.

"I listened to your album," I tell Jeff, my fingers comfortably cradled between his.

"Yeah?" He turns to me, a great smile lighting his features as bright as the neon sign above his head. "What did you think?"

"It's amazing — and I'm not just saying that because I know you. I'm legit gonna recommend it to customers at work."

"I'm so glad you like it. A lot of you went into it."

"Really?"

"Yeah, I mean, I worked on it while we were apart, so I pulled a lot of inspiration from what we had. Because, you know, before you, I only had one long-term relationship. Mia." He lets out a long sigh.

"Ah, the elusive Mia…"

In the first half of our relationship, I asked Jeff about her, but, other than the Cliff Notes I got on our first date, he'd refused to elaborate. He said he didn't want to bring old baggage so soon into a fresh relationship.

"Guess I should tell you now, right?" He shrugs. "For the sake of starting anew and honestly?"

I nod. "If you feel ready."

He takes a deep breath. "We were together for two years, but the last nine months were spent apart. She got a scholarship to study in Belgium. Told me she was leaving two weeks before the fact. Barely enough time to get used to it, you know? I finally ended it because she kept talking about nothing but her roommate. A Greek artist. I mean, who can compete with that?"

"I'd take my Montreal bassist over the Greek hipster anytime," I whisper in Jeff's ear.

He looks at me with misty eyes. "You know, you taught me I could love again."

Now it's my turn to get teary-eyed. I pull him against me and kiss him — a kiss full of hopes and promises.

Around us, Montreal sleeps. The blissful, unknown hour between the bars closing and the early birds leaving for work. Stars and city lights alike blink at us, two lovers, owners of the city. Our feet take us to the top of Mount Royal. We sit on the grass and watch the sun rise over the city, a work of art for our eyes only.

We fall asleep curled up on top of the world as it wakes up, birdsong our lullaby.

TWENTY-NINE

On our way to Gaspésie, Mitch is at the wheel of the grey Toyota Yaris we all pitched in to rent. Alex, Georgie and Cory are squeezed up in the back. I'm in the passenger seat, feet propped up on the dashboard because we had so much luggage that we had to cram some under my seat.

I managed to get shotgun because I'm the only one who doesn't mind serving as a human GPS for Mitch. This also grants me DJing privileges. I take my duties seriously, choosing music that will please everyone: old school punk rock for Alex, disco for Cory, classic rock for Georgie, and pop for Mitch.

My navigating duties don't keep me too busy: the road to Gaspésie is pretty much just two highways, so I'm mostly needed at the beginning and the end of the trip. This leaves me free to text Jeff: we've spent as much time together as possible since we reunited, but the last night before the trip was David's, so I already miss him.

He texts me inside jokes, silly emojis, and risqué stuff, so, of course, I blush and giggle. The others make fun of me, as they do every time I meet someone.

Alex joins in with them, but her jokes are stiff, forced. Our friendship is slowly returning to normal, but it's the first time we talked about who I'm seeing since she came back. I can tell she isn't crazy about it, but doesn't want to spoil the fun. She definitely isn't happy that my open relationship is now about love as well as sex.

I hope this trip will bring us closer. It's a good way to start anew, to get over the past and rekindle our friendship with new memories.

Eager to drive the conversation away from my love life, I put on "Bohemian Rhapsody" — it's impossible not to sing along to this song. I turn around in my seat to shoot an apologetic glance at Alex. She smiles and nods — I know she understands, though she might not like it.

The drive is ten hours long, so we left at dawn — well, eight o'clock. We drive non-stop until lunchtime, when we grab sandwiches at a rest area. Sometime around four, we lose cellphone reception — right after Jeff texts me: I'm still sad you didn't spend last night with me.

I don't get a chance to reply, sadly, and I ask around if anyone still has reception, but nobody does. I put my phone down with a sigh and turn around in my seat to see what everyone's up to.

Cory's asleep on Georgie's shoulder. Georgie's playing a game on his phone. Alex is reading a queer zine. Mitch is focused on the road, bobbing her head and mouthing the words to "Don't Stop Believing."

The road is sinuous, full of turns and hills. We weave through forests and coastal villages constituted of nothing, but a tiny school, a church, a general store and two farms. The Murray's cabin is in a village almost at the very tip of the Gaspésie peninsula.

We make a left at a fork and leave the main road. Houses are scarce, but colourful — red, blue or even yellow, beautiful against the sparkling backdrop of the gulf. We take a dirt track next to a boarded-up garage and follow it up a hill, until we finally see the cabin, surrounded by trees.

The place is a smallish, A-frame log house with a porch running all around it. The façade is entirely made of windows. A little path winds around the house, leading to a picnic table and a fire pit.

We grab our luggage and follow Mitch inside. She flicks on the lights and we can see how gorgeous and cozy the place is. Mismatched armchairs and couches covered in quilts stand in front of the fireplace. The wooden beams are exposed; the kitchen is tiny, but welcoming.

Mitch claims her usual bedroom — the one with a single bed — Georgie and Cory take the masters' bedroom, and Alex and I each take a bed in the mezzanine bedroom. We drop our stuff and dig into our bags to find socks and sweaters: the nights are pretty chilly so close to the ocean, even in June.

Georgie grabs the case of beer, I take the marshmallows, and Mitch follows us with an armful of blankets. In the backyard, which is basically a clearing between the cabin and the woods, Alex is starting a fire in the pit near the picnic table. Cory hands her branches and newspapers. When Alex has got it big and roaring, she sits next to me on a tree trunk laid on the ground. She pulls on my blanket to join me underneath it.

"I didn't know you could build a fire." I hand her a marshmallow on a stick.

"The only thing my dad ever taught me." She pauses, staring at her rapidly browning marshmallow. "Well, that and 'Men always leave.'"

I keep quiet. Alex never talks about her father. She told me he left when she was ten, but I know better than to ask about him. Instead, I gently bump her shoulder with mine — a way of letting her know I'm here without her closing up.

She gobbles up her blackened marshmallow and cracks open a beer.

"I brought Trivial Pursuit!" Mitch offers.

"Oh, thank god," Alex mutters.

She's never been one to open up, so this must have been especially hard for her, considering our still shaky relationship.

We take turns asking trivia questions without the game board, because who cares? We laugh at the way-too-hard questions about people no one's ever heard of. Georgie aces all the cinema questions and I manage to answer a few of the music ones — working in a record store has its perks.

After a while someone tells an anecdote and we forget the game. We start telling old childhood stories, and soon, the beer case holds more empties than full bottles. My words are slurred, but so are everyone else's. It feels so good to spend time with them again — just friends and nature, no drama — I almost don't miss my boyfriends.

Drunk and filled with affection for my friends, I don't think before saying it out loud. Everyone shuts up at the mention of my boyfriends, turning to Alex to see her reaction.

"Cut it off, guys." She shrugs and looks away. "I'm over you, anyway."

Cory cheers and raises his bottle, spilling some on Georgie's knees.

"To getting over people!"

We start drinking to increasingly stupid stuff — *To friendship! To Gaspésie! To Mitch's parents' cabin!* — until the beer is all gone and we're off to bed.

THIRTY

I wake up the next morning around seven — I definitely didn't get enough sleep, but I hate sleeping in on holidays. The cabin is silent except for the steady breathing of my friends and birdsongs outside. I make my way downstairs as quietly as I can, cringing as the wooden steps creak under my feet. The first rays of sunshine warm up the kitchen floor, filtered through yellow flowered curtains.

I make a cup of tea in a World's Best Grandma mug and grab my boots and a plaid blanket on my way out. On the back porch, I sit down and put on my boots without having to worry about making noise. I wrap the blanket around my shoulders and take a few sips of scalding Earl Grey.

The morning air is crisp. Dew clings to the blades of grass. I grip my mug tightly for warmth and take the path that opens into the woods behind the cabin. Mitch said last night it leads to the beach. I follow it slowly, enjoying the nature around me: birds singing, waves crashing on the shore beyond the woods, the smell of wet leaves and dirt, the way the sun trickles through the leaves, creating a green-lit dome above my head.

I emerge from the woods onto a pebble beach, deserted except from a flock of seagulls searching for food. Waves crash against the rocks. A slowly dissipating fog hovers above the sea — like dozens of spirits trying to find their way back from our world.

I sit down on a flat rock a few feet from the sea, waves lapping at the toes of my boots. The atmosphere is perfect for introspection, and, judging by the rise of the sun in the sky, I must spend about an hour sipping my tea and thinking.

I think about Jeff. It's so hard not to see him all the time. Whenever we have to say goodbye feels like pure torture; whenever he asks me over and I have to decline is like tearing out a piece of my heart. I know he doesn't mean to make me feel guilty, but when I see how tired he looks — he says he has trouble sleeping without me — I always regret spending nights away from him.

But I also have David. One of the main rules of our relationship is making sure we don't neglect each other, no matter who we meet. Lately, I have dropped the ball here. We haven't dined-and-dished in a while. I spend a lot of nights with Jeff, and David has a hard time coming home to an empty bed this often. I get it: it was hard for me to wake up alone this morning, without his warm body pressed against mine. I wish he could have come along. He'd love it here — everything is gorgeous, like it was made for the sole purpose of being photographed.

I hear footsteps behind me and turn around to see Mitch, wrapped in a blanket and clutching a Christmas mug playing a tinny-sounding, distorted version of Jingle Bells — the batteries will probably die soon. She sits down on the rock next to mine and presses her hand to the bottom of her mug to shut it up.

"Good morning." I welcome her with a smile.

"Morning," she says softly.

We sit like this for a while, sipping in silence.

"So, I'm kind of glad Julia couldn't come," she finally says, setting her mug down on a rock.

I nod and drain the last drops of tea from my mug. "Yeah, you guys haven't gotten along that well lately, right?"

Mitch shrugs and looks away. "She keeps trying to set me up with guys…"

"She's doing it to be a good friend, I'm sure — "

"She just can't believe someone can be single *and* happy. I swear if she were here, she'd try to set me up with one of the fishermen down at the cove." Mitch fiddles with her Hufflepuff wristband, turning it over and over around her arm.

"It never used to bother you that much, no? You'd laugh about it…"

"I'm asexual."

She drops this like a bomb and waits, staring at me defiantly, waiting for me to freak out or something. I smile at her and put a hand on her shoulder.

"I have no interest in dating anyone she introduces me to, and probably nobody else, for that matter," she continues when she sees I'm not freaked out. "I might be aromantic, too."

"What about Justin?"

"He knows. He's the first one I told, and he took it really well. We agreed to stay friends. Well, not really friends. Platonic soulmates is more like it. It's difficult to define."

"I'm happy for you. Julia can fuck off. Anyway, it's not like we still see her a lot nowadays."

Mitch gives a grateful smile and nods.

"I think she latched onto me because I was the only other straight person on your Island of Queer Toys."

"Yeah, she could forget about my bisexuality because I was dating a guy, but as soon as I came out with the open relationship thing, she started to bail."

"I guess no one really stays friends with their childhood best friends."

THIRTY-ONE

Amy Evans — I miss you so much… <3
Message failed to send

Of course I knew I wouldn't have cellphone reception on this trip. But in the back of the general store down in the village, my signal is at one bar, so I figured I'd give it a try and text David.

I hit refresh a couple more times, to no avail. I pocket my phone with a sigh, grab a case of beer and a box of linguine and make my way to the register. I stop by the magazine rack and notice they have one of these teenage girl magazines full of quizzes and horoscopes. Perfect for tonight.

I hand the cashier a twenty and our hands brush as she takes it. Our eyes meet, and her looks strike me: a long, bright blue braid, a lip ring, a tattoo peeking under her uniform shirt — miles away from the other girls I've seen so far in this village.

She smirks as she hands me my change. *"Bonne soirée,"* she chuckles.

"Merci!"

I leave, conscious that the teen mag and beer combo is odd, but convinced that she is somewhat interested. I hope I'll see her again, and vow to volunteer for all errands for the two weeks we're here.

I get back to the cabin as Cory sets up a board game on the dinner table.

"Hey, you're just in time for a game of Life before dinner!"

"I want the red car!"

I put the beer in the fridge and join the others. As usual, we all choose same-sex partners when we get to the wedding. Alex wins, even though she spends the whole time criticizing the glorification of capitalism and heteronormativity.

Georgie and Mitch get up to make dinner — pasta carbonara with a Greek salad.

"I got a surprise for you guys!" I pull the magazine out of my bag.

"A quiz mag! Hun, this is gonna be amazing after a few beers!" Cory exclaims.

"My thoughts exactly."

I decide to give them a little preview by reading the titles of the quizzes aloud.

"Is he The One for you? What does your nail polish says about you? Does he have a secret crush on you?"

I catch Alex staring at me and quickly looking away, pretending to be engrossed in the rolling of a joint. I can't help wondering if it means anything. Was she telling the truth when she said she was over me?

She looks awkward for about half a second before scoffing.

"Look at the heteronormative bullshit they force-feed our youth. Disgusting."

"Come on, it'll be fun!"

"Sure, I've always wondered if you and I were astrologically compatible BFFs."

She frowns, but I know it's just for show and that she'll have fun with the rest of us, mocking these quizzes.

After dinner, we gather on the living room couches, armed with copious amounts of beer and chips, and the quiz mag. We toast to the mocking of patriarchal values and I turn to the first quiz.

"Which Chris is right for you?" I announce. "Evans, Hemsworth, Pratt or Pine?"

Follows a series of questions like 'How do you let your crush know you're into him?'; 'Your bestie and you both fall for the same guy; what do you do?' and 'Describe your dream wedding.'

We drink and answer the questions. Wise Mitch notes our answers on a pad to facilitate the result-compiling process. We all end up with Chris Evans, except for Alex, who gets Hemsworth.

"Figures the lesbian would get the hunk…" She rolls her eyes.

"Sorry to break it to you, honey, but they're all hunks," Georgie points out.

"You guys know what I mean." Alex shrugs and downs her beer.

We take a few more quizzes, (What kind of kisser are you? Which Starbucks drink are you? What does your favourite flower reveal about you?) getting progressively drunker. I finally get to 'Does he have a secret crush on you?' It might just be my imagination, but Alex seems to actively avoid my gaze. She looks like someone who's got something to hide, like maybe an unresolved crush?

I'm beginning to think maybe she's not as over me as she said she was.

I answer all the questions with Alex in mind, hoping it might help me figure it out, even though these tests are pretty dumb. I get a final result over 46, which, according to the magazine, means 'He is 100% smitten with you — make a move!'

Alex promptly gets up for another beer.

"This is dumb," she declares, plopping down on the couch. "Let's do something else."

"What about that bar you told us about?" Georgie asks Mitch.

"I could go for some pool," I say.

"Don't get your hopes up, guys," Mitch replies. "This is a true small town hole-in-the-wall — four customers is rush hour for them, and they are all regulars. And they tend to close around eleven because no one stays out past that time."

"No time to waste, then." Alex shoves her wallet in the pocket of her cut-off shorts and heads out.

We all follow her down to the village. The bar is right above the general store. The only way you can even tell there's a bar is the Budweiser neon sign in the far right window. As far as I know, the place doesn't even have a name.

Inside, we're immediately greeted by four pairs of eyes staring at us intently. One of them belongs to the barmaid, and only one of them isn't filled with a mix of hate and curiosity: a pair of gorgeous brown eyes belonging to Blue-Haired-Girl from the store downstairs.

We walk up to the bar. All eyes are on us, except for Blue's, whose focus is back on her pool game. The middle-aged, leather-clad barmaid looks at us, eyebrows raised, daring us to order something.

"What beers do you have?" Cory asks bravely.

"Beer," the barmaid barks, as if there were no such thing as different kinds of beer.

She pours five beers from the only tap in sight, never even stopping to ask if one of us wanted something else. We sit at a table near the bar — well, the place is so small that all of the tables are near the bar.

"This sucks," Georgie sighs, sipping his beer. "I really wanted to play pool, it's been ages."

The place, of course, only has one pool table, and Blue already claimed it to herself.

"Leave it to me." I take a big gulp of beer and make my way towards her. I channel my sexy walk, just to make sure the odds are on my side.

I can hear Alex groan, but I try not to pay attention. I'm off to flirt my way to a pool table, not get married.

"Hey." I lean against the table as Blue sinks the cue ball and curses under her breath in French.

"*Câlisse. Oh, allo!*"

"*Penses-tu qu'on pourrait jouer avec toi?*"

A huge grin illuminates her features — perhaps one of the prettiest smiles I've ever seen. I already thought she was cute when I met her at the store this morning, but she's even more gorgeous without the mandatory polo shirt. She's wearing a black polka dot dress — very retro, love it — and her cherry red lips just make me want to kiss her right here and now.

"*Pas de trouble,*" she answers, handing me a cue stick. "*Moi, c'est Marie-Ève.*"

"Amy." I shake her proffered hand. "*Merci!*" I smile at her and motion to the others to join us.

"*Marie-Ève, je te présente Cory, Georgie, Mitch et Alex. Guys,* this is Marie-Ève."

They all greet her. Mitch thanks her in French for letting us play. Alex just looks away, draining the rest of her beer.

"Oh, you are Anglophones? We can talk English if you want!" Marie-Ève speaks in an adorable, thick accent.

We start playing — Marie-Ève, Mitch and I versus the boys and Alex. Every time Marie-Ève says something in English, I want to melt because she's just too damn cute. She does that thing I noticed in a lot of French Canadians when they speak English. She doesn't pronounce the letter H where there is one, and puts one where there is none — like *'ello, hi'm Marie-Ève.* David used to do this when we first got together. He still slips into it when he's nervous or distracted, and it never fails to charm me.

The barmaid soon comes to see us, and, seeing we're friendly with a local, she switches into Caring Auntie mode, giving us pet names and chatting with us.

"*Une autre bière, ma pitoune?*" she asks Alex, who has done little but drink and play in silence since we got here.

Alex has no idea what a *pitoune* is, but she nods.

"*En fait, Ginette on prendrait un pichet, s'il te plaît.* On me, guys!" Marie-Ève smiles.

"*Parfait, ma cocotte!*" Ginette disappears behind the bar and quickly comes back with a huge pitcher of beer.

After a few games, Marie-Ève grabs her beer and heads to a table.

"I'm gonna sit this one out, guys," I tell the others.

They remake the teams so they're even and Alex breaks, hitting the cue ball so hard she almost cracks her cue stick. She turns her back to us and Marie-Ève pulls her chair closer to mine. I catch Georgie and Cory looking from Alex to us, puzzled and gossip-hungry.

"So what's the deal with Alex? Is she always this..."

"Rude? Not usually. It's a long story."

"I have all night." Marie-Ève leans in, ready to hear it.

I shrug and refill my beer. "She's jealous."

"Why?"

"Because I'm interested in you." I figure there's no point in hiding the truth — the tension is already thick between us, so why delay the inevitable?

Marie smirks — I recognize the feeling; the one you get when you successfully guessed someone's intentions. "And you're not interested in her?" She sneaks a glance at Alex, bent over the pool table to take a shot. Marie is obviously appreciating the view, and I can't blame her — Alex's strong thighs peeking from her cut-off shorts are, indeed, quite a sight.

"Well, the truth is, I can't give her what she wants."

"Which is?"

"Exclusivity."

Marie gives a sympathetic smile. "That's rough. Been there."

"Yeah?"

"Yeah, I just got out of a relationship with my girlfriend of three years. She wanted to open the relationship, and I couldn't deal with that."

"It's not for everyone," I agree.

"For now, I kinda see the appeal, though. I mean I definitely want to settle down with the right girl someday, but, for now, I just want a summer fling, you know? No strings attached."

"Something like a two week fling, maybe?" I ask innocently.

"Yeah, something like that." She winks and clinks her glass against mine.

We play a few more rounds of pool with the others as the bar gradually empties of its regulars. At twenty past eleven, Ginette starts putting chairs up on tables, sweeping the floors and turning off the music.

"Let's get out of her hair, guys," Mitch suggests.

"*Bye Ginette, bonne soirée!*" Marie calls.

We file out of the bar in a chorus of "*Merci!*," an exhausted grunt from Ginette her only response. My friends start in the direction of the cabin, but Marie-Ève and I lag behind.

"Wanna go for a walk?" she asks.

"Go ahead, guys, I'll meet you there later."

Alex bolts silently, not waiting for the others.

"I thought things would get better between us," I sigh, following Marie behind the general store.

Where in Montreal there would be a dark, reeky back alley, here you can find piles of milk crates strewn over a vacant lot, overgrown with weeds, running up to the beach.

"She said she was over me," I continue.

"Maybe she thought she was." Marie shrugs. "You know, sometimes you genuinely think you're okay, but then you see them with someone and it all comes crashing down."

"You're probably right."

"I usually am." She winks.

We laugh as we kick off our shoes to walk in the soft sand, stark white under the moonlight. The salty ocean wind plays with Marie-Ève's undone hair; so blue the breeze probably thinks she belongs to the sea. Sprinkles of laughter still adorn her eyes, pulling me towards her by the heartstrings.

She walks up to the very edge of the tide, her feet leaving clear imprints in the wet sand, and lets the waves lap gently at her toes, trying to claim her. I stand at her side, marvelling at the sheer number of stars visible in the night sky, and their twins like diamonds bobbing along the waves.

We stand so close together I can feel the warmth emanating from her body, our shoulders almost brushing together.

Just a spark is all it takes. A catalyst.

Between us, there is no denying it, it would happen sooner or later. We just didn't know what would start it.

Turns out, it's her.

She drops everything, every pretence and every convention, to light fireworks deep in my soul.

Nearly tears me apart.

She presses her forehead against mine, takes a deep breath and closes her eyes. Her actions are forward and daring, but, at the same time, she looks flustered, her rosy cheeks hinting that she can't quite believe she's doing this.

Cherry red lips press against mine, soft but determined. Feet planted fast in the surf, I wind my arms around her waist, pulling her closer and closer still. We sway together as the tide comes and goes. I try to catch my breath and the salty taste in the air conjures up this image of Marie-Ève as a mermaid, luring me to the depths of the ocean.

Somehow, I don't think I'd mind.

THIRTY-TWO

I wake up the next morning with a smile on my face. The sun rays peeking through the blinds and the sound of someone whistling a peppy tune in the kitchen both perfectly match my mood. I get up quietly, careful not to wake Alex — she gets cranky whenever she has to wake up before ten, and I figure she's already grumpy enough with Marie-Ève around.

Marie-Ève.

I tiptoe down the stairs, unable to contain a grin.

"Good morning!" I sing-songily greet Georgie and Mitch.

"Someone's chipper," Mitch remarks, cracking eggs into a mixing bowl.

"Someone came home late last night..." Georgie stops whistling to answer.

I shrug innocently and start filling the kettle. "Tea? Anyone?"

"Don't change the subject!" Mitch chides.

"Dude," Georgie pipes up, "you look like a freakin' heart-eyes emoji."

I'm pretty sure by now I look more like a blushing emoji, so I hide behind a cupboard door, pretending to look for tea bags.

"Morning," Cory mumbles sleepily as he walks in.

"Even asleep, Cory can feel when there's gossip happening. It's like a gift." Georgie kisses him hello and immediately hands him a cup of coffee.

Half a cup later, Cory's eyes seem brighter and he no longer has to lean against Georgie for support.

"Okay, I'm awake," he says. "Dish."

I take my sweet time pouring hot water in a Rocher Percé mug. "We kissed, that's all."

"Until two a.m.?" Georgie raises an incredulous eyebrow.

"We took a long walk." I shrug, unable to hide my smile.

"Are you gonna see her again?" Mitch asks as she stirs her pancake batter.

"We intend to make the most out of the next two weeks."

"A summer fling!" Cory exclaims. "How very 'coming-of-age movie' of you!"

I take a sip of tea. "What's bumming me out, though, is *her* reaction." I nod towards the ceiling, above which Alex is hopefully fast asleep and not listening to us. "I feel like she's this close to another disappearing act."

"She's a big girl," Mitch says. "She said she was over you. You can't stop living out of fear of how she might react."

"I don't want to lose her again, is all." I fiddle with the string of my tea bag.

"Maybe this is none of my business," Georgie says, chopping strawberries, "but I don't feel like this thing between the two of you is very healthy. Like, you welcomed her open-armed, no questions asked. You never held her accountable for the — I have to say — pretty shitty way she acted. You're the one walking on eggshells around her, scared of doing anything that might set her off again."

"Yeah," Cory nods. "And that might be why you can't go back to the kind of friendship you had before. It's not 'cause you had sex — it's 'cause you're not equals anymore. The whole dynamic is off-balance."

"You know," Mitch muses, "I think you got something there. One pancake or two?" She thrusts a plate at Cory.

"Two, please."

"Yeah, but, with that said, what am I supposed to do?"

"Confront her. Tell her how you feel." Georgie answers.

"But what if I lose her?"

"Hun, you can either clear the air and retrieve what you once had, or lose her completely. You have to ask yourself if you'd rather stay in this miasma of a friendship or if you take the risk."

"I think you're right." I drain the last of my tea, already drafting a speech in my head.

"Mmm, smells good." Alex steps into the kitchen.

"Slept well?" Mitch asks.

"Like a log. I was actually glad I got home before you guys, because I can never fall asleep with Miss Snores-a-Lot in the same room," she adds, nodding at me.

"I don't snore!"

"Um, we've had enough sleepovers for me to be an expert on your sleep habits. You do." She winks.

What a turnabout. Is she sorry for her behaviour last night? Did she hear us talking just now? What's her game? Maybe a good night's sleep was all she needed to shed the stress of the semester. Whatever it is, I'll take it while it lasts — I'll keep my speech in mind in case she acts out again.

¤

That night, after a truly decadent seafood feast, I join Marie-Ève at the general store at the end of her shift. She's waiting for me, leaning against the hood of a pick-up truck as blue as her hair. She drives me to her place, a weathered bungalow on the other side of the village.

"This is my parents' place. I rent a flat in Gaspé during the school year, but I always come back for the summer. The whole basement is mine. Don't worry, though, they're visiting my sister in Quebec City for the week."

We enter by a side door that leads directly to the basement stairs. Her apartment is exactly how I expected her habitat to be: retro, vibrant and cozy. Old vinyl records on the walls; a corner of the room has been converted into a kitchenette, painted yellow with a cyan retro fridge. The bathroom has a sailor theme going on, with red and white stripes and navy anchors — a sailor pin-up poster even hangs above the toilet.

"Beer or wine?" she asks as she opens the refrigerator.

"White wine, if you've got some."

"Coming up!"

I cozy up on the black and white polka-dot couch. She joins me, propping her feet up on the coffee table, hugging a throw pillow against her chest. She presses a few buttons on a remote and music fills the room. I instantly recognize the first notes of my favourite Beatles album, *Rubber Soul.*

"Beatles fan?" I raise my glass.

She clinks hers against it, beaming. "Of course. Last year in school, we put on a whole show around their music."

I must look puzzled because she instantly clarifies it.

"I teach at a circus school."

"Seriously?"

"Yeah!" She blushes. "I'm an acrobat."

My mind short-circuits and it must show on my face — Marie-Ève laughs.

"This info tends to have that effect on people, I don't know why…" She scrunches her face in mock naïveté and looks so adorable I can't help pulling her closer.

She shuffles over to straddle me and, at this point, I'm doubtful my lungs even work anymore. The way her dress rides up just takes my breath away. She takes our drinks and sets them down on the coffee table behind her. I run my hands up and down her thighs.

"You look amazing," I breathe out.

"So do you," she replies in a whisper so hot it might be the cause of global warming.

I grip her bottom lip between my teeth, fiddling with the hem of her dress. She cups my face in her hands, looks straight in my eyes and kisses me, hard. Again, her kiss feels like it could save me from drowning, but also lure me to the bottom of the ocean — and this time I follow it blindly, without interruptions.

Short, frantic breaths mix together, incredulous reactions to an amazing situation. This kind of sensual summer adventure usually only happens in books, so we both want to savour it all.

I grab the hem of her dress and pull it up. She lifts her arms to help me. I fling the dress across the room and let my fingers run wild across the tides of her body. I pepper kisses like raindrops across the waves tattooed on her clavicle. My gaze is drawn irresistibly to the reproduction of Botticelli's Venus spread on her thigh.

Marie-Ève chuckles. "Yeah, that always gets a big reaction."

"It's amazing!" I trace the details of the seashell with the tip of a finger, mesmerized.

"Come on." She stands up and takes my hand. I follow her to the other side of the room, where a curtain separates the bedroom area from the rest of the basement.

She kneels on the bed and bounces a bit, pulling me by the hand. She looks so eager, like she's having so much fun, it's enticing as hell.

"God, I just wanna eat you up."

THIRTY-THREE

Flames dance before my eyes, but I don't see them.

Chatter rises around me, but I don't hear it.

I can't pay any attention to my friends or the campfire — my entire brain is busy reliving last night. Slow motion shots of Marie's best moves. Her moans, her breaths, replaying in a loop, hair rising on the nape of my neck all over again.

I grip my bottle of beer tight, its cold, hard surface a stark contrast to the phantom of her warm skin my mind has conjured up all day.

A sharp elbow in my ribs brutally pulls me out of my reverie. I blink the mermaid's smile out of my eyes and turn to Mitch with a pointed, "Ow!"

She gives me an apologetic smile. "Wanna go for a swim?"

Alex is already completely naked, standing defiantly in a crumpled pile of clothes. "Skinny dipping, actually," she corrects.

"I never agreed to that," Georgie pipes up.

Alex doesn't try to hide; she just stands there at the edge of the sea, her slender form provocative and unapologetic. Her skin is pale under the moonlight, creamy white striking against the pitch black of her tattoos, dark as the sky behind her.

In my mind, every bump and dip of her skin blends together with Marie's. A ballet of tattoed limbs fills my head, pink and blue hair tangled together — last year and last night blending into a highly volatile, highly dangerous temptation.

I strain my eyes on my beer label, reading *Blanche de Chambly — Bière sur lie — 5%* over and over until the images fade away.

I hear a big splash, followed by cheers, so I finally allow myself to look. Alex dives under the waves and kicks her legs, the rest of her invisible under the dark mirror of the sea. I gather the few shreds of self-control that didn't leave me when Alex stripped, and join the others standing at the edge of the tide.

"It's good," Alex calls to us. "Come on!"

Her stare drills straight into my eyes. I swear she just asked me to have sex right there and then. Under her toxic gaze, I nod, like in some kind of trance. A second later, she's laughing with the others, who are all in different states of undress. Mitch nudges me in the ribs and I don't get what is happening.

"Are you coming?"

I snap out of it and see Cory and Georgie already in the sea, in their underwear. Mitch is standing in front of me in a blue bra and Deadpool boxers. Alex joins me on the shore, an eyebrow raised in a 'what's wrong with you?' way, paired with a smirk that says, 'I know exactly what's up with you.'

I quickly try to look as though nothing's going on. I kick off my shoes, pointedly avoiding Alex's gaze. I pull my dress over my head, leaving it on the rock behind me. Her stare is heavy on me as she grabs a beer from the case. I'm standing right in front of her in nothing but old panties and a mismatched bra, and her eyes are boring into me.

I stare straight ahead at the guys in the sea. If I so much as look at her, there's no telling what kind of delicious mistake we'll make. I run towards the waves, giving Mitch a playful nudge as I swim by her.

We swim and kid around for a while. On the surface, I'm having fun, but deep down, I'm stuck in a whirlwind of *what-ifs* and *what-could-happens* and *should-Is*. The battle is as good as lost as soon as Alex drains her beer and wades back towards us.

I swim as far away as possible while still in earshot of the group. I kick my legs and float on my back, cradled between the waves. The steady hum of the water in my ears cuts me from the world outside and allows me to wrangle my urges. My body is tingling all over. If I listened to it, I'd be dragging Alex to a secluded spot to see what would happen.

This past year's heartache, the near loss of our friendship, all of this has apparently done nothing to quell my desire. I know it would be a mistake, though, which is why my mind is battling to keep my body in check.

"Guys," Mitch calls out, making her way back to the beach, "I'm an all-you-can-eat mosquito buffet, so I'm gonna head back."

"I'm freezing," Georgie says through chattering teeth, "I'll come with."

The current brought me further than I thought, so it takes me a while to swim back to shore. By the time I reach the campfire, only Alex is left outside, huddled near the dwindling flames in a too-small, ratty towel that barely covers her panty-clad ass.

Fuck.

My gaze resolutely fixed on the fire, I pat myself dry with the last towel as well as I can, before putting my clothes back on. My dress clings to my damp skin, and my bra is soaked through, the padding heavy with seawater.

Alex throws a half-smoked cigarette onto the coals and stands up, letting her towel drop to the ground. She bridges the two steps of safe distance I've kept between us. Alarm bells go off in my head, but fail to drown out my lustful thoughts.

What happens at the cabin stays at the cabin.

She said she's over you.

What's the worst that could happen?

Alex stands so close to me I can feel the heat of her body, more potent than even the fading flames. She smirks and raises an eyebrow. Daring me to stop her.

My mind battles with itself, trying to summon the strength to walk away. To leave before making this mistake a second time. But my feet are rooted to the ground. I can't even turn away or close my eyes. I can only emit a feeble "This ain't a good — "

Alex silences my protest with a kiss. "Shut up," she mumbles against my lips, fingers digging into my hips.

My breath stutters in my throat, and I close my arms around her waist, a split-second show of weakness before my brain catches up with the events. I push her away, knowing I can't stay strong with her this close, wearing nothing but a bra and thin, almost sheer panties.

Finally snapping out of my daze, I manage to run back to the cabin. I sit on the back porch, trying to regain control of my whirlwind of thoughts.

Alex emerges from the woods a few minutes later, a pair of cut-off shorts hanging loosely from her hips, but still in her bra.

"Eager to go up to our room?" she drawls.

"You know that can't happen." I steel myself, determined not to succumb.

Alex pulls out a lighter and a joint from her back pocket. "Uh-uh. And why is that?" She lights the joint without one look at me, as if the discussion was but a formality.

"Because last time — "

"Was different. I was heartbroken. Drunk. Hooked on you."

"And now?"

She takes a long drag, and a sweet, acrid smell, reminiscent of skunks, fills my nostrils. "I saw you watching me. You are so completely turned on."

Her smirk pulls at my very core, but I must stay strong. "I still can't give you what you want."

"A good time?"

"Exclusivity."

"Maybe I don't care anymore." She shrugs, a bold gleam in her eyes.

"Okay, say we do this. Say we go up to our room right now and have sex. What's next? We'll have a summer fling for the next week before returning to Montreal, and then what? You're not the sharing type. As soon as you see me going back to David or Jeff, you're gonna bail. You can't just fuck me whenever you're horny and upthrow our entire friendship in the process."

"Sure, cause flings are only okay with small-town sluts!"

"Flings are okay with people who can deal with open relationships! And slut shaming? That's a new low, Alex."

She throws the butt of her joint at my feet. "Look, you can fuck the entire world, for all I care. But why is it that when it's me it's always a fucking mistake?"

"I don't know, maybe because it always ends up like this?"

"You know what, I don't need this." She climbs the three steps to the cabin door, which she slams. I hear her storming upstairs, the wooden steps creaking so loud they might collapse.

At my feet, the joint is still smoking. It took less time for our friendship to go out than a fucking blunt.

I step on it, putting it out of its misery.

THIRTY-FOUR

I wake up the next morning, my back creaking almost as loudly as the stairs. I spent the night on the living room couch — a brown plaid thing, probably older than me. There was no way I'd spend the night in the bed next to Alex's.

I get up and stretch the cricks out of my back, when I notice a few things missing from the hooks next to the front door. Alex's denim jacket is gone. So are her purse, flip-flops and Docs. Slowly, I thread upstairs, afraid of what I might — or might not — find there.

Two unslept beds and my luggage are the room's only occupants.

Alex Bell has bailed again.

¤

"She left."

Mitch doesn't need to hear more. She's at my side in an instant, offering her arms and a friendly ear. She follows me out on the porch, where I tell her what happened, trying hard to keep my anger in check. Alex is her friend too and the last thing I want is to turn everyone against her.

"This is it. There's no coming back from this. I don't think there's a friendship to salvage anymore."

"You never did manage to go back to how it was, uh?"

"I thought we might, the other day, when she was all upbeat, but then she tried to make a pass at me."

"She was jealous."

"Maybe I shouldn't have pursued this thing with Marie-Ève ..."

Mitch shrugs. "Maybe. But, I mean, Alex did say she was over you. You couldn't stop living out of fear of angering her. If it hadn't happened because of Marie, it would have done so sooner or later — because of Jeff, or someone cute you'd meet in a bar ..."

"I just can't believe it's over. Just like that. After I tried so hard to make it work."

Mitch drapes an arm around my shoulders and I cuddle in close.

The tears don't come.

I don't know if they ever will. The serial crier in me is surprised, but maybe I already exhausted all the tears I had for Alex.

The thought is somehow comforting.

THIRTY-FIVE

The next week passes in a flash of swimming, hikes and canoe rides with my friends, and dates with Marie-Ève, tainted only by the occasional wistful pang when something reminds me of Alex. Overall, though, I think I feel relieved. I don't have to walk on eggshells anymore, scared of doing or saying the wrong thing and setting Alex off. A huge weight has vanished from my shoulders.

On our last day, we drive to Percé — Georgie had never seen the Percé Rock before, and we wouldn't let him leave Gaspésie until he did. We leave the cabin not long after dawn, and we're alone on the road, so we get to enjoy the early morning fog, the first few sun rays piercing through the canopy of leaves, the nocturnal chill still present in the air.

This is probably the most touristy thing we've done this whole trip, but at least we get there early so we beat the crowds. We take a ferry to Bonaventure Island and the view is breathtaking. The Percé Rock looks majestic in the morning sun, all pinks and oranges, with the waves crashing against the shore.

Cory is bracketing Georgie against the railings, head tucked into the crook of his neck. Georgie looks at the Rock in awe, and the whole scene seems so intimate I turn away to let them have their moment. I walk over to Mitch, pulling out my phone.

"Selfie?"

We turn our backs to the railings, pull funny faces and I take a picture, making sure the Rock is in the frame.

"I'm glad we're doing this," Mitch says. "Somehow, far from the cabin, it doesn't seem as weird that Alex isn't here."

"Yeah, I get what you mean."

"Like, you've got Marie, and Cory and Georgie are — well — *Cory-and-Georgie* — so I feel a bit fifth-wheely, you know?"

I hadn't thought about that. I'd been so caught up in the whirlwind of my summer romance — in the coming-of-age movie feel of it all — that I never realized I was neglecting my friends.

"Oh my god, Mitch, I'm so sorry. I totally ditched you, didn't I?"

She shrugs. "I get it, you know. Well, not the rom-com head-over-heels for a stranger part of it, but, like — trying to keep your mind off Alex. When we're all together, her absence is more obvious."

I nod, gripping the railing until my knuckles turn white. This is exactly what I did with Jeff, the first time Alex left. I clung to him, and when that fell out, what was left?

Mitch.

Mitch, and Cory, and Georgie — my friends who keep putting up with my bullshit, and somehow still love the fuck out of me.

"How do you know me so well?" I chuckle, pulling her into a side hug.

"Well, after a while you start to notice that Amy Evans tends to follow patterns."

Wow. Called out.

¤

We get off the boat and hike a trail that takes us around the island to see gannets — thousands of them. Cory just about loses his mind. He's always been way into penguins and I guess gannets are the next best thing.

"Oh my god," his voice gets even more high-pitched than usual, "can we keep one?"

"Sure," Georgie deadpans. "I bet Ms. Reuben would love that."

Ms. Reuben, Cory and Georgie's downstairs neighbour, has been on the warpath ever since that night Cory tried to do death drops in five-inch heels at three in the morning after clubbing.

Cory is still making grabby hands at the birds when we decide to resume our hike.

"I'll buy you a stuffed one at the gift shop," Georgie offers.

We return to the mainland around lunchtime and gorge ourselves with fish and chips from a tiny restaurant in a shack. Cory clutches his stuffed gannet — he named it Gannet Paltrow — and Georgie looks at him fondly, like he does whenever he thinks we're not watching.

"So, big date tonight?" Cory asks me.

It's our last night, my last chance to see Marie in months — or maybe forever — and we intend to make the most of it. As I remember our conversation on the ferry, I turn to Mitch, suddenly feeling guilty.

"I could stay with you —"

"Don't you dare! You have one last night with this girl, you better enjoy it! I'll be fine."

"Yeah, you'll be with us!" Cory grins, draping an arm around her shoulders and shoving Gannet Paltrow against her chest.

"Just, please, don't act so married, alright?"

Georgie makes a big show of sliding away from Cory on the bench. "Cory who? I don't know her."

Cory gasps, clutching at his non-existent pearls. "The shade!"

¤

We drive back to the cabin and have time for one last swim before Marie picks me up.

I'm climbing in the passenger seat of her blue pick-up truck when I hear Mitch's voice calling out.

"We leave at seven thirty tomorrow morning — don't be late!"

"Yes, Mom." I roll my eyes at her, but I blow her a kiss so she knows how much I love her mothering us.

Marie waves Mitch goodbye and kisses me hello. It's a simple kiss, and we've already slept together a few times, but it still sends shivers up my spine and a wave of anticipation builds in my stomach.

"So, what did you have in mind for tonight?"

She told me yesterday not to worry about a thing, that she'd take care of everything to make my last night in Gaspésie unforgettable. The only hint she gave me was to bring warm clothes, so I guess we'll be outside.

"Look in the back." She jerks her head towards the back of the truck, an enigmatic smirk on her face.

I turn in my seat and peek through the rear window. In the bed of the truck is a wicker basket covered with a red and white checkered tablecloth. Next to it are a bunch of sleeping bags and blankets, and a long, black carrier bag I can't identify — some musical instrument? Sports equipment?

"A picnic?" I turn back to her, grinning.

"Not just a lousy picnic," she scoffs. "I'm taking you to the best viewpoint around. We'll have a picnic, watch the sunset, and we'll camp in the bed of the truck and stargaze."

"What's in the bag?"

"My dad's telescope. I don't know a lot about astronomy, but it's always impressive even if you don't know what you're looking at. Dad said we might get to see the Northern Lights and some shooting stars."

Marie looks at me expectantly, eager to see if I like the idea. I grin and squeeze her thigh — her hand is busy with the gear stick.

"I can't wait."

She drives off the highway onto a beaten path weaving through the woods. The path is so narrow the branches scrape against the car and she has to drive really slowly to avoid bumps, rocks, and the occasional bunny or bird strolling across the road. We drive into the woods for fifteen minutes or so, until the trees become scarce and give way to tall grass. She parks the truck in a patch of wheel tracks — she's been here before, I guess.

I follow her out of the truck. She grabs the picnic basket and hands me the telescope carrier. She finds a trail through the grass and leads me to a large expanse of flat rock. At our feet is a rocky ledge dropping about fifty meters into the sea.

A surge of vertigo hits me and I grab Marie's hand to steady myself. She pulls me a step back and places a grounding arm around my shoulders. The vertigo passes and I let out a deep breath.

"Are you okay?" she asks, eyebrows knitting into a frown. "We can go elsewhere …"

"No, it's alright." I take a few steps back. "I just need to keep away from the edge. I'm fine here." I crack a smile — but she still doesn't look convinced.

I grab the tablecloth and spread it on the ground, making sure to be at least a meter away from the edge. I sit down on it, cross-legged, to stop the wind from blowing it away.

"See? All good!"

Marie sets the basket down to stop another corner dancing in the wind. She rifles through the basket and produces a bottle of wine and two metal camping mugs. "This should take the edge off," she says, her voice muffled by the cork between her teeth.

I gesture at the cliff drop. "I think the edge is okay where it is, if you don't mind."

Marie laughs and drops the cork. It rolls away into the tall grass. "Well, would you look at that? Now we'll have to drink all the wine!"

I shake my head in mock outrage. "Bummer…"

The wine is delicious and so is the dinner she prepared: lobster rolls — she calls it *guédille* — made with lobster caught this very morning by her uncle.

"You couldn't leave before you had a real *guédille*. Or a real sunset."

She nods at the horizon slowly turning pink. We watch in silence, cuddling together as the burning disk drops into the sea, setting the sky ablaze. The sky turns slowly dark blue, and as the stars begin lighting up, Marie-Ève sets up the telescope.

In the beam of the large flashlight, her blue hair sets off her pale skin perfectly. I am again reminded of a mermaid, in the fluid way she moves and how her hair flows around her face in the wind.

"If you ever come to Montreal, you should pose for my boyfriend. He's doing a mermaid photography series."

She looks up, eyes as glinting as the newborn stars. "You think I look like a mermaid?"

"You clearly belong to the sea."

She chuckles and rubs the thigh of her jeans, where her Venus tattoo is hidden. "I've always felt a deep connexion to it. Probably why my favourite colour is blue."

She fiddles with the telescope and waves me over. "It's working! C'm'ere."

I press my eye to the telescope and gasp. A cluster of stars. So many of them. Used to Montreal's night sky with its five or six visible stars, I can't quite believe what I'm seeing.

"This is amazing," I breathe out, still glued to the telescope.

Marie chuckles. I feel her hand nestling at the base of my neck, fingers combing through my hair. She plays with a strand and caresses my scalp in feather-soft touches. A shiver runs down my spine and I turn to her. She gives me the cutest half-smile ever, her eyes brighter than anything I can see through the telescope. I boop her nose and press the softest kiss to her lips, eliciting a breathy laugh.

"Wow," she whispers. "I know we came here to watch the stars, but I kinda just wanna watch you." She looks away, her cheeks reddening. "Was that too cheesy?"

"Not at all." I shake my head and laugh. "Well, it was, but who says it's a bad thing?"

Marie giggles and pulls me to lie on the ground next to her. "I can spot *la Grande Ourse* — how do you call it?"

I cozy up to her side. "*Ursa Major*. The Big Dipper."

After we run out of the three constellations we know — the Big Dipper, Cassiopeia and Orion — we start making some up.

"The Mermaid!"

"The Acrobat!"

"The Lesbian Lovers!"

By this time, we're laughing too hard to even be able to point up at the sky. Laughter echoes down the cliff, carried on the strong wind, and dies down on the rocks among the crashing waves. Marie's hand finds mine, but immediately recoils.

"Your hand is freezing!"

I suddenly notice how cold I am. Strong wind bats at my sweater and I can barely keep my stomach covered. "That's alright, I'll just have to put it somewhere warm." I snake a hand under her shirt and she shrieks at the touch.

"Come on, back to the truck." She stands up and puts the telescope away in its carrier, while I gather the picnic basket, wrestling with the tablecloth as it flaps in the wind.

The way back through the tall grass is harder to find in the dark, with the wind sending the grass swinging at us, but we finally manage to find the truck. We build a nest out of blankets and sleeping bags in the bed of the truck, but no matter how close we snuggle, my teeth won't stop chattering.

"I've got just the thing for you." Marie scrambles out of the nest and digs through the basket to find a thermos.

"God, you're the best!" I exhale loudly.

She offers me a plastic cup filled to the brim with hot cocoa. I cradle it between my hands, my skin prickling at the contrast in temperature. I burn my tongue on the first sip, but don't even slow down — I need the warmth trickling down my throat and spreading through my chest.

Halfway through the first cup, I can feel my toes slowly thawing, and I finally stop shivering. "Can't believe this time tomorrow, I'm gonna be sweating through insomnia in the forty degree Montreal heatwave."

"Can't say I envy you," Marie chuckles.

After the second cup, I still feel a bit chilly, but I am now on a sugar high of considerable proportions. Marie snuggles up closer and looks at me with very cheesy bedroom eyes.

"I know a game that will both warm us up and spend all that pent-up energy."

"My favourite kind of game."

¤

My alarm wakes me up at six the next morning. I snooze it, letting myself enjoy Marie-Ève's warmth a bit longer before waking her up. I bury my face in her blue hair, trying to commit her scent to memory — ocean air and campfire, exactly the way I'll remember Gaspésie.

She stirs in my arms and tangles her legs through mine. "I hope you know I'm not letting you leave," she mumbles, sleep blurring her consonants.

She weaves her fingers through mine around her waist and holds me in a surprisingly strong grip for someone who hasn't even opened her eyes yet. I chuckle and pepper kisses across her shoulder.

"I'm gonna miss you," she whispers, so low I don't know if I'm supposed to hear it.

"Me too." I kiss the top of her head.

"Gimme your phone."

I unlock it and hand it to her. She types her name and phone number into my contacts. "If you're ever in Gaspésie again…"

"I don't think I'll wait this long to talk to you. You better prepare for a lot of texting."

"I can live with that." She chuckles in the crook of my neck, sending shivers down my spine.

She notices the goose bumps, giggles and trails her hands up and down my sides, excruciatingly slowly. I grab her and kiss her, hard.

"We better go, or else I'll have to fuck you again."

"That's not a good incentive — it just makes me want to never let you go."

"You'd think for someone in an open-relationship, I'd be better at one-night-stands and goodbyes. I just get too attached — unless the person is a jerk, of course."

"You sleep with jerks?"

"Sometimes I don't realize they're jerks before it's too late."

"Been there. But, hey, if you ever miss me too much, call me. I've been told I'm incredible at phone sex."

"Sounds interesting. I may take you up on that." I wink at her.

I sit up and untangle myself from the blanket nest. The crisp morning air hits me like a blast and I instantly cuddle back to Marie.

"Nope. You're right. Never leaving this cocoon."

She giggles. "Hey, I don't want to suffer the wrath of Mama Mitch."

I let out an exaggerated sigh. "Fine."

The ride back to the cabin is silent. What can you say when you fall halfway in love and all the way in lust with someone? When there's nothing left to say but goodbye?

Marie casts glances at me while she drives, covert looks reflecting my own pain, my own questions. At last, she parks her pick-up truck in front of the cabin, heaving a sigh as she turns off the engine.

"I don't wanna go," I say in a small, desperate voice.

"Then don't," she pleads.

I shake my head — as much as I want to stay here, bathe in the sea with her and make love to her, I have a life to go back to. A life that, at the moment, seems utterly unattractive — but I remember David. Gorgeous, amazing David, the love of my life.

I grab Marie-Ève's face in my hands and kiss her — a kiss full of pressing, unsaid things.

I wish for more.

I'll miss you.

I could love you.

Unspeakable things. Everything went by too fast — you're not supposed to say these things to someone you've only known for two weeks.

Especially if you're leaving.

My heart tightens up. I breathe out a sigh against her lips, hug her close, and get out of the truck before my heart can convince me to stay.

I watch my mermaid swim away in her truck, blue as the waves, blue as her hair, and tears fill up my eyes like seawater.

I walk in the cabin without a word as my friends finish packing up. I get in the shower. I can't go on a ten-hour drive smelling like her — the memories would just kill me.

The shower helps, a bit, even though it acts up, like it did all through our stay, and refuses to give me any hot water. At least it allows me a good cry without anyone seeing or hearing me. I need that, or else I'll spend the entire ride trying to hide my tears.

I can't believe I'm crying this hard for someone I didn't even know existed fourteen days ago. I don't know if it's the setting — gorgeous Gaspésie, an exciting summer fling — or if she's just an amazing person, but in just a fortnight, Marie-Ève dug herself an enormous place in my heart.

I wouldn't have it any other way.

THIRTY-SIX

As we get closer to home, I get cellular reception again. All the text messages I missed this week start coming in. I ignore them. The real world can wait until tomorrow. The sound of alerts dings every few minutes until I get sick of it and put my phone on plane mode. Let's pretend I don't have reception for a bit longer.

We make a few stops to eat and pee, and finally get home around eight, exhausted. Mitch drops me home first to pick-up Gaspard. Hopefully he didn't torture David too much in the past two weeks.

I lug my suitcase to the door. Never have I been so happy to live on the first floor. David's waiting for me in the kitchen with a big glass of white wine and a steaming bowl of mac and cheese — and he makes *the* best mac and cheese this side of the St. Lawrence River. I fall into his arms, half-laughing and half-crying.

"I missed you terribly," I mumble into his shoulder. "And I have so much to tell you."

"Good or bad?"

"Too much of both."

"Eat, shower and sleep. You can tell me all about it tomorrow — you must be exhausted."

I reluctantly leave his comforting embrace long enough to scarf down his delicious meal and take a long shower. You never appreciate the amazingness of hot water until you go someplace where you have to stand on your head and sacrifice a virgin or two to get the tiniest amount of lukewarm water.

I step out of the shower and am greeted by David, holding a huge bath towel fresh out of the dryer, ready to wrap me up in it. I let him burrito me and pat me dry. I'd forgotten how great it is to be pampered.

I slip into one of his old tees — one that smells like him, like black tea and our fabric softener, but, most importantly, like home. I follow him to the bedroom. The sight of our own bed almost brings tears to my eyes. Not to mention *my pillows*. Soft, warm, fluffy. I climb into bed and David barely has time to kiss me goodnight before I'm whisked away to dreamland.

I wake up the next morning, around eleven, to the scent of warm pancakes. I pad away to the kitchen where David has set the table with a tablecloth, orange juice in champagne flutes, a teapot full of steaming Earl Grey and fresh flowers.

"Dude, you went all out!" I whistle in appreciation.

"I missed you," he says with a bashful smile.

I pull him closer. "Good morning," I mumble through a kiss.

He hugs me tight, like he never wants to let me go, but then he realizes his pancakes are starting to burn and runs to the stove. He fixes me a plate with non-burnt pancakes, maple syrup and fresh fruit while I pour us a cup of tea.

While we eat, I tell him about everything: Alex, Marie-Ève — "Of course you met someone, called it!" — and how I didn't realize it would hurt so bad to leave her — but also about the good stuff: the village, the beach, the cabin.

"We should go to Gaspésie together one day, you'd love it. The landscapes are amazing — so photogenic."

"Did you eat seafood for me?" He asks eagerly, a forkful of pancake suspended halfway to his mouth, forgotten.

David is the biggest seafood nut I know. He spends most of his paychecks from September to December on oysters.

"You bet. Clams. Shrimp. The best smoked trout I've ever had."

"Lobster?"

"Marie-Ève made me an amazing *guédille*."

"Oh my god." David's face right now looks so much like his orgasm face I have no choice but to laugh.

"So when are we going?" He's at the edge of his seat, almost ready to leave on the spot. He's already mentally drawing up the menu for a week of seafood feasts.

"I haven't even unpacked yet!" I laugh.

"Great — you won't need to pack, then." A twinkle shines in his eyes.

"David, are you serious? I can't take any more time off work." I giggle and climb in his lap.

"Fine, but we're going next summer for sure?"

"Promise." We seal the deal with a kiss, and he carries me back to bed, breakfast forgotten in favour of a more interesting activity — one we both missed so much these past two weeks.

¤

Jeff Williams — Miss you already

Jeff Williams — Can't sleep :(why aren't you next to me?

Jeff Williams — Dunno if you got a signal at the village or something, but if you get this, call me, I miss you <3

David Paradis — Allo chaton, just wanna say je t'aime, just in case you get reception at the village or whatever <3 <3 <3 Oh and tell Mitch Gaspard misses her!

Jeff Williams — Guess you really don't get reception. Call me as soon as you do. Can't wait to hear your voice <3 <3 <3 <3 <3

David Paradis — 9 hours of D&D, still going strong!

Jeff Williams — Heyyy I'm drunk ans snot the samm w/out u — whyy did u leavee we jist got back 2gethr :(

David Paradis — Jason's rogue just died o_O

David Paradis — shiiiiiit a dragon just ate my mage!!!

Jeff Williams — Forgot 2 say I miss u :P

Hugo Gibson — oops. the whole party's dead. pretty sure your bf hates me as a DM

Julia Tyler — Hey, call me, I got great news!!!

Julia Tyler — I just realized this is the week you're at Mitch's cabin isn't it? You probably don't have cellphone reception. Well, call me when you get back! Great news!!!

Julia Tyler — Oh, heck, I can't wait! Jason popped the question! I can't wait to tell you all about it!!! Wait til you see The Ring!!!

Hugo Gibson — i just played a 30min set at a sold-out venue and the crowd was amazing! wish you were here <3

Charlotte Evans — u never told me hugo was such an amazing musician?!

Jude Harrison — Shifts w/out you & G are the epitome of boring. Come back at once xox

David Paradis — Un dodo before you come back <3 have a good ride home chaton

Michelle Murray — Tell David thx for cat sitting :D Man, my bed is awesome :P

Marie-Ève Provencher sent you a friend request.

I quickly accept Marie-Ève's friend request — and I stare at her profile picture for way too long: she's kneeling in the ocean, waves lapping at her thighs, like the flawless mermaid she is. I 'like' the picture, as a way to say 'hey.'

I then start answering my text messages. One text to Jeff should do the trick, even though he completely missed the point of no cellphone reception.

Amy Evans — Hey sweetie! I just got back last night! I missed you too <3 <3 <3 Wanna get together tomorrow night?

To Julia, I send a quick congratulations text and we arrange to get together for coffee next week. Julia and I may have drifted apart in the last year, but she's my oldest friend, so I'm genuinely happy for her. She's always dreamed of the classic 'happily ever after' ending, and she's been with Jason for three years now. I've seen her plan her wedding for the last decade or so, and I know how important it is to her.

I text Charlotte and we go back and forth until I promise to tell her next time I'm going to one of Hugo's gigs.

I send the applause emoji to Hugo and tell him I miss hearing him play. He sends me a demo of some stuff he's been working on and that pretty much makes my day — I really missed his voice.

¤

David and I take advantage of the fact that we both have tomorrow off to have a date night. We cook dinner together — mussels to assuage his seafood craving — take a long bubble bath, make love (again), and he tells me all about their twenty-hour long game of D&D.

"I swear, Hugo must be the most ruthless dungeon master I've ever seen. Georgie is an angel compared to him. I mean, we all lost characters we've played for over a year!"

"He said he thinks you hate him."

David chuckles. "Of course not! I like him better as a player than a DM, though. Jason was glad his rogue was killed early — he went home and planned his proposal to Julia."

"You knew about that and kept it to yourself?"

"He told us just before the game; you were already gone. Plus, I didn't think you'd care, you're not as close to Julia as you used to be."

"I'm still glad she and Jason make each other happy, though."

"Oh, definitely. You should have seen the look on Jason's face when he told us what he'd planned. It made me miss you even more."

"I think these two weeks apart were a good thing," I say as he tries to make me a beard out of bath foam. "I think we've forgotten 'us' a bit these past months. We failed to keep our New Year's resolution. We haven't even dined-and-dished in weeks."

"We were really busy. With wedding season, I have shoots and meetings almost every day." He laughs at his bubbly masterpiece.

"Yeah, but we're never too busy to go on dates with other people. And when we're together, we're so exhausted we don't even 'Netflix and chill' anymore. We just 'Netflix and crash.'"

"Okay, how's this: Sunday through Wednesday is ours, and we can see other people on Thursdays, Fridays and Saturdays?"

"Sounds great." I beam at him and wipe away the beard. "Although I've already made plans with Jeff tomorrow night…"

"Of course, you just got back. Let's say this new schedule starts next week, alright?"

"Perfect." I fashion him Princess Leia buns out of foam. "And, can we make exceptions for like, birthdays, or if the person is shipping out tomorrow, or whatever?"

"Sure, but we have to balance it out with an extra you and me day the following week."

"Deal." I hold out my hand for him to shake.

"I love you," he says, as seriously as he can with foam buns on either side of his head.

"I know."

"Geek."

THIRTY-SEVEN

The bright June sun is out. People are rushing to terraces for a happy hour pitcher of sangria to celebrate summer. The excited, elated vibe reaches me and I'm filled with anticipation. I can't wait to see Jeff. He lives a twenty-minute walk from Quarante-Cinq, but I can't bear the thought of being underground in the subway on such a beautiful day, so I decide to walk.

I almost run the last few blocks to Jeff's place — the last minutes apart seem more excruciating than the whole two weeks I was away.

When Jeff opens the door, he flashes me the brightest smile and pulls me into the biggest hug.

"Finally," he breathes out. His body slumps into mine, as if it tensed up without me and now it can finally relax.

"I've missed you," I say with a small laugh. I love seeing him this happy.

"God, 'miss' isn't strong enough a word. I don't even know how I got through these two weeks."

I take a closer look at him — his eyes are sunken, circled in purple shadows.

"I wrote a song about you while I couldn't sleep."

"Really? Wow, no one has ever written a song for me before!" I kiss him and follow him to the kitchen. "Mmm, something smells good!"

"Shrimp skewers with mango salsa."

"I feel so spoiled!"

"You deserve it." He kisses me, soft and tender.

"Here, I brought wine." I hand him a paper bag.

Jeff pours two glasses and we go sit on his balcony where he can keep an eye on the grill. We eat outside and catch up — I tell him all about the cabin and how pretty Gaspésie is.

"So, did you meet anyone there?"

"A girl. Marie-Ève. We're gonna keep in touch on Facebook, but unless one of us moves, I can't see much of a future."

Jeff makes a face and quickly changes the subject.

"Anyway, the band got a gig this weekend! We're playing the Matchbox, you should come! We'll probably play your song." He grins. "I just have to finish it."

"Of course I'll be there! I can't wait to hear it!"

We spend the rest of the night outside. The wine is cold on my tongue, but warm in my veins. My brain feels fuzzy, but in a good way — like nothing exists or matters but Jeff's hand lazily resting on my thigh and the way he looks at me under heavy lids.

Jeff breaks the comfortable silence. "So how come you waited so long to text when you came back?" he asks, his words a bit slurred from the wine.

"Well, during the ride back I wasn't feeling well because I had to leave Marie-Ève and I had a fight with Alex. Then, when I got home I was exhausted and David took care of me. And yesterday we spent the day together."

"So how come you went to see *him* first?"

The way he says *him* sets me on edge — he bites into the word like he wants to kill it.

"He's my boyfriend."

"So am I — or at least you said so."

"Yeah, but I live with him. Of course I went home first."

"Oh, so he's always gonna come first because of his roommate privileges?"

"Look, I don't wanna fight. But this is something you've gotta understand, if we want this to work. You agreed to be with a girl in an open relationship. This means I can't give you all of my time. I don't want you to make me feel guilty when I spend time with David — or with anyone else, for that matter."

Jeff shrugs and looks away.

"Can you accept that?"

Another shrug. "I guess."

"Look, I think you need to process what this kind of relationship entails. Before I left, we talked about it, but we were hurrying to pick up where we left off so we didn't get the chance to see if we can make it work. I think you need to sleep on it and we'll talk tomorrow." I stand up, but Jeff takes my hand to stop me, a puzzled look on his face.

"You said you'd spend the night." He makes it sound like I owe him. My stomach churns, but he seems to realize what he's saying. He gives a sad smile. "I missed you."

I look in his wistful eyes and my determination wavers. One night can't do much harm, especially if he decides he can't do this afterwards. I smile and sit down.

"You have to promise you'll take the rest of the week to decide if you can be in that kind of relationship."

Jeff nods enthusiastically. "You got it!"

We spend the rest of the night steering away from sensitive subjects, like David. Or Marie-Ève. Or anyone I've ever been remotely interested in, for that matter. We end up going to bed for dizzy, drunken sex.

The next morning, I wake up early. I have to go to work, but Jeff keeps a firm hold on me as I try to slip out of the covers.

"Stay," he whines, his voice drowsy with sleep.

"I can't, I have to be at the store at nine."

"Kiss me and I'll make you breakfast."

I indulge him and head to the bathroom with my overnight bag. When I get out, breakfast is on the table, along with a steaming mug of tea.

"Thanks, sweetie."

"Thank *you* for the best sleep I got in a week. I can't sleep when you're not here."

There it is again. The sound of entitlement in his voice. Like I owe him something because I call him my boyfriend. I decide to give him the benefit of the doubt. He probably just missed me. He'll go back to the sweet, loving Jeff I know once we see each other more often.

We eat mostly in silence — I know he's anything but a morning person, so making and eating breakfast before eleven is huge for him. I gather my things, thank him and leave. I'm pretty sure he's back in bed before I even close the door behind me.

THIRTY-EIGHT

"Guess what?" Mitch sets four Le Trèfle ceramic mugs on the table and sits down with Cory, Georgie and me.

Cory perks up, his gossip-hungry face lighting up. "What?"

"Alex was supposed to work tonight and she just called to say she quit, without so much as a day's notice."

"What?" Georgie exclaims.

"This is so not like her — she loves this job," Cory points out.

"Has anyone heard from her since we came back?" Mitch asks, pulling her phone out of her apron pocket.

Cory shakes his head no, scrolling on his phone. "She unfriended me on Facebook!"

"Me too!" Mitch notices.

They all turn to me, realizing I've been silent for the whole discussion. I scrunch up my face.

"I hoped it wouldn't come to that. Our last fight, the night she left the cabin, was because she hit on me and I turned her down. I didn't want a repeat of last year, y'know?"

"So why did she…?" Georgie shakes his phone, indicating Alex's locked Facebook page.

Mitch sighs. "I guess she finally realized she couldn't get over Amy if they still saw each other all the time."

"Yeah, probably." I take a sip of my latte. "I think she needed a clean slate, so she got rid of everything reminding her of me."

"Us," Cory concludes dejectedly.

"I'm so sorry, guys. I didn't mean for you all to get caught up in this mess."

"It's okay," Mitch says. "This was Alex's decision. What matters is that she's doing what she needs to get better, and we'll be here if she decides she wants us back in her life."

¤

On Wednesday morning, my phone reminds me I have a coffee date with Julia after work.

"Ugh." I make a face and David chuckles. "I just hope she won't be — you know — all *Julia*."

Let's just say, after everything that happened with Alex and Marie, I'm not up for judgemental looks and snide remarks about my life choices.

"Knowing her," David points out, "she'll be too busy talking about her wedding and Jason's proposal to even think about judging you."

"Oh god." I bury my face in my hands. "She's gonna be a total bridezilla, isn't she?"

¤

I step inside the Starbucks and spot Julia waving at me from a table near the window. I nod in her direction and get a large London Fog before joining her.

"Hi!" she squeals as I sit down in front of her.

She immediately extends her arm, presenting the unmissable diamond sparkling proudly on her perfectly French-manicured left hand.

"Gorgeous!" Not my type of ring at all, but this is obviously what I'm meant to say. "Congrats, you must be over the moon!"

"Yes! Oh my god, Jason is the *absolute* best. He surprised me at work with flowers and an actual horse-drawn carriage! We took a ride to the park where we first met, and he popped the question at the exact spot where we first saw each other — can you believe it? And he hired a professional photographer — who was hiding, of course — so we've got perfect memories of the proposal! And then we had dinner at Orphée, where we had our first date! Isn't he the best?"

"That's amazing!" I'm honestly overwhelmed, but you know, that's Julia for you. "I'm so happy for you guys — "

"So, there is *so* much to do," she interrupts me, flipping open a huge pink binder. From what I can see, it's full of calendars, colour swatches, and pictures of flowers, cakes and dresses.

"The wedding will be on the third Saturday of next May, of course, because I've always wanted a spring wedding. That leaves us only ten months to plan everything. The theme colours are honeysuckle and gold. We haven't chosen the venue yet, but my mom has a cottage in Vermont that would be just perfect. But then there's Jason's parents, who also have a gorgeous place up in Tremblant — you know how families can be when you plan a wedding…"

Sure, because I planned dozens of them. I nod politely, not that she notices, with her head buried in her wedding binder.

"So anyway, I've found a few dresses for you guys — "

"I'm sorry?" I pause, bewildered, my mug suspended midway between the table and my lips.

"Oh my god, I'm *such* an idiot! Amy, will you be my bridesmaid?"

"Um — yeah, I guess — "

"Oh my god, thanks! Okay, so my maid of honour is my sister Olivia, and the other bridesmaids are Sophie — you know, from high school? — and Brittany, who I went to McGill with."

This comes as an absolute surprise. We barely see each other anymore — I mean, she skipped my birthday for the first time in years, so I never thought she'd ask me. I know this probably isn't the best idea — I have trouble keeping up with Julia most of the time, so imagine her as a bride — but she *is* my oldest friend and she put me on the spot, so…

"Great!" I give a reluctant smile and hide my awkwardness behind a sip of tea.

"Oh, and I can't believe I'm saying this to you, and not to Jason's groomsmen, but please behave." Her face is scrunched up in a lousy attempt to hide her disgust.

"What do you mean?"

"Don't sleep with them," she stage whispers, lest she scandalize someone by talking about my harlot ways.

"I won't."

"I mean it, Amy. This is *my* day, it is *sacred*, and I won't have it ruined by — by your usual slutting around!" Julia turns a page in her binder, looking satisfied, as if this was just another thing to cross on her to-do list. Slutshame Amy, *check!*

I sit in front of her, unable to emit any kind of reply — how do you even begin to explain things to someone with such a different outlook on life they might as well live on another planet?

You accepted to be dragged into Julia Tyler's Bridal Extravaganza, now suck it up.

"So," she continues, her flashiest grin back as if nothing had just happened, "these are some ideas for your dresses."

She pushes the binder towards me and I flip through a few pages of bridesmaid pictures, all wearing pale shades of pink, which I gather must be the aforementioned honeysuckle, all sporting various amounts of lace and ruffles.

"Obviously, nothing's set in stone yet, and we'll have to hold a few meetings, to make sure everyone's on the same page, but you can sleep on it, you know, to get an idea of what you like."

"Alright — "

"And I'll send you guys some Pinterest boards with ideas, so make sure you check that out."

Is she actually giving me *homework*?

"Alright, I have to run, Mom and I are meeting with caterers after lunch! Oh, and honey?" She rests a sympathetic hand upon mine. "Don't worry. David *is* gonna ask soon. I'm sure of it. Okay, *ciao!*"

She kisses me on both cheeks and departs, along with her binder and most of my sanity.

THIRTY-NINE

Matchbox is almost empty — everyone is outside on the terrace, enjoying the warm summer night, save for an old guy playing pool alone. Mitch and I have our pick of tables, so we choose one near the stage. We order a pitcher of sangria to avoid having to get up during the set.

"Man, I'm so excited," I tell Mitch. "I haven't seen them play in so long!"

"You're gonna love it — they've gotten so much better!"

"Jeff says he wrote me a song."

"Really? That's so nice! I wish Justin would do that. But then again, songs for ace platonic soulmates are kinda niche, don't you think?"

"You never know, maybe there's a huge ace fanbase waiting for a pop-punk band to cling to?"

The place slowly fills up as we talk about the band's album and Julia's wedding. The bar is almost full by the time Jonathan taps a countdown with his drumsticks and Jeff starts strumming a rhythm on his bass.

"What's up Montreal? WE! ARE! THE! J-WALKERS!" Jenkins shouts into his microphone.

Jeff waits for the applause and cheers to die down a bit and leans into his microphone. "Hey guys, this one's for the love of my life and it's called *513 Miles*."

Mitch gasps and elbows me square in the ribs.

"What?" I exclaim as she almost makes me drop my glass.

"Love of his life?"

"What?" I shrug. "Jeff's always been a little intense, you know him…"

"I think he's far more in love with you than you with him… He's bound to get hurt — "

"Can we talk about this later? He wrote this for me, the least I can do is pay attention."

"Fine," she mumbles, and turns her attention to Justin.

Indeed, Jeff is looking at us with a worried frown, but I smile and tap my foot to the beat, which makes him smile again. He jumps around with his bass, sharing the mic with Justin for the chorus.

You're 513 miles away
Why would you think that's okay?
Why would you rather be out there?
In the fucking middle of nowhere

"I don't know for sure but I bet 513 miles is the exact distance to my parents' cabin."

"Mitch!"

"Right. Later." She crosses her arms and turns away.

Are you thinking about me?
I can't think of anything else
Life means nothing without you
You're 513 miles away

The melody is great — the band as a whole has indeed greatly improved since I last saw them, but Mitch is right. The lyrics are veering past intense into creepy territory. I mean, there's a line between 'I miss you' and 'I can't survive without you,' and this song enthusiastically crosses it.

I decide to worry about it later and enjoy the rest of the show. The other songs are not better per se, but, you know, saner. They're about random girls — read: not me — or at least girls Jenkins knows, not Jeff. And they're about fun, normal things: car rides, skinny-dipping, rooftop parties.

Halfway through the set, Mitch seems to thaw: she refills my glass, smiles at me, and comments on the music, like, "This one's my favourite on the album!" or "Isn't Justin really coming into his own as a singer?"

I'm glad, because I really don't want to fight with Mitch on top of everything. We've gotten tight-knit over the last few months — of course, she can't replace Alex, but she has taken a bigger place in my life, and I'm so grateful for that.

After the show's over, Mitch and I step outside and secure a table on the terrace for the band and us. They pack up everything in Joanna's van and join us afterwards, armed with several pitchers of beer.

"Great gig, you guys!" Mitch and I holler and clap when they get to us.

"Thanks, love." Jeff takes me in his arms, his grin spreading across his face. I just love the way his eyes light up when he smiles.

When everyone is settled around the table with a beer, chatter rises around us, sounds of praise and congratulations. Jeff is silent, but looks at me expectantly. He obviously wants to know what I thought of my song.

I hesitate a quarter of a second. Jeff is clearly so proud of it, and, of course, he hopes I liked it. I don't want to bring him down right now — not when he's on his post-gig high, in front of all his band mates.

But Mitch is right. I'm baffled at the intensity — clinginess, even — of the song, and the fact that he said I'm the love of his life. I'll talk to him later, when we're alone. For now, I'll just try to focus my praise on the rest of the show.

"Amazing gig! I'm so proud of you!"

He beams. "Really? You liked your song?"

So much for not talking about it.

"Of course!" I hug him so I can hide my face in his shoulder — my sister keeps saying you can always tell I'm lying with one look at my face.

"I'm so glad! I was worried you wouldn't like it. This is exactly the push I needed to finish the other ones I wrote for you."

"The other ones?"

"Yeah, you told me to think about us this week, and when I think, I compose!"

"I can't wait to hear them!" I hide my faint enthusiasm by taking a sip of beer.

At the first occasion, I join Mitch and Justin's conversation. Next time I look, Jeff is chatting away with Jonathan and his boyfriend.

Confident I managed to push back the unpleasant talk, I enjoy the rest of the night talking and drinking with everyone.

People keep coming up to the band to congratulate them on a great show. Most of them look at me and smile, head cocked to the side. I swear they're all thinking, *aww, she's the love of his life.* Jeff's arm around my shoulders does nothing to dispel this idea.

At the end of the night, I pretend to have a headache combined with an early morning the next day to get out of spending the night at Jeff's. I don't want to go home with him without having a serious talk, and tonight, neither of us is in the right mindset for that. We're both tipsy and he's still on his post-gig rush, so I don't have the heart to bring him down.

¤

If Jeff's illegible 4a.m. text — which I can only assume meant 'I love you,' but can't be sure — is anything to go by, I'm guessing they kept partying well into the dawn. Knowing him, there's no way he'll be up any time before five in the afternoon.

I decide to drop the issue for the weekend — a hung-over Jeff is not any fitter for a serious conversation than a drunk Jeff.

On Monday night, David has a photoshoot and I have no plans, so I start on my 'homework' for Julia. I make myself a nice dinner, pour a glass of wine, and enjoy it all on the couch with my laptop, browsing through endless pages of frilly dresses, elaborate flower arrangements and gravity defying cakes.

After a while, my cellphone rings. The screen lights up with Jeff's face and name.

"Hey, love. What are you doing?"

"Bridesmaid duties. I have to check out dresses and floral arrangements."

"You're gonna be a bridesmaid?"

"Yeah, for my friend Julia."

"When's the wedding?"

"I haven't got the invitation yet, but sometime in May, I think."

"Tell me when you're certain and I'll reserve my weekend."

"Um, I'm going with David — "

"What? This could be our first official event, you know, as a couple!"

"Well, all these people know David and me as a couple and they're not really — "

"That's 'cause you won't introduce me as your boyfriend!"

"Look, to these people, *David* is my boyfriend, and he's their friend too. He's Jason's best man — it just makes sense!"

"Are you ashamed of me?" Jeff's tone is accusatory, but his voice cracks mid-sentence.

I heave a sigh. "I'd rather not discuss this on the phone, nor while you're mad. I told you to think about it, to see if you're ready to be in this kind of relationship. All you're proving to me is that you're not."

The thing with a smartphone is that you can't slam it down when you're angry. I cut the call and throw the phone on the couch as hard as I can. Really lacks catharsis.

I take a quick shower and go to bed, turning my phone off because Jeff keeps calling back. I know if I answer right now, the fight will just pick up where we left off. We both need to sleep on this.

The next day, I feel somewhat better. My anger has calmed down during the night, although I'm not sure if my relationship with Jeff is salvageable.

When he calls at lunchtime, I tell myself I have to give us a chance and answer.

"Look, love, I'm so, so sorry. I was way out of line. Of course you're going to the wedding with Dave."

"David."

"Yeah. So, do you think you can forgive me?"

"Sure." Relationships take work. I didn't break up with David at the first fight. I'm determined to work things out with Jeff.

"Awesome! Look, I really want to see you. Are you free tonight?"

"It's Tuesday — I'm staying home with David."

"But — " I can tell he wants to argue, but he probably doesn't want to start another fight so soon, so he shuts up. "Alright, what about Friday?"

"Karaoke with Mitch and the guys."

"Can I come?"

"I — " I'm about to refuse, but then I realize that in a public setting we won't have to get into long explanations and a potential fight. I know we have to talk about this, but for now, I just want to have fun with him — to go back to why we're together in the first place.

"Yeah, it'd be great. I'll text you the details."

"Oh, by the way, we have a gig on Saturday. Maybe you could come?"

"Yeah, why not?"

"Great! Love ya!"

"Me too," I answer automatically, wondering if I still mean it.

FORTY

"Jeff's coming with us to karaoke on Friday."

Mitch hands me my latte and starts to make another for the next customer.

"Great! So you guys fixed things up?"

"Not in the slightest. I'm hoping being with others will force us to pretend we're okay."

"Sure, cause that'll work." Mitch shakes her head in despair, looking at me like I've lost it.

"Look, I don't know if Jeff is the type of guy who can be in an open relationship. We have to work on it if we want this to last. I just need one night of fun with him, to remind myself how great we are together when we're not fighting."

"Just be careful not to string him along if you don't love him. Like — look at Justin and I. Things are going great — he knows and *accepts* that I'm ace, so he doesn't entertain expectations I can't meet, but we love each other and we're really enjoying our platonic relationship. Look, I can't believe I'm saying this to you of all people, but communication is the key, sweetie. Make sure you're both on the same page."

To be honest, at this point, I'm not even sure we're in the same book.

¤

Karaoke night at La Pharmacie is always such a blast. They fully own the fact that karaoke is cheesy and over the top, and they run with it. The third floor of the bar is dedicated to it and they go *hard*. I'm talking cyan walls, year-round dollar store Valentine's decorations, mic-stands decked in feather boas. I'm talking drag queens partying with us and bringing the house down. I'm talking the most fun we've ever had, every single time.

We sit at our usual table, closest to the stage, and immediately start flipping through the catalogue for our favourite songs. I feel a pang of nostalgia and sadness as I turn a page and see songs by Queen. Alex and I always used to sing at least one of their songs, usually "Killer Queen." Karaoke night definitely won't be the same without her.

We've all chosen several songs when Jeff walks in. I do my best to look happy to see him, but the truth is, I feel like I have to walk on eggshells around him — like anything could be the spark to light up another fight.

In fact, I feel exactly like I did with Alex towards the end.

The realization hits me like a brick through the chest and I take a large gulp of beer to shake it off.

The look on Jeff's face as he stares at the drag queens, visibly uncomfortable, is not helping.

Lord, give me the strength to deal with straight boys.

The bar starts filling up and the DJ officially kicks off the night with one of Mitch's songs: ABBA's "Take a Chance on Me," successfully getting the party started. Cory follows with his flawless rendition of "Toxic" — complete with choreography, and, as always, I am completely floored. I mean, he's got this diva in him that just screams to be let out, and when he does?

He brings the house down.

A few drag queens come by to congratulate him afterwards.

"Honey baby, my wig? Snatched. We're waiting for you on the main stage whenever you want!"

"I'd be honoured to be your drag mama — you've got *it* already, you just need a wig and makeup, believe you me."

Cory's blushing, hiding his face in his hands, and Georgie beams so wide he lights up the whole room. "I'm so proud of you, baby."

The next table — a dozen people our age — sing a few songs, and they have great taste: 80s classics and cheesy pop, just my style.

Jeff and I sing "Total Eclipse of the Heart" and it's utterly ridiculous and awesome. I'm reminded why I like him in the first place. It's been a while since we just had pure, unadulterated fun together, without thinking about our relationship, without overanalyzing every single word the other says.

A few beers later, the first notes of "Don't You (Forget About Me)" start playing. I always sing this song at karaoke — it's one of my favourites. I run to the stage to grab a microphone. A girl from the next table takes a mic at the same time.

"Um, I requested that song …?" she asks, puzzled.

"Duet?"

"Sure!"

We each grab a mic and start singing. It's *so much fun*. She sings really well and looks like she's enjoying herself, dancing around, beaming. At one point she even throws her fist in the air, just like in *The Breakfast Club* — which is where I first fell in love with that song.

By the end of the track, she stares straight into my eyes while we sing. I can feel my cheeks heat up. The girl is super cute. She's this tiny, curvy Black girl with amazing curly hair and dark, velvety eyes.

At the end of the song, we leave the stage, laughing like old friends.

"Oh, my god, that was amazing!"

"Right? Thanks for the duet."

"I'm Amy." I hold out my hand.

"Emma." She shakes it, but after a duet this amazing, this kind of formality feels weird. I lean in to kiss her cheeks.

We share a look that lingers a bit too long — we don't want to leave, but standing here between the tables is just awkward.

"Well, I should join my friends," she suggests, but doesn't move.

At this moment, I realize I'm still holding her hand. Her soft, warm hand. I swear I can feel her pulse.

"Right." I smile and return to my seat in the most self-conscious way ever. I'm convinced everyone can see how flustered and red and smitten I am right now.

As soon as I sit down, Jeff drapes a possessive arm around my shoulders. Mitch notices and frowns.

"I'm out of beer," she says. "Come with me to the bar?"

Grateful for the escape, I follow her.

"That duet was great," she says as soon as we're out of Jeff's earshot. "She seems nice."

"I don't know, maybe." I shrug in that 'casual' way that fools no one, especially not Mitch, the resident cartoon angel on my shoulder.

"You like her!" Mitch says triumphantly.

"Is that so obvious?" I hide my face in my hands desperately.

"Now, yes. But she is really pretty."

"Stop looking at her! She's gonna know!"

"Oh god, this is so high school! Just ask her out!"

I am saved from having to answer by the first notes of "Love Shack" and Georgie coming to get Mitch for a duet.

I end up at the bar alone, so I order beers for Mitch and I.

After Cory's heartfelt rendition of "It's All Coming Back To Me Now," I weave my way through the crowd to go to the bathroom. Emma comes out of a stall just as I enter.

Oh god.

"Hey!" she greets me, her smile the only thing I can focus on because it's just too damn bright and gorgeous.

As if she's happy to see me.

Good god, you have to say something!

"That was great back there… I love that song."

Well, duh, you sang it at karaoke. Get a grip, for fuck's sakes! Flirting is your thing!

"Oh, me too! I mean, isn't *The Breakfast Club* just the best movie ever?"

"Oh, definitely! I must have seen it like ten times."

"We should watch it together sometime."

Damn, she's good.

"I would love that! Let me give you my number…"

I enter my number in her phone and she puts hers into mine. I turn to leave before I further embarrass myself.

"Didn't you have to go to the bathroom?"

"Right!"

Great, now she thinks I went in there just to corner her.

She blocks the way to the stall with her body and takes my hands.

"Relax," she whispers, looking right into my eyes. "You're doing great. Don't worry about me changing my mind. I'm really interested in you and I don't like playing games. You know the whole 'She'll think I'm too eager' thing or whatever? None of that."

I let out a relieved sigh and smile. "Thanks."

"I'll call you." She presses a soft kiss to my cheek and leaves.

The rest of the night passes by in a blur: I cheer with everyone when people sing; I'm pretty sure I sang one or two more songs, but, from the stage, I could see no one but Emma. I leave with the others in time to catch the last train, blowing a kiss towards her.

As soon as I'm out of the bar, no longer acutely aware of her presence at the next table, my mind clears up.

Jeff lives within walking distance, in the opposite direction to the subway station, so he says goodnight to everyone and looks at me expectantly.

"Actually, I think I'm gonna head home…"

"Are you kidding? You haven't spent the night in like two weeks!" he says pointedly. Clearly, 'spent the night' is a euphemism for sex.

"I know, I'm just — so tired."

"You know I can't sleep without you…"

I refuse to be moved by his puppy eyes.

"So sorry. Goodnight."

I kiss him on the cheek, but he holds on to my hand when I try to leave.

"I want to talk about this."

"I'm gonna miss my train! We'll talk later. Tomorrow, after your gig." I free my hand and run after my friends.

FORTY-ONE

"The J-Walkers!" The announcer's voice resounds through the bar, above the clapping and cheering. "And now, please give a warm welcome to… Hugo Gibson!"

I was halfway out of my seat to join Jeff backstage. The name glues me to my chair. I haven't seen Hugo since my birthday — not for a lack of trying, but life kept getting in the way — it's pesky like that, especially when you're trying to juggle two boyfriends.

I flag the waitress to get another beer and settle back down as Hugo walks on stage. He sits down on a stool, center stage, adjusts the microphone at the right height and strums a chord.

"Hey, how's it going? I'm Hugo Gibson and this is a brand-new song."

He starts singing and scans the crowd. His face lights up as he notices me and the song picks up a definitely cheerier mood. He nods in my direction and I grin and wave at him.

If possible, he looks even better than he used to — more slender than lanky, he fills his shirt nicely. His hair is shorter — clipped on the sides, but still an irresistible cloud of curls on the top. I wish I could be buried whole in this chestnut mess. I'm suddenly hit with a vivid memory of the way his breath hitches in his throat when I pull his hair. The air in the bar seems to grow ten times hotter — and so does Hugo.

The memories come flooding back. I can't believe we let it go this long without seeing each other. I miss him so much. I miss our long talks — the way he gets me, the way everything is so simple with him.

I need to leave with him tonight.

A hand on my shoulder makes me jump. Jeff sits down besides me.

"What's going on?" he asks, visibly annoyed.

"What?" I'm unable to look away from Hugo.

"I've been waiting for you backstage. For like, fifteen minutes," he adds, looking at his watch.

I manage to tear my gaze away. "Oh! Sorry. Hugo's a friend of mine." I nod towards the stage. "I didn't know he was playing tonight."

"They called him last minute to fill a spot. Let's go." He gets up.

I can feel Hugo's gaze on us. Standing up in the middle of a set? As a musician, Jeff should really know better.

"I wanna see the rest of his set. Come on, sit down." I pull him back in his chair.

From this moment on, Hugo's eyes never leave mine. I'm not sure Jeff notices; he's playing Candy Crush under the table.

When Hugo says, "Thanks so much! You've been a great crowd!" Jeff is on his feet before Hugo has even left the stage.

"Come on," he says impatiently when he sees I'm not getting up.

"I'm gonna go say hi. Haven't seen him in months."

Jeff looks at his watch, sighs and nods. I drain the last of my beer and we wait outside the backstage door for Hugo to come out.

"Great set!" I say when he finally emerges.

"Thanks!" He hugs me, tight, and kisses me on both cheeks. "I didn't know you were coming!"

"Jeff is the J-Walkers' bassist." I introduce them to each other.

"Hey, man. Good gig." Hugo smiles and shakes Jeff's hand.

"Yeah." Jeff keeps an eye on his phone screen, barely acknowledging Hugo's presence.

"So how have you been?" Hugo turns away from Jeff, cocking an amused eyebrow.

"Great! Busy — it sucks we haven't been able to get together…"

"Yeah, well with the West Coast tour, I couldn't really — "

Hugo pauses to say goodbye to another musician who's leaving, and turns back to me.

"Wanna go get a beer and catch up?"

"She's with me." Jeff finally puts away his phone and stares at Hugo defiantly.

"No worries, man. Come along — I'd love to get to know Amy's new... boyfriend?" Hugo looks at me inquisitively.

"Come on, it'll be fun!" I plead with Jeff. "You guys can talk music."

Jeff shrugs and pulls me aside. "But, love, it's been so long... I thought you were gonna spend the night." By this point, Jeff sounds downright whiny, and Hugo's smirk at this childish behaviour is attractive as hell.

"Look," I say sternly. "I haven't seen Hugo in months. I'm going. Now, you can either come with, in which case we'll probably go home together afterwards, or stay here and whine."

"Stop talking shit, let's go home." Jeff grabs my arm forcefully.

"Okay, man, I think you need to go." Hugo steps between Jeff and me. I disentangle my arm.

"Amy's my girlfriend. Mind your own business."

"Jeff, what the fuck? I can't talk to my friends, now, is that it?"

"A friend? You clearly wanna fuck him." Jeff is almost screaming now.

"Look, Amy and I are old friends. We just wanna catch up, and you clearly need to brush up on your 'acting decent' skills. Just go home, man." Hugo stands half a step in front of me. He straightens up his tall body to look even taller.

Jeff's rage and determination seem to waver. He looks absolutely lost.

"Goodbye, Jeff." I turn and walk away.

"Call me!" All anger is gone from his voice — now he just sounds desperate.

I ignore him and get out of the bar, followed by Hugo. We head to La Belle Province for poutine and hotdogs — Hugo's always starving after a gig.

"So, was that your boyfriend?" Hugo asks once we're settled at table.

"Not after what he just pulled. But yeah, David and I are pushing the open relationship to another level. More than just hook-ups, you know?"

"Cool. Although, this guy?"

"Jeff was great, at the beginning. He's a little intense." Hugo shoots me a look. "Okay, a lot intense. He thought we'd spend the night together. We haven't been alone together in like two weeks."

"So why aren't you with him right now?"

"I missed you."

Hugo raises an eyebrow. "I mean, I'm not complaining, but it was a bit shitty of you to ditch him for me. Before he got aggressive, that is."

I take a long sip of soda to avoid looking at him — he's always been able to call me out on my bullshit, and, frankly, I love him for it, but that doesn't mean it feels good.

"Yeah… I guess at this point I was just looking for any excuse to make my exit."

"Well, then, I think you got what you wanted."

"Between this and Alex, I just wish things would go smoothly, for once." I tell him everything that went down at the cabin and he lets out a long whistle.

"Tough shit."

"Tell me about it." I sigh and look at him fondly. "Why is it that with you, it's always so easy?"

"Because we both want the exact same thing: sex and a great friendship. I think you tend to hook up with people who want more."

I make him scoot over to sit on his side of the booth and lay my head on his shoulder.

"I wish it were easy like this with everyone else."

"Ah, but then, you and I would be nothing special, you see?"

I chuckle and lightly punch him on the shoulder. He puts his arm around me and pulls me close. I lean into his warmth and let go of everything else. I'll deal with it later. For now, I'm happy just tilting my face towards Hugo for a much-needed kiss. Back to his place, later tonight, he'll make me forget everything else, including my own name.

FORTY-TWO

For our first date, Emma suggests we have dinner at La Banquise for some poutine, followed by an open-air 80's movie festival: she shares my passion for John Hughes movies. Her laid-back choice of restaurant confirms she was serious about not being interested in playing games. She's not trying to impress me: she legitimately wants us to have a good time.

I wait for her in front of the restaurant, enjoying the warm September sun. Emma almost passes me by; she's walking with her head buried in a book and looks up at the last second to avoid bumping into a woman walking her dog. She apologizes profusely — to the lady and to the dog, aww — and, as she puts her book back in her bag, our eyes meet.

"Oh, hi!" she exclaims, slightly out of breath.

We share a laugh and I greet her with a kiss on both cheeks.

"Was that Deathly Hallows?" I ask, curious about the flash of golden-yellow I caught before she closed her bag.

"Yeah — I'm almost at the final battle and I was hoping no one would die before I got here. Tears on a first date; real turn-on, right?"

"I would have cried along with you, to be honest." We chuckle. "Shall we?" I nod at the restaurant door, since we're standing in the middle of the sidewalk and passersby have to go around us.

Once we're seated, we can barely stop talking about our Hogwarts houses. The waitress has to ask if we're ready to order twice before we decide to look at the menu.

"Whoa. I didn't know there were so many kinds of poutine in the world." My eyes widen at the sheer length of the menu.

"I've never ordered the same one twice." Emma beams. "I think tonight I'm in the mood for something weird. Let's see… Pulled pork, coleslaw and sour cream," she declares, triumphant.

"On top of the gravy and cheese curds? That's just wrong."

"Pretty sure it's gonna be delicious."

"I'll just stick to the original recipe, thanks."

"Your loss." She winks, looking absolutely adorable.

The waitress comes to take our order and we also ask for two bottles of Cheval Blanc.

We wait for our food, comparing the merits of Ravenclaw and Hufflepuff. Our plates arrive and, as expected, her plate looks like a pile of goo — more than poutine usually does, that is.

"Oh my god," she exclaims after her first bite. "You have to try this!"

She hands me her fork, on which she was careful to balance a sample of every flavour, 'so I get the full experience,', as she says.

I close my eyes and shove it in my mouth, wanting this to be over quickly. I swallow and chase it with a big gulp of beer.

"Not my cup of tea." I shrug. She's beaming at me like I just made her day, so I can't help smiling with her.

After dinner, we walk to the park for the movie festival. Emma pulls a blanket out of her leather backpack and spreads it on the ground so we can sit down. She rummages in her bag again and retrieves a thermos and two plastic cups. She fills them with red liquid and hands me one.

"Homemade sangria," she explains.

"Delicious," I answer after taking a sip. "You're a lady of many talents, aren't you?"

"You haven't seen half of it." She winks.

She's sending me all kinds of signals — god, just the way she *looks* at me! It would be a shame to let that go unnoticed. I scoot over to sit closer to her.

The sunset filters through the trees to illuminate her dark brown skin with deep copper flecks. Her eyes stare into mine, lit with a mischievous glint. She opens her mouth to speak, but the first movie starts.

Lucky for us, it's *The Breakfast Club*. Emma holds out her hand and I high five her, but I keep her hand in mine, instead of letting it go. She makes no effort to free it.

"God, I've always had such a huge crush on Molly Ringwald," she whispers as the actress' face fills the screen.

"Are you kidding? *She* made me realize I'm bi!"

"Me too! Well, I'm pansexual, but you know. She's the first girl I ever liked."

"She's the reason I dye my hair red." I hold up a lock of my hair, redder than ever in the last straggling sun rays. "Well, her and Anne of Green Gables."

We giggle and a nearby couple shoot us a stern look. "Some of us are trying to watch the movie," the man whispers.

"Sorry!"

We giggle again. The more we try to keep quiet, the more we laugh. We have to look away from each other to be able to calm down. Once we've managed it, we both get into the movie.

I can feel Emma shifting to lean into me. Her hand melts in mine, as if it had always been there — a natural part of my body, as natural as my own hand.

As the movie comes to an end, we both sing along to "Don't You (Forget About Me)," fist proudly brandished in the air like Judd Nelson's. We sit still during the credits, as if moving would break the spell woven between us. The credits end and give way to a message saying that *Weird Science* will begin after a fifteen-minute break.

Our eyes meet. We both explode in laughter at the same time.

"Seriously?" Emma asks, indignant. "That's what they went with?"

"Should we get out of here?"

"Hell yeah."

We gather our stuff and leave, deploring the poor movie choice.

"I mean, they could have gone with any Molly Ringwald movie!" Emma sighs. "*Sixteen Candles, Pretty in Pink...*"

"*St. Elmo's Fire*, even though Ringwald's not in it."

"Oh, definitely."

As we get out of the park, Emma slips her hand back in mine.

"You know," she says as we cross a small, quiet street, "I live like six blocks down that way."

We stop on the corner, hesitating.

"Wanna come over?"

"I'd love to."

Her building is a very cute brownstone with a wrought iron staircase, shaded by an enormous maple. We climb up to the second floor and she unlocks the door to let us in. From where I stand as I drop my bag and take off my shoes, I see a long corridor leading up to a kitchen at the far end of the apartment. The white walls are lined with prints and family photos. On the right side are two doorways.

"Do you live alone?"

"Yeah, I had a roommate once and I bailed after three weeks. Not for me."

She guides me into the first room.

"Welcome to my world," she says, flicking on a light switch.

The living room is bright, even though it's dark outside. Three walls are white and the one behind the couch is canary yellow. I spot several vintage items: an antique rocking chair painted bright blue, an aqua turntable, and various picture frames. The whole place is covered with books: open paperbacks laying face down, precarious piles of hardcovers, even some peeking out from under the couch.

"I love it!"

"Thanks! I basically live in thrift shops and book stores."

She closes the drapes and gestures towards the couch.

"Make yourself at home. Oh, sorry!" She chuckles and gathers a pile of books, setting them haphazardly on the coffee table. "Do you want a beer, or something?"

"Yeah, beer would be nice."

She exits the room and I walk up to the shelf holding her turntable. I go through her extensive record collection, and find a Dean Martin album. Perfect. Smooth, but classy; not too suggestive.

Emma comes back with two bottles of Raspberry Saint-Ambroise and I show her the record.

"May I?" I ask, because her turntable looks pretty old.

"Go ahead." She smiles and sits down on the couch while I put the record on.

The warm voice of the crooner fills the room, dissipating some of our awkwardness. This date feels radically different from pretty much every other one I've been on. Usually, the date either flops for some reason, or I get to their place and we can't keep our hands off each other.

With Emma, sex isn't the main goal. I don't think that's why we're here. This could be the beginning of something more. In fact, I feel exactly like I did on my first date with David: dizzy with anticipation, like my whole life is on the edge. Something tells me I should take it slow with her — relish it.

Emma lets out a content sigh. "I love old music so much. It's so full of history, of memories. Like, can you imagine how many people had their first dance to this song?"

She closes her eyes and sways to the music. I'm irresistibly drawn to her, closer and closer, until I can almost taste the blissful smile on her lips. Her eyes blink open, full of a tantalizing tenderness.

"Can you imagine how many people fell in love to this song?"

Electricity fills the room.

My fingers inch ever closer to the smooth skin of her shoulder.

I close my eyes.

My phone chirps with R2-D2's signature beeps.

Fuck.

Emma turns away; her smile falters.

"So sorry — I'll turn it off."

I pull my phone out and turn the ringer off. A glance at the screen reveals a text from Jeff.

Jeff Williams — Come over?

I heave a sigh. After Jeff's violent behaviour, I considered our relationship to be over — I got the confirmation that what I had with him wasn't worth saving, so I decided to stop feeding time and energy into this relationship. I assumed he'd get the memo, with the cold, final way I said goodbye and left with Hugo. Apparently not.

Amy Evans — Sorry, I'm on a date.

"Sorry," I tell Emma. "Guess there's a few things I should tell you before we begin anything."

She turns towards me and sits crossed-legged, nodding so I can go on. I fiddle with the label on my beer bottle. There's never a good time to say this.

"I'm in an open relationship. I have two boyfriends, and our arrangements allow us to see other people. Things haven't been great with one of them recently, though."

"I'm sorry," Emma says, putting a comforting hand on my shoulder.

"Thanks. I don't think he's cut out for open relationships. He's jealous. The last time I saw him, he became aggressive."

"Are you okay?"

"Yeah, he just grabbed me. I left before anything else could happen. I'm gonna end it."

My phone buzzes in my hand.

"I'll arrange to talk to him tomorrow and then I'm all yours. Sorry again."

Jeff Williams — WTF???

Amy Evans — Look, can we talk tomorrow? I could come over around 3?

Jeff Williams — If you want to.

"Ugh, he drives me crazy! He's so passive-aggressive!" I take a gulp of beer to calm down. "Sorry. This has nothing to do with you."

"Hey, I don't mind. I've been told I'm a great listener, so…"

"I kinda killed the mood, didn't I?" I scrunch up my face apologetically.

"Well, correct me if I'm wrong, but I feel like we both want to take things slow?"

"You don't mind that I have other partners?"

"Absolutely not. I date other people too. I love making new experiences. That includes not being tied down to one person."

"I'm glad you understand. I feel like — okay, this is probably not the best thing to say on a first date — but I feel like this has the potential to be about so much more than just sex."

"I feel the same," Emma says softly, pushing a strand of hair behind my ear.

I close my eyes and lean against her hand, kissing the inside of her wrist. We sit like this for a long time, sipping our beer, listening to the music. When the record ends, she pulls out her phone and plays her favourite 80's power ballads — "Love Is A Battlefield," "Heaven Is A Place On Earth" and so on.

We push the coffee table against the wall and improvise a dance floor in the middle of the room. Emma dims the lights and we dance around the room, belting out the lyrics. She looks so cute when she dances — eyes closed, hands in the air, waving her bouncy curls around. I come to a stop, forgetting to dance, unable to do anything but stare shamelessly at her.

Emma notices I stopped singing and opens her eyes. She answers my sheepish grin with a beam of her own and holds out her hand. I thread our fingers together, her warm palm spreading a cozy glow up my arm, straight through my heart.

She pulls me in, close, closer, and presses a tiny kiss to my nose. A flick of her wrist and she sends me twirling. I laugh as a dizzy spell hits me.

I can't tell if it's from the twirling or the kiss.

¤

I leave in time to catch the last subway train and she walks me to the station. Just before we reach the turnstiles, I pull her close. She buries a hand in my hair and smiles — crinkles crease the corners of her eyes, again. I'm falling hard for that smile. I take a deep breath — she smells like pears. Our lips touch and we both sigh and melt into it. She's still smiling and I part my lips to taste her.

I hear the train coming, so I hug her close one last time and start running.

"I had a great time!" I shout as I pass the turnstile and she waves and laughs.

I sit on the subway, electrified and happy. I literally can't stop grinning. I can't remember the last time a first kiss felt like such a big deal — not since David, anyway.

FORTY-THREE

The good mood doesn't last.

I go to Jeff's place the next day, dreading seeing him after the way he behaved last time. Hugo comes with me — I asked him to accompany me in case Jeff gets violent. I don't think he will, but, then again, I never thought he'd act so aggressively before last time.

"I should come up with you," Hugo insists as I press the doorbell to Jeff's place.

"I think your presence would just anger him more. I'm not looking for a fight here — I just need to make him understand it's over. But here —" I press Hugo's name in my cellphone to call him, and shove it down my pocket. "I'll call your name if I need you."

Hugo answers the call and nods, a frown on his face.

"Thanks." I kiss him on the cheek and open the door when I hear the unlock buzz.

Jeff lets me in, a glum look on his face. I follow him into the living room. The place is a mess. Lyrics sheets and beer caps litter the floor. The coffee table is lost under piles of empty bottles and Thai food containers.

I move a bass guitar to its stand so I can sit in the armchair and Jeff drops down on the couch in front of me. He looks away, arms crossed and mouth shut. I have no idea how to start this conversation.

"I can't believe it!" he shouts, mostly at the wall. "You were on a date last night? With that douchebag Hugo, I suppose?"

"Not that it's any of your business, but no. I was with Emma. You know, that girl I sang with at karaoke?"

"I thought you and I were on a date that night, but what — you were just there to pick up chicks?"

"I didn't plan this, you know. We just clicked —"

"You're so fucking greedy. What, two boyfriends aren't enough for you? You still need to go whoring around town?"

I take a deep breath and steel myself, determined not to let him drag me into a fight.

"You agreed to be in an open relationship —"

"I accepted that you had another boyfriend, but if even that isn't enough for you —"

"I asked you, again and again, to reflect on whether or not you could handle this type of relationship."

Jeff opens his mouth to retort, but I don't let him.

"This means, yes, that I have two boyfriends, but also that I was gonna keep dating other people. I need that in my life. I need to make discoveries. It's like music. You wouldn't want to just play one song for the rest of your life, right?"

Jeff scoffs.

I stand up. "I gave you time to decide if you're okay with that, but you're obviously not. It's over, Jeff."

I dig the copper feather earrings out of my pocket and drop them at his feet.

FORTY-FOUR

David's home when I come back. One look at my expression and he opens his arms to me. I bury my face in his chest and heave a long sigh.

"It's over with Jeff."

"*Chaton*..." he says soothingly, rubbing my back softly. "What happened?"

"It's been a mess for a while now. He's been clingy and jealous and last night he freaked out because I was on a date with a girl."

"I'm so sorry..."

"I thought it could work, but some people just aren't meant for open relationships."

"Not everyone can keep their jealousy in check." David goes to the kitchen and comes back with two cups of tea.

We settle down on the couch, close together — I need him so much right now.

"You know what?" I break a long silence. "I'll just stop seeing other people. I mean, you're free to continue, I don't mind, but think about it. Pretty much all this has brought me in the last year is pain."

David looks at me, puzzled. I elaborate, counting on my fingers as I go.

"Well, first there was Jeff. Then Alex, of course, and it ruined our friendship, twice. Then countless douchebags, like the one who wasn't mature enough to deal with my period —"

"The married man," David adds.

"Right, him too. The girl who outed me to Charlotte. I mean, it's just insane. You, you have it good. Things are going great with Jude, smooth, no drama, even when you meet other people."

"Speaking of which, I have a second date tonight —"

"Really?"

"I can cancel if you want me to stay with you —"

"No, I was just surprised cause it's been a while since you've met someone new. Go, I don't mind — I'll call Mitch and we'll rant about guys."

"Well, if you're sure…"

"I am. No sense in spoiling your night as well as mine."

David looks torn, but I can tell he's excited for this date. His eyes never lie. He's so smitten.

"Go!" I insist. "I'm happy for you. Good luck!"

He kisses me goodbye and leaves.

¤

David comes home the next morning with a huge grin on his face.

"This girl!" he gushes. "She's so interesting and funny."

"You're so cute! I haven't seen you so smitten since Jude!"

"Are you kidding? I'm smitten like this every day I wake up next to you."

"Aw," I pull him closer and kiss him. I'm met with a familiar scent — other than his own — that I can't pinpoint.

"So, will you see her again?"

David nods excitedly. "Next Thursday. We're going to a concert — you know, this new electro band I told you about?"

I scrunch my nose. I hate electro. "I'm glad you found someone to share this with you."

"Yeah, and we found out we both had tickets for a gig next month. We decided to go together." David grins brightly as he takes off his clothes to take a shower.

"That's great!" I exclaim, trying to sound as sincere as possible.

It's not that I'm jealous — I wouldn't be in an open relationship if I were the jealous type. It's just that seeing him gush like that makes me miss it. I genuinely love the thrill of new relationships, when you're utterly crazy about someone.

But I'm just sick of getting hurt. I'm not sure the bliss of first dates is worth the pain of break-ups. I just need to stick to my decision and, eventually, I won't miss it so much.

FORTY-FIVE

Emma Lewis — Hey sugar :) I miss you

Emma. I completely forgot about her when I took that big decision.

Emma, the best thing to happen to me in a while.

Emma, who makes me believe pain couldn't possibly exist.

Emma, the embodiment of all the good left in this fucked-up dating world.

I can't stop seeing her.

Which is probably why my brain conveniently decided not to bring her up when I made my decision — it just didn't want to consider a world where I have to stop seeing her.

I figure she at least deserves an explanation — or maybe I'm trying to find an excuse to see her one last time. I type up a quick reply and we make plans to get coffee later.

I meet her in an artsy café halfway between her place and Quarante-Cinq, after my shift. She's already there, at a window table, sipping a latte. She looks amazing — her dress is my favourite shade of blue and her face lights up as I walk in.

Fuck, I missed her.

I grab an Earl Grey at the counter and walk over to her. With every step, I change my mind: *You have to break it off — oh, one last date couldn't hurt — no dating at all — but, good god, look at her!*

I'm at *You can do this; you're a big girl* when I reach her table. She stands up to greet me with kisses on the cheeks. My resolve falters with the stutter of her fingers on my hips — I almost drop my tea.

We sit down and make some small talk until I finally breach the subject.

"I can't postpone it anymore. I wanted to meet for coffee because I need to talk to you."

Emma's brows furrow. I almost change my mind again — seeing her with anything but a beaming smile on her face shatters my heart. I take a deep breath. *Alright, you can do this.* I fiddle with the string of my teabag; anything to avoid her worried gaze.

"Listen, I really like you, and it kills me to do this. I decided to stop dating altogether. I realized I just can't be in an open relationship anymore."

Emma stares out the window, seemingly absorbed by a woman walking her dog, but she's tearing the carton sleeve from her cup to shreds. She sighs and finally looks at me.

"Can I ask why?"

"Well, it used to make me happy, but lately — for the past year or so — I've gotten nothing but hurt. I've lost my best friend and neglected my main relationship. It ended badly with pretty much everyone I've dated this year."

By now, my eyes are filled with tears. Emma takes my hand and I try with all my might not to start bawling.

"Look," she says, holding my hand tightly and looking deep in my eyes. "I'm not saying you *have* to give me a chance. But I genuinely like you. I'm curious to see where this could go, if we let it. I have a feeling we've got something pretty great here. And I promise I'm a hundred percent okay with open relationships."

A tear silently rolls down her cheek — I know she means it. This is one of the hardest things I've ever done, and I'm not even certain I want to do it. Emma looks at me earnestly; this is hurting her as much as me. Why am I fighting so hard for something that's causing both of us this much pain?

Before I can fully make up my mind about it, I find myself nodding, trying to smile through my tears.

"Let's try," I say softly.

She wipes her tears on her sleeve, takes my hands in hers and looks straight in my eyes, beaming. "I was so not ready to say goodbye to you."

"Me neither. Coming here took all my strength."

¤

That night at dinner, I announce my decision to David.

"I went to see Emma today, to tell her I decided to stop dating."

"How did it go?"

"I couldn't do it. I realized I can't cut myself from happy experiences just because I'm scared of getting hurt."

"Makes sense. So then what happened?"

"So I decided to give it a try. I think I could really love her. We went for a walk on Mount Royal afterwards and we shared disastrous dates stories. She is *so* funny!"

"Wait — did you say her name was Emma?"

"Yeah — Emma Lewis, why?"

"Lewis? Wait a minute. What does she look like?"

"She's short, Black, afro hairdo, cutest smile…"

"Like this?" David pulls up a picture on his phone and hands it to me.

The picture is a selfie of David and Emma, heads close together, laughing at the camera.

"You know her?"

"She's the girl I've been seeing — the electro fan…"

I freeze, a forkful of couscous suspended midway to my open mouth.

"You're kidding! We're dating the same girl?" I let out an incredulous laugh.

"Apparently! Isn't she amazing?"

"Tell me about it! I can't get enough of her — like, I can't believe I almost ended it."

"So what does this mean?" David asks more seriously.

"What do you mean?"

"Well, do we tell her? Do we keep dating her separately? Or do we have, like, three-way dates?"

"I guess we should ask her? I'm seeing her on Friday — I could bring it up."

"Sounds good. Man, I can't believe it!"

FORTY-SIX

Friday couldn't come fast enough — I missed Emma so much. I meet her at Camellia Sinensis, a cozy and quiet tearoom. I feel giddy as I wait for her in front of the shop — I can't wait to tell her the news. By the time she joins me and we walk in, I'm literally bouncing with anticipation.

The quiet atmosphere in the room calls for whispering, so we're using it as an excuse to sit as close as possible in our booth. The waitress comes with our tea and I wait until we take our first sip before I break the news.

"I've got something to tell you," I whisper excitedly.

"Is it another 'something' that will leave us both in tears?" Emma asks, cocking an eyebrow.

I chuckle. "No, don't worry — it's actually pretty mind-blowing."

"What is it?"

I pull out my phone and show her a picture of David. "You know that guy, right?"

"Um, we went out a few times, why?"

"He's my boyfriend."

Emma's jaw drops. "I'm dating your boyfriend?"

"Yeah. David and I realized the other day." I'm grinning so hard my jaw actually hurts.

"And you don't mind?"

"We both think you're amazing, so we just find it a hilarious coincidence."

Emma still looks astonished, but a smile is creeping its way into her eyes. "So where do we go from here?"

"That's what we were wondering. We weren't sure if you wanted to keep dating us separately —"

"Or maybe I could date you both together?" She's full-on beaming by now.

I wasn't prepared to be this aroused by her saying that. She bites her lip and fiddles with the lid of the teapot, perfectly playing the 'coy but sexy' part. I tilt her chin towards me and kiss her softly.

"This has definitely come up when David and I discussed it, so I think he'd be up for it. He's home right now, should we call him?"

"Not tonight," she whispers right at the edge of my ear, her breath tickling my earlobe in a very deliberate way. "You see, I've already slept with David. Before I'm with the both of you, I'd like to know you — alone."

I can feel the heat spreading from my cheeks to my ears, down my neck — and, of course, down between my legs. I nod, not trusting my voice.

"So, I know we said we'd take it slow, but I really have trouble waiting." Emma grazes a hand across my thigh. My legs spread apart of their own volition. "What do you say we finish our tea and then skip the movie?"

I don't even have the slightest clue what movie we were planning to watch anymore. I gaze into her eyes eagerly. "Yes, please."

I pour myself another cup of tea in an attempt to finish it quickly. Of course, I burn my tongue with the first hurried sip.

"Careful," Emma says, and kisses the burn away.

I smile through the kiss and pull back.

"We can't start this here or I won't be able to stop."

"Hurry up and drink, then, cause I can't keep my lips off you much longer."

Emma pours herself another cup, noting happily that the teapot is almost empty. We manage to finish it and pay in less than fifteen minutes. We also succeed in not jumping each other's bones on the subway back to her place, but the ride is excruciating.

At her door, I reach unprecedented levels of anticipation as she rummages for her keys in her bag. I just want to take her right here, right now, even if we're standing on her front porch on a relatively busy street. At last, she manages to get the door open. As eager as I, Emma pulls me in by the hand and kicks the door closed behind us. We scramble to her bedroom, haphazardly scattering our shoes and purses on the floor along the way.

We tumble down on her bed at last, heaving relieved sighs as we press our bodies as close together as possible. I run my hands all over her, needing to take it all in, to discover all of her. Her fingers flutter on my hips, searching for the hem of my dress. She grasps it with a smile and pulls it over my head. I lift my arms to help her and she takes a moment to look at me. Her breath catches in her throat and her face lights up.

"You look amazing."

I kiss her, bashful but beaming. The way she looks at me makes me feel like a queen.

I pull her on top of me and kiss her, pulling entrancing moans out of her throat. My fingers travel up and down her back. We breathe together, deeply, as if we had been holding our breath all this time we weren't having sex.

Her kisses mark a trail down to my neck; she bites my earlobe lightly. I arch my back, pressing my thigh between her legs. She grinds against me urgently.

"Please," she moans.

We take off the rest of our clothes and throw them across the room. Emma is naked before me, looking sexy and regal, but, above all, breathtaking. Her curves, her soft skin, her pleading eyes are all calling to me, begging me to touch her. I trail my hands down her sides, watching in delight as goose bumps appear on her dark skin. She bites her lip and looks at me coyly. She pushes softly at my shoulders so I lay back on the bed.

She kneels above me, kissing a path down my neck to my breasts. The tip of her tongue teases my nipples, making them hard. She drives me crazy — the way she darts her tongue between her lips while staring straight into my eyes is absolutely insane. A contented 'mmm' escapes her mouth.

Heat pools between my legs. My brain stops working for a second — I can't think cohesive thoughts; I am nothing but sensations.

When, at last, we collapse side by side, we are both exhausted, but blissful.

"Oh my god!" I chuckle breathlessly.

"I know! That was amazing!"

"Why did we wait so long?"

"No idea." Emma turns on her side to face me. "Imagine that, but with David…"

"Are you trying to kill me?"

I try to picture my two best lovers at the same time, but all my sexual energy is spent for the moment, so my brain short-circuits.

Emma chuckles. She settles in the crook of my shoulder and trails her fingers on my skin in mindless patterns.

"You make me so happy," she sighs blissfully.

"You too." I cup her cheek, tickling her behind her ear.

"So, how do you think it should happen? Should we go on, like, a three-way date or something?" Emma looks up at me and the angle makes me notice how long her eyelashes are. Yet again, I get lost in how gorgeous she is.

"Maybe you could come over for dinner one night and we'll see how things go?"

"I'd love that. Much more personal than going to a public place."

"Yeah, that's what I thought."

"Oh my god, I can't wait to see your place!"

I laugh and pull her closer. We cuddle and talk for a while, until we fall asleep in each other's arms.

FORTY-SEVEN

David and I are in our kitchen, cooking dinner for tonight's date with Emma. I'm making a huge lasagna and David's tossing a fancy salad: spinach, raspberries and bacon with a maple balsamic dressing and caramelized onions.

I've always liked cooking, but there's something about preparing a meal with David for someone we both really like that is different, amazing. I think it's bringing us closer together as a couple — something we've missed lately, focused as we were on our other relationships.

I start giggling as I spread sauce and ricotta cheese over the first layer of pasta.

"What?" David asks.

"I'm just so excited! I still can't believe it, y'know?"

"It's incredible. I mean, what are the odds of us both dating the same person — who's pretty perfect, by the way — at the same time?"

He pulls me into a warm embrace, but I keep my hands up in the air.

"Hug me," he whines playfully.

"I'm covered in sauce and cheese!"

"I don't care," he mumbles in my neck, his stubble tickling me right where I'm sensitive, "I haven't changed yet."

"Sure you don't care, I'm the one on laundry duty!"

He laughs and twirls me towards the sink. "Wash your hands, then."

I oblige and he whisks me off my feet towards the bedroom. I shriek with surprise and laughter. "That's not what I call making dinner!"

"We'll just have to eat slightly later." He lifts my shirt above my head.

"Save some for Emma," I protest.

David looks at me mischievously. "Oh, I see you have big plans for tonight, huh?"

"I mean, maybe — probably. The three of us already had sex with each other, so — I mean, do you think it's too much of a stretch to expect something will happen?"

"Of course not, I'm just messing with you."

"Come on, then." I put my discarded shirt back on, not without putting on a bit of a show. "The lasagna won't make itself."

David chuckles.

The doorbell rings just as I take the dish out of the oven — David and I got changed while it was baking. David answers the door and I overhear their greetings.

"Hey, how are you?"

"Great — a bit nervous — you?"

"Good. You look amazing."

"Thanks!" Emma laughs bashfully. "The place looks great!"

David brings her to the kitchen and I can see he was right. She looks absolutely amazing. In a yellow sundress that sets off her dark skin perfectly, she looks like a sun goddess. David stands next to her in a royal blue button-down and I can't get over how gorgeous they look together. It makes me insanely happy.

Emma and I greet each other with kisses on cheeks. She hands me a bottle of red wine with a smirk. I glance at the label distractedly while I rummage in a drawer to find a corkscrew. I dissolve into laughter when I see the name.

"*Ménage à Trois*? Really?" Emma is folded over laughing. David reaches for the bottle to have a look. Soon, he's cracking up with the two of us.

After we've calmed down, I open the bottle and pour three glasses.

"To a wonderful coincidence." David raises his glass and clinks it against ours.

I serve the lasagna and we sit down to eat. David dims the lights to set the mood.

"Everything looks delicious," Emma says. "I feel spoiled."

"You deserve it," David replies. His voice gets low and deep and he looks straight into her eyes.

Whoa. Blast from the past. I'd forgotten what it looks like when David flirts. And I realize just now how much of a turn on it is to be a spectator while he flirts with someone else. A coy smile lights up Emma's features and she takes a sip of wine.

"Thanks for having me, seriously." Emma looks at both of us and takes our hands.

We take a moment to look into each other's eyes — take it all in, basking in the joy this night brings us.

"Well, dig in!" I finally break the moment. "It's getting cold."

"*Bon appétit*," David says. Emma draws in a sharp breath and bites her lip.

"What's going on?" I ask.

"I just love it when he speaks French," she giggles.

"Yeah?"

"Turns me on," Emma cracks a shy smile.

"*Vraiment?*" David presses, eyebrow cocked, and we all crack up.

"Save it for later," Emma says suggestively.

We eat and chat and it feels natural — like the three of us have been dating for a long time. We're still talking long after the food is gone, when the second bottle of wine is half empty. By now, the air around us feels thicker — warmer — and a certain tension fills the space between us.

At the beginning of the night, it was all about the three of us having dinner and flirting. Now that dinner is over and we're all a bit tipsy, I bet we are all thinking the same thing: what might happen next.

Obviously, no one wants to straight up ask 'So, should we fuck, now?' It has to come naturally, but I hardly think this setting — dining table like a wall between us, straight wooden kitchen chairs — is ideal for that.

I grab my glass and the bottle of wine and stand up. "I think we might be more comfortable on the couch."

David and Emma take their glasses and follow me to the living room. The couch is a bit snug for three — especially with mine and Emma's full hips — so we have to sit close together: perfect. I sit with my back to the armrest, my legs in Emma's lap. On her left, David is sprawled out, legs on the coffee table, arm slung around her shoulders.

We sip our wine for a while, quietly enjoying the closeness of our bodies. Emma runs her finger up and down my bare legs, each time daring to move a bit closer to the hem of my skirt. My toes curl in anticipation.

David sets his glass down on the table, turns towards Emma and buries his face in her neck. I set down my glass and Emma's as well. I kneel beside her to lean in and kiss her.

Her lips are soft and warm. Her tongue tastes of red wine — like mine — as she smiles into the kiss. She splays a hand over my thigh, under my skirt, and breaks the kiss. I whimper at the loss, but she nudges at David's chin to capture his lips. Suddenly, I don't mind the loss. I marvel at how comfortable they seem to be with each other. Of course, they've already slept together a few times, so it's not that surprising — but they just fit together.

David tilts his head to the side to deepen the kiss and Emma bites his bottom lip softly. I cannot look away. It's enthralling, like a well-rehearsed dance, like they already know what makes the other tick. Emma's hand on my thigh inches higher and higher.

Her eyes widen as she feels how aroused I am. She breaks the kiss and moves to whisper something in David's ear. His eyebrow twitches and he reaches across Emma to slide his hand up my skirt.

"You so want this." David's voice is but a rumble in his throat, deep and enticing.

"So do you." I look at both of them and they nod eagerly.

"Bed?" Emma suggests.

David jumps to his feet instead of answering. I kiss Emma softly before we follow him to the bedroom.

"I'm really glad this is happening," I whisper.

"Me too."

Emma takes my hand as we enter the bedroom. David's already lying on the bed, his shirt rumpled on the floor. I make to join him, but Emma stops me with a hand on my shoulder. She stands in front of me and drags her fingers down my sides, slowly. With a sly grin and a glance at David, she grabs the hem of my dress. She pulls it over my head, taking her sweet time and clearly enjoying it. She tosses it on the floor and splays her hands on my ass to bring me closer.

I wrap my arms around her, enjoying the silky fabric of her dress caressing my skin. She pulls down my bra straps, peppering kisses on my shoulders. Her breath spreads goose bumps over my neck and down my arms. She reaches behind me and unclasps my bra, letting it fall to the floor between us.

David and Emma both gasp sharply. Shivers run down my spine; I can't quite believe the simple sight of my half-naked body provokes that kind of reaction. I reach around Emma to unzip her dress. It pools swiftly around her feet. She looks like some kind of fairy, perched in the middle of a bright yellow flower, in her underwear.

David and I glance at each other, grinning at how beautiful she looks — a goddess, really. David suddenly kneels on the bed, practically bouncing.

"Alright, I can't take it anymore, c'm'ere." He gestures to us.

Emma and I quickly strip off the last of our clothes, not bothering to put on a show for these last garments. David's clothes follow ours on the floor at once. In sync, we pounce on the bed, landing next to David in a haphazard pile of naked limbs, laughing.

I'm surrounded by skin — the pale plains of his, the dark hills and valleys of hers. I don't know where to begin.

And it feels glorious.

¤

When I wake up the next day, the sun's shining through the drapes. Emma looks beautiful in the soft light, still lying between me and David, who's curled up against her side. She stirs, stretches her arms above her head, and finally opens her eyes.

"Morning," she whispers, grinning.

"Good morning!"

"My god, you're beautiful," she exhales.

"So are you." I lean in to kiss her. She still tastes faintly of sex — sweat and juices — and it awakes tingles inside of me.

"You're both goddesses," David pipes up, propped on an elbow to look over Emma's shoulder.

"I just feel so good with both of you," Emma says. "Like, you feel like home to me."

David and I squeeze her in a hug, spreading kisses wherever we can reach.

"We should go to brunch and talk things over," I suggest. "Y'know, like boundaries, where we want this to go."

We get dressed reluctantly — David tries to pull off each item of clothing to tickle us while we're putting them on — and walk to Emma's favourite brunch place. After we get our food, we start talking about how we see this going — the usual first, of course: communication, honesty, trust. We kind of tiptoe around the main question for a bit until Emma bites the bullet and asks it, spearing a piece of waffle with determination, as if it held all the answers.

"How about seeing other people? Would we be a closed triad, or...?"

"I don't think I'll keep dating," I reply. "For now, anyway. I mean, yeah, I still like to discover new people, but I really need a break. I've hit a bit of a rough patch before I met you, Emma, and it kinda turned me off the whole dating scene for the time being."

"Yeah, that's valid," David agrees. "As for me, things are going great with Jude, so I kinda got my hands full with three gorgeous people," he adds with a smirk.

Emma shakes her head, fondly exasperated at the praise. "I've got a few other partners — nothing steady, but, yeah, I'd like to be free to see other people. Is that okay with you?"

"Of course!" I lay my hand on hers on the table. "We don't want to change you, or force you into anything you're not comfortable with."

Emma beams. "Thanks for saying that — that's something I struggled a lot with in past relationships. I mean, some of them tried to change me, but I also tried to fit into a mold that wasn't me, because I felt like I had to? To please them? Man, you don't know how many times I've tried to make myself monogamous for a cute girl."

"I'm so sorry you had to go through this. It sounds pretty rough," David says, taking her other hand. "I hope you know you can be yourself with us."

Emma brings his hand to her mouth, kisses his knuckles gently. "I think so. Like I said, you two feel like home."

"Speaking of home," I pipe up, "we should finish our plates and go back home, there's a nice bed in it just waiting for us."

"Don't tell me you already wanna go again?" David chuckles.

"Oh, you're one to talk, Mr. I-Won't-Let-You-Get-Dressed."

FORTY-EIGHT

After work one late October day, I take a walk to the queer bookstore where Emma works, to take the subway home with her. She's having dinner with us and spending the night, like almost every night since the three of us have gotten together. I bump into David, who had the same idea, since he came from a shoot in the neighbourhood.

We walk in the bookstore, the bell above the door uselessly signalling our presence — Emma's sitting behind the counter, absorbed in a book, and gives no indication that she heard us. David's about to say something, but I elbow him and put a finger to my lips with a wink. I want to see how long it'll take for her to notice us. I walk up to her, not even trying to be stealthy — I even lean against the counter, watching Emma intently.

After a minute or so, I can't keep it in any longer — I burst out laughing. Emma jumps almost a foot in the air and sends her book flying.

"Oh my god! Sugar, you scared me half to death! How long have you been standing here?"

"About a minute. You really didn't hear us?"

"God, I'm a mess today. I came in twenty minutes late cause I was reading on the subway and missed my stop."

"*Today*?" David teases, quirking up an eyebrow.

Emma's always late everywhere, and it's always because she was reading. It's endearing, really.

A flush heats up her cheeks. "Okay, fine, all the time. But it's worse today — this book is unputdownable."

On the train, we manage to find three seats together — a feat, during rush hour at Berri-UQAM station. Emma sits with her arm around me and holds David's hand. They're talking about the calendar shoot he did for the roller derby team she coaches, which is how they first met.

I look up and see *her* across the wagon.

Alex Bell.

Looking at the three of us like she doesn't know if she should barf, punch us, or run away.

Emma notices me tensing up, so she looks up.

"Hey, Alex!" She smiles and waves at her.

Alex comes over, visibly against her better judgement.

"Hey, Emma," she says through gritted teeth.

"You guys know each other?" David asks, bewildered.

It finally dawns on me and my jaw drops.

"*She* is your Emma?!" I ask Alex.

"Apparently, she's *yours* now." She shoots a snide look at David's and Emma's intertwined hands. "And *his*." The word is but a hiss.

"*Station Place-des-Arts*," the P.A. system announces as the doors open. Alex pushes past the crowd and gets out without another word.

David looks at me, puzzled.

"Remember Alex's girlfriend from last year? The one who wouldn't commit to a monogamous relationship?"

"That's you?" He looks at Emma, eyes wide in disbelief.

She nods. "How do you guys know her?"

"She's my — she used to be my best friend."

"Right, I remember her talking about an Amy. Why aren't you friends anymore?"

"We had one drunken night together, when you two broke up. She was in love with me, but I couldn't give her exclusivity any more than you could." My eyes fill with tears. I miss Alex so much. Seeing her now, months after our fight, brings all the pain back, a tsunami rushing over me.

Emma pulls me closer. "I know how you feel. It broke my heart that I couldn't give her what she wanted. She's a great girl."

I nod. "Every time something good happens to me, or I see something I know she'd like, it physically hurts not being able to call her."

"I know, *chaton*," David says softly. I can see in his eyes how much it pains him not being able to make me feel better.

"Thank you both so much for being here."

"Hey." Emma gives a soft smile. "This is the whole point of this relationship — we're here for each other."

"Thanks. I love you." My heart aches with how true this has come to be in the past few weeks.

"So how come you never told me you were Emma Sculation?" I ask, eager to switch to a happier subject. "Cause I gotta say, it's the greatest derby name of all time."

Emma winces. "I love coaching, but since my knee injury, I wasn't sure I could ever play again, so I didn't wanna dwell on it."

I nod and rub her knee. "I'm so sorry. It sounds like it was a big part of your life."

She cracks a smile. "Actually, I didn't wanna say anything until I was certain, but I might be able to go back soon."

"Really?" David squeezes her hand earnestly.

"I haven't told the team yet, but I've been practicing on my own and I'm almost back to last year's level."

"The girls will be so glad," David says. "During the shoot they all talked about your exploits — you're kind of a legend to the team."

Emma scoffs. "I couldn't do it without them, really. I'm happy I could inspire them, but the team is just as good without me. The other jammers are amazing, you should see them."

Out of the subway, in the middle of the street, David and Emma recreate the highlights of the game he shot. I trail after them, safe on the sidewalk, shaking my head.

I love these dorks.

FORTY-NINE

"Amy, we've been patient, but this is ridiculous." Mitch shakes her head.

I grab onto my latte, unsure what this is about. Georgie, Cory and Mitch are all towering above me with expectant looks on their faces.

"You and David have been with Emma for two months."

"Two months!" Georgie echoes.

"And we have yet! To! Meet! Her!" Cory continues, clapping to emphasize his words.

I let out a relieved sigh. "Oh, that's it? With the way you guys were ganging up on me, I thought I messed something up again."

They sit down at my table, frowning in mock disapprobation.

"It's unacceptable, is all we're saying." Mitch sums up.

I chuckle. "This relationship is so fresh and amazing, we barely realized it had been two months already."

Cory takes a sip of kombucha, trying hard to keep up the offended façade. He scoffs.

"Stop being such drama queens! You can come over tonight."

We arrange for them to come over at eight. Emma goes home to grab some clothes — she hasn't been to her place in like a week — so David and I eat dinner alone.

Emma and Mitch arrive at the same time. Emma lets her in — she already has her own key, since she spends more time here than at her own apartment.

"Hey guys!" David greets them while I open a bottle of wine in the kitchen. "Emma, this is Michelle. Mitch, Emma."

"Yeah, we've already introduced ourselves," Mitch says. "I recognized her from karaoke night."

"Oh, right! Well, come on in!"

I hug them hello — and kiss Emma — when they come in the kitchen. Mitch hands me a bottle of rosé wine.

"I can't believe you were Alex's elusive Emma too!" Mitch says. "You know, I've wanted to meet you for, like, a year now."

"Yeah, what are the odds that Alex, David and I would all date the same person?"

"That's queer dating for you, sugar," Emma answers with a grin. "I can't tell you how many friends of exes or exes of friends I've hooked up with along the years. It's a tight-knit community."

Cory and Georgie arrive at this moment, with a bottle of wine each.

"Are you here to meet Emma or get her drunk?"

"Both, of course," Georgie replies.

I introduce them to Emma before she hands me a pile of envelopes.

"You guys had mail."

"Thanks." I rifle through the flyers and bills and find a pink envelope with our address etched in gold letters.

"Oh, this must be the invite to Julia's wedding!" I exclaim, trying to open the envelope without wrecking it — it probably cost more than the wine we're drinking.

"Oh, right, I got mine this afternoon," Mitch recalls.

"Crap," David says, reading the invitation over my shoulder. "This is addressed to both of us, no plus ones."

"Well, that's pretty standard when you invite a long-term couple."

"Yeah, but we're not a couple anymore. We're a triad."

"Julia doesn't know that," I say. I cast an apologetic glance at Emma. "Sorry, every time we speak lately is all about the wedding; I didn't break the news."

"Yeah, but can you picture how she'd react if you did?" Georgie points out.

Cory takes on this grating Valley Girl voice that sounds nothing like Julia, but we all laugh anyway. "You mean, like, you and David, like, have a girlfriend? Like, the both of you? Isn't that, like, illegal? Anyway, gross." He scoffs and examines his nails.

"Julia is the perfect stereotype of closed-minded straight. Like she's okay with gay marriage, but as soon as you get deeper than that, she bails," Mitch explains to Emma.

"Polyamory, asexuality, trans people, to name a few," I add.

Emma cocks up an eyebrow. "So, why are you guys friends with her?"

"I've known her since we were kids. I think we stayed friends mostly out of habit. And her fiancé is a good friend of David's."

"Yeah, maybe I could talk to Jason." David throws the invitation on the kitchen table. "He's a good guy."

"I doubt he has a say in it," Cory points out.

Georgie nods. "We got our invite today, too. She deadnamed me on it. Come on, I play D&D with your fiancé, we've been hanging out for years. I know you know my name."

"Ouch." Emma cringes.

"Yeah. Not sure I wanna go, at this point. I mean, she didn't invite me, did she? She invited Cory, and some girl with my last name."

"That is so shitty." I sigh.

Georgie shrugs. "I don't mind not going, really."

Emma wraps an arm around my shoulders. "Neither do I, sugar."

"No, you know what? I'm so fed up with Julia trying to impose her monosexist and transphobic views on us."

Mitch laughs. "Honey, you sound like Alex." Emma nods.

"Yeah," David sighs. "This is Julia's wedding, though. If she wants it to be an allocishet-fest, there's nothing we can do."

"Unless..." Mitch trails off, mysteriously looking at us over her glass of wine.

"Unless?"

"Unless I bring Emma as my plus one!"

David and I beam at her.

Emma looks worried. "Don't you want to bring your own date?"

"I'm asexual. The only other person I'd like to bring is on tour in the UK with his band. I'd rather take someone my friends and I will have fun with than someone who will expect this to turn into something more. Plus, I kinda wanna see Julia's face when I show up with a girl after years of her trying to set me up with guys."

"In this case, I'd be honoured." Emma says, raising her glass gracefully.

"Now, this, I gotta see!" Cory exclaims, looking eagerly at his boyfriend. Georgie just sighs and nods.

"Yeah, okay. But I'll talk to Jason. No way I'm having my deadname on the place card."

"Let's queer the fuck out of this wedding!" Cory hollers. "Group hug, bring it in!"

¤

I don't have to wait very long for Julia's reaction. As soon as she gets Mitch's RSVP card, she texts me in a frenzy.

Julia Tyler — Did you know Michelle's a lesbian??? She's bringing a girl to my wedding!!!

I'm so glad she did this via text message: that way I don't have to hide my hilarity. I send a quick, No she's not — probably just a friend, barely able to type because I'm laughing so hard.

Pizza and beer — the usual promises when you help someone move, but even without it, I'd still be here. My baby sister — I should probably stop saying that, she's an adult, now — is moving out of our parents' house to her first apartment.

I spend the whole day debating whether to tell her about Emma. At first, the point is moot — Dad's here to help move the bigger pieces of furniture, and there's no way I'm coming out in the middle of moving day. He leaves around dinner time, but then the place is full of her roommate Lauren's friends who came to help her, too.

I'm still indecisive about it when it's eleven and only Char, Hugo and I are left. Hugo carries the last few boxes in while she and I are filling her bookshelves. He knows about Emma, so I could absolutely speak in front of him, but I'm unsure. Somehow, it still feels too fresh? Like something precious I should protect. The same instinct that made me wait so long before introducing her to my friends is preventing me from mentioning Emma now.

She probably would be too distracted to listen to me anyway. I've noticed her ogling Hugo's lean frame in his increasingly sweat-damp T-shirt — she's basically drooling at this point.

We're almost done filling the shelves when he brings in the last boxes, dropping on the bare mattress with an exhausted grunt. He wipes the sweat from his forehead with the bottom of his shirt, exposing inches of tanned skin. Charlotte drops a heavy Tolkien box set, barely missing her foot.

I mean, I get it. Hugo is incredibly hot and charismatic. But, somehow, I feel like that chapter of my life is over. We haven't hooked up in months, not since that time I ditched Jeff for him. He's still one of my closest friends, but since Emma came into my life... I don't know, I feel like the only thing I want is to spend time with her and David. This is probably just the new relationship energy — who knows, perhaps I'll go back to dating and hooking up eventually, but for now, I'm sick of this scene. I've got everything I could ask for with those two.

Char and I collapse on whatever surface is available in her still crowded room — she on the bed next to Hugo, I on her desk chair, with my feet up on the bed. We finish our beers while Charlotte tells us her plans for decorating the room.

I'm definitely going to tell her about Emma. Just not tonight.

When I stand up to leave, so does Hugo. Charlotte's face falls, but she manages to school her features into a somewhat credible smile when he turns to her.

"Make sure to call me when you want to set up these shelves," he says, puffing out his chest, pulling the trigger of his electric drill to make it whir, in what he probably thinks is a badass cowboy move.

Charlotte giggles — she probably agrees about the badass cowboy move. "I will!"

I hug her goodbye. "I'm so proud of you, Char — your own place at last!"

As soon as Hugo and I are out of the building, on our way to the subway station, I bump my shoulder against his.

"I think she was hoping you'd stay."

He heaves a long sigh, shoves his hands as deep in his pockets as his skinny jeans will allow. "I know. I — real talk? I wanted to."

"Why didn't you?"

He stops in his tracks, eyeing me up and down in a *Are you for real?* way, eyebrows raised.

"Don't let me hold you back."

"You sure?"

"I mean, you and I… that's in the past, right? I'm not about to tell you who you should date — that's never been our style."

"But still… your sister."

"Look, if you're not okay with it, don't do it. I'm just saying, if the only thing stopping you is me, you should just go for it."

Hugo nods pensively. "A'ight, then. I'll see where things go from here…"

We reach the station and hug goodbye before going our separate ways. He kisses me on the forehead.

Yup. The sexual part of our relationship is *definitely* over.

FIFTY

Later that week, I get a message from Marie-Ève on Facebook. Even though we said we'd keep in touch, I haven't heard much from her since June. We sexted a few times, but it just wasn't the same, and then she got busy training for a big audition, and, frankly, with everything that happened, my summer went by in the blink of an eye.

A thrill goes up my spine as I click to open her message. One look at her profile picture brings back all the excitement and bliss of our too-short summer fling.

Marie-Ève Provencher — Hey :) I'm in Montreal for a week for auditions. Wanna get a drink and catch up?

My fingers are flying over the keyboard, typing a reply of their own accord — Sure! — before I can even think of what this means.

Is it just catching up between old friends? Will we just pick things up where we left them? Is it a date? Do I *want* it to be a date?

Not this again, I tell my overanalyzing brain.

¤

We meet the next day at La Brunante, grateful for the cozy atmosphere shielding us from the icy November wind. I still have no idea what Marie wants this to be. She kisses me on both cheeks when she gets here — affectionate, but nothing more than friendly.

She sits on the opposite side of the table and makes no attempt to touch me — no holding my hand or anything of the sort.

I decide to bury my worries and just enjoy her company — I'll deal with whatever happens if and when it does.

"So, what's the audition for?"

"Le Cirque du Soleil." Marie shrugs as if it's no big deal, but she blushes a little.

"No way! That's huge!"

She nods, fiddling with her coaster. "I'm so nervous. I got on the first call-back list, but there's three more rounds of audition to get a spot on the troupe."

"I hope you get it." I squeeze her hand. "I'll send good vibes your way."

"Thanks. And thanks for meeting me, by the way. Otherwise, I'd be stuck in my hotel room, freaking out about my routine and overtraining."

"Glad I can be of help."

After we finish our beer, Marie suggests we leave the bar and go for a walk. "My audition's at eight tomorrow — I can't be hungover."

I take her on a tour of my favourite places in town. It's only her second time in Montreal and she's mostly been to the tourist spots.

"So, what's new with you?" she asks, threading her fingers through mine as we walk the cobbled paths of the lesser-crowded streets in the Old Port.

My hand goes still against hers. This is it. The make it or break it point.

"Well, it's been kinda crazy since I came back. My boyfriend and I started seeing someone — a girl — we're a triad now."

"Really? That's so great!" She flashes a sincere smile at me, but doesn't let go of my hand.

"Yeah, in fact, I decided to stop dating around and enjoy this fresh new thing. I got sick of the heartache, you know."

She squeezes my hand in agreement, then stops in her tracks.

"Oh. Right." She drops my hand. "I didn't mean — I mean, I didn't expect anything to happen. Of course, it would be nice if it did, but this can totally be a platonic thing. It just felt nice holding your hand, is all."

I stop her rambling by taking her hand in mine again. "Nice to see I'm not the only one freaking out about this." I chuckle.

Marie knits her eyebrows together, puzzled.

"I didn't know if you thought this was a date — if you wanted to pick things up where we left them, and since I stopped dating, I didn't want you to take it the wrong way."

"To be honest, I can't really afford to think about romance right now — my entire mind is on the auditions. This is just two friends catching up. I only wanted to see Montreal and give my mind some rest for a night."

I grin. "Once again, my anxious brain managed to make me freak out for no reason whatsoever."

We resume our stroll, hand in hand, weaving through old stone buildings and street performers, until we end up in front of her hotel.

"However," Marie says with the most mischievous glint in her eyes, "I wouldn't be *totally* opposed to a goodnight kiss."

"I think that can be arranged."

Our lips meet, a delicious reminder of our idyll, with a tiny bit of tongue thrown into the mix to sate any remaining hint of lust.

"Do you need a good luck kiss, too?"

FIFTY-ONE

Being jerked awake by "Don't You (Forget About Me)" — my ringtone — is not a fun experience. I extricate myself from between David and Emma, both still blissfully asleep in a warm cocoon. The only thought that permeates my sleepy brain is that we really need a king-sized bed. When I notice the hour and the caller's name, a terrible sense of dread fills me.

3:42a.m. — Phillip Evans

"Dad?" I answer shakily, bracing myself for bad news. "Is everything okay?"

"Your mother's in the hospital. She fainted when she was getting ready for bed. She's in a critical condition. We're not sure if —" He trails off, his voice strangled in his throat.

"Shit." I sit down on the bed, speechless and now fully awake. "Um. What can I do?"

"She's in the ICU at Sacré-Coeur. She can't have visitors at this hour, but I'm spending the night here in case the situation changes."

"Do you want company?"

"No, you get some rest. You can come by during visiting hours tomorrow."

"Then why'd you call me in the middle of the night?"

Dad stays silent. He'd never ask help from Charlotte and I; I know he wants to be strong for us, but he needs me right now.

"I'm coming over."

Dad heaves out a huge sigh and hangs up. I'm halfway through getting dressed when Emma stirs.

"'s goin' on, sugar?" she mumbles.

"My mom's in the hospital." My voice cracks. Saying it out loud is harder than I thought it would be.

I sit back down on the bed and tears come to my eyes. Behind me, I feel Emma shake David awake.

"Amy?" David sits up and pulls me into a warm embrace.

"Her mom's in the hospital," Emma explains. I'm grateful for it because I don't have the strength to say it again.

"Alright, let's go," David says, pulling jeans over his boxers.

He never thinks twice when I'm in need.

Emma's also getting out of bed.

"Emma? I'm grateful for your support, but — well — my parents don't know you exist."

"I know, sugar. But I can't possibly go back to sleep now. I'll stay here and send out good vibes. Call me if you got news or if you need anything, alright?"

"You're the best. I love you." I lean in and kiss her.

David calls a cab while I pack a bag of stuff that might be useful — snacks, crosswords, etc. Dad has been there all night and probably left in a rush. I feel restless waiting for the taxi to arrive, so I hurry outside. David runs after me, handing me my forgotten coat and boots.

"It's snowing," he points out.

The cab ride is excruciating. I have nothing left to do but wait. The most horrible *what-ifs* swim around my brain, dark reminders of my worst fears.

What if Mom isn't home by Christmas?

What if she dies?

Tears fill my eyes again and for the first time since Dad called, I let them fall freely. David takes my hand. I know if he weren't here I'd crumble to a sobbing mess in the back of the cab. Despite David's — perfect, amazing David — best efforts to be here for me, however, Emma's absence is especially hard to bear.

What if Mom dies without ever knowing about Emma?

A rush of certainty comes over me as I realize Emma is the love of my life, just like David is.

Mom cannot die before she meets her.

My tears dwindle, distress replaced by a resolved anger. I'm angry at myself for never having the courage to tell the truth to my parents.

When the cab stops at the hospital door, I've made up my mind. If Mom gets better — no, not *if,* I have to convince myself she'll get better, or else I won't be able to keep going. As soon as Mom's better, I'll tell her and Dad about Emma.

David and I follow the signs to the ICU to find my father pacing in front of the doors. He's picking at an empty paper cup until the rim unravels. His eyes are sunken in dark purple circles. He looks about ten years older than the last time I saw him.

"Dad!" I call when he doesn't notice us.

"Amy!" He envelops me in a tight, warm hug. I can tell the embrace is meant to comfort him as much as me. I rub his back, feeling as if I'm parenting my own father.

God, it must be so hard for him. I can't even imagine what I would do if anything happened to David or Emma, and my parents have been together for thirty years. Dad's chest stutters against my cheek and I can feel warm droplets falling on my head. His hands grip my winter coat like a lifeline.

"Come here, Dad. We should sit down." I guide him to a nearby sitting area — in view of the ICU doors, so they can find us if anything happens.

"I'll go get some coffee," David whispers in my ear before leaving for the cafeteria.

The main reason he's leaving us is to preserve Dad's intimacy. David knows my father isn't the emotional type : to cry in front of his daughter's boyfriend is a big deal. I'm glad David respects that.

Dad explains how the doctor thinks it's a pulmonary problem — maybe emphysema.

"In the last few months, she was getting winded more quickly, she even had trouble eating because she couldn't breathe at the same time."

"I noticed last week she's lost a lot of weight," I recall as we sit down.

He nods bleakly. "Tonight, she got so winded while preparing for bed, she fainted."

I squeeze his hand. "Does Charlotte know?"

"I'll call her tomorrow. No need waking her up on a school night." He makes an apologetic face. "You're the oldest. That's why I called you."

"Don't worry about it, Dad. I'm glad you called me."

"I — I couldn't wait alone." His voice breaks, and my heart along with it.

"I'm here." I rub his hand soothingly.

David comes back with three coffees and a newspaper.

"I figured you might want to take your mind off things, sir."

"That's very nice of you, David. Thanks for being here for Amy."

"It's the least I can do."

Dad starts reading and we keep quiet for a while. I think he even falls asleep for a few minutes, hidden behind the sports section. He and Mom got here around midnight, so he was up all night.

A nurse comes up to us. I introduce myself as Phillip and Geneviève's daughter. Dad stands up at once, eager for information.

"Your wife's situation is stable, but we want to keep her under observation. We're moving her to Observation Room B on the third floor."

Dad nods and thanks him, and we gather our things to relocate to another waiting room.

"You should go home, Dad. Get some sleep and come back tomorrow." I glance at my watch. Four thirty. "Well, later today."

"I should stay here in case —"

"David and I will be here, and if anything changes we'll call you."

"But…" Dad rakes a hand through his thinning hair. I've never seen him look so lost. A distraught look haunts his eyes, his shoulders slouch, defeated. The love of his life almost died and he can't bring himself to leave her. My heart clenches and I blink back a few tears.

Dad sits back down, tightening his grip on his rolled-up newspaper, as if he was holding a shield. David sits next to him.

"Sir? The last thing we need is for you to collapse from sleep deprivation. Geneviève needs you well-rested and healthy."

Dad heaves a long sigh. "You're probably right." He stands up and pats David's shoulder. "Take care of my girls."

"I will."

As soon as Dad is out of sight, I collapse into David's arms.

"Thank you," I mumble into his shirt. "I didn't have the strength to do that."

"That's why you have me. And Emma."

"Speaking of, I should call her."

She answers at the first ring.

"Hey, how is she?"

"Not better, really, but stable. She's out of the ICU, at least. They're keeping her under observation. I convinced my dad to go home and rest, so David and I are gonna be here a while."

"I'm glad things are looking up."

"Yeah, I was really scared for a while. And I made a decision. I'd like you to meet my parents."

"Yeah?"

"I thought about it and I couldn't stand the idea of Mom dying before she could meet one of the loves of my life."

Emma's voice is choked up when she speaks. "This means a lot to me, sugar. I look forward to it."

"Me too. I love you, sunshine."

"I love you too."

"I love you too!" David leans in to speak into my phone.

Emma chuckles. "Tell David I love him too."

We hang up and David's eyes widen.

"You're gonna come out to your parents? Shit, that's... that's so big."

David looks surprised, but, beyond that, I can't read him. I have no idea how he feels about it.

"Don't you agree?"

He beams. "Of course I agree, *chaton*. I'm just surprised because you always said it was none of their business."

"It's none of their business who I sleep with. But Emma is so much more than that. She's with us for the long run."

¤

Dad's back at the hospital at eight o'clock sharp, gigantic cup of coffee in hand and almost as huge bags under his eyes.

"Have you slept?" I ask in lieu of greetings.

He shrugs and stifles a yawn. "How could I? Anything new?"

"Still under observation. They said we could see her around noon."

"I'm gonna call your sister."

¤

Charlotte skips her morning class and joins us a bit before noon. She clings to Dad's hand hard, but I notice Dad is holding on just as much. My eyes fill up with tears for the millionth time since yesterday, but I wipe them on the back of my hand. I wanna be strong for my sister. Fuck, I mean — she's only nineteen. She's just too damn young to lose her mom.

I grab her other hand between mine, to show her that I'm here, that she can lean on me. Dad has enough to worry about; I have to take some weight off his shoulders.

Char pulls me closer and buries her face in the crook of my neck. I can feel a few tears trickling down my clavicle. I know my sister, she's always been more like Dad — she doesn't want him to see her cry. She wants to prove that she's an adult, that her world didn't shatter around her when she got that damn call.

I rub her shoulders; trying to make her understand that I'm here for her, that she doesn't have to act strong for me. If she falls apart, I'll pick up the pieces and, together, we can both be strong for our parents.

I gaze at David over her head, a silent look of thanks. I know when it's my turn to fall apart, he'll be there to build me back up. Him and Emma.

When we're finally allowed in the room, my knees buckle under me. I don't know if I'm ready to see Mom like this. David tightens his grip around my shoulders and guides me through the door.

The first thing that hits me is how tiny she looks. She's like a child, lost in this cold hospital bed, tangled into tubes and scratchy blankets and an ill-fitting hospital gown. She seems to be sleeping, but she cracks open an eye when David and I come in.

"Hi," I whisper, my voice hoarse from all the crying.

I don't know why I'm whispering. The hospital is hardly a quiet place — machines beep, people talk and cough and cry — but it's like I'm scared I'll startle her and she'll disappear. She already looks so thin and pale she's almost transparent, a wisp of a woman.

Her bony hand quivers over the covers and she looks at me imploringly, the corner of her mouth stretching feebly into her closest approximation of a smile. I close the two steps to the bed and take her hand gently, nervously, like you handle a priceless artefact threatening to crumble.

"Amy," she croaks, and I see the movement of her lips more than I hear the sound come out of them.

"I'm here, Mom." I don't know what else I can say. Every thought passing through my head is along the lines of 'Help me, Mommy, I'm scared', but what good is that when she's the one who's sick? Who's probably as scared as I am?

I decide to just say nothing. Stand there and hold her hand, smile at her, send some strength so she gets better.

After a while David squeezes my shoulders and I realize it's Charlotte's turn. I lean in to hug Mom, and it's awkward, but I manage not to pull on any tubes. I kiss her on the forehead — the only part of her that doesn't show how much weight she's lost.

"I love you, Mom."

FIFTY-TWO

The first thing I do when Dad calls with the news that Mom is out of the hospital, after a week, is to wrap her Christmas gift.

All the other presents are already sitting under the tree, nicely wrapped. I couldn't bring myself to wrap hers. The set of mandala colouring books and colour pencils I got her is still in its plastic bag on the upper shelf of my wardrobe. I think it will be perfect for her recovery, to pass the time before she can go back to work. I know it sounds lame to focus on a Christmas present when my mother came so close to dying, but I guess it gave me the illusion I could control at least *something*.

It also allowed me to stop worrying about the inevitable: telling Mom and Dad about Emma. I decided to wait until January. Mom's still weak, so we only planned a small Christmas dinner — my parents, Charlotte, David and I. For once, I won't have to put up with my uncles.

It kills me not to spend our first holidays together with Emma, but I just can't drop that kind of news at Christmas, nor while Mom is still frail.

I tie a neat golden bow on top of the plaid wrapping paper and place the box underneath the tree, satisfied. Emma comes home at the same moment, announced by her traditional knock before entering.

I keep telling her she doesn't need to knock — we gave her a key so she can come and go as she pleases.

"I don't live here. It's just polite," she always says.

I chuckle at how adorable she is. "Wherever David and I are, you can call it home. You know that."

She smiles and kisses the tip of my nose. "Of course, sugar. How was your day?"

"Mom's out of the hospital!"

"Really? That's so great!" She pulls me in her arms and bear-hugs me.

"I'm so glad she'll be home for Christmas."

Emma glances at the new gift under the tree and the scraps of paper and spools of ribbon surrounding us. She nods knowingly. David and she have spent a few nights comforting me while I worried about the gift and what we would do if Mom had to spend the holidays in the hospital.

"I'm so relieved you'll get to have a nice family Christmas. I'd have hated to leave knowing you're spending it in an hospital room."

Emma's spending the week in New Jersey, where her family on her dad's side still lives. She gets to celebrate Kwanzaa with them for the first time in years.

"When you come back, we'll have a sweet New Year's Eve, just the three of us." I take her hands and pepper kisses all over them.

"I can't wait."

¤

The sight of Mom on Christmas Eve gives me quite a shock. Her sunken eyes and hollow cheeks, the way her bones nearly jut out of her skin, somehow didn't seem so out of place in a hospital bed, hooked to all these machines. Now, however, against the backdrop of the fairy-lit Christmas tree, wearing a navy blue velvet dress that hangs loosely on her frame rather than hugging her curves like it used to, she makes a striking, worrying image. I grip David's hand for comfort and his thumb rubs soothing circles onto my wrist.

Her motherly smile hasn't changed, however. She can't stay on her feet for too long and sometimes she runs out of breath mid-sentence, but she's still warm and comforting as ever.

Dinner's delicious. Charlotte made the whole feast with Dad, forbidding Mom to help, insisting that she sit down and rest. I notice how they fill her plate way more than usual, and during dinner, we all watch not so subtly, to make sure she puts some meat on her bare bones.

Mom chuckles and spears a big piece of meat pie with her fork. "You can stop watching me," she tries to reassure us. "I still can't eat without getting too out of breath, but at least I got my appetite back."

We all laugh and self-consciously direct our gazes to our plates.

"The *tourtière* is amazing, Char," Mom adds. "Just like Mamie Lucille used to make it!"

When we exchange our gifts after dinner, she thanks me profusely for the mandalas and colouring pencils.

"This is perfect for my new resolution. I want to take up yoga, relax, and take care of myself. I'm not in any hurry to go back to the hospital."

I notice with glee that there isn't a single ashtray or pack of cigarettes visible in the house. Looks like Dad is doing this with her. He keeps looking at her like he's not quite sure she's there, that she's alive. Like he came so close to losing his soulmate and now he can't believe that he didn't. I know he'll do everything he can to nurse her back to health. I know because that's exactly what I'd do for David and Emma.

FIFTY-THREE

David helps Emma with her luggage while I make hot cocoa. Her bus got stranded in the snowstorm — she was supposed to come home yesterday.

"Here, I thought you'd be cold." I hand her a fuming mug, toppling with marshmallows, just the way she likes it.

"Thanks, sugar." She cradles the mug between her still-gloved hands, stepping closer to me for warmth.

"There's also a warm blanket waiting for you in the dryer," David adds as he hangs up her coat.

"You guys are perfect," Emma sighs into her cocoa.

"We're not gonna let our girl die from hypothermia on New Year's Eve." I hug her and rub her back, trying to warm her up.

"Or any other time, for that matter."

After Emma's warmed up — which may or may not have involved naked antics — we all get dressed up in fancy clothes and pop open a bottle of prosecco.

"So, we went a bit crazy with the food…"

I open the fridge to take out the trays of hors-d'oeuvres David and I prepared yesterday.

"We've got so much stuff," he says. "Oysters —"

"Of course," Emma answers with a knowing grin. She knows they're David's favourite.

" — shrimp cocktail, fine cheeses, bruschetta, mini-quiches …"

"David kept adding more stuff to our cart, saying, 'Ooh, Emma would *love* that!'"

"I'm guessing we won't have to buy food again until Valentine's?" Emma replies, eyeing the trays covering every inch of the kitchen counter. "You do realize there's only three of us, right?"

David, already stuffing his mouth with oysters, can't emit a reply, but answers with a sheepish grin. Emma and I join him, and all three of us eat more than a reasonable amount. We realize soon afterwards that we've barely made a dent in the ludicrous amount of food on the table.

"I say we bundle up, take a long walk to help this all go down, then come back to eat some more," David suggests.

"Do you mind going back out in the cold?" I ask Emma.

She presses her nose against the frosted windowpane, her breath fogging the glass. "Nah, look how pretty the night is!"

We go out into a proverbial winter wonderland. The streets are deserted and silent. Snow falls slowly in tiny flakes. Christmas lights turn the snowbanks into stained glass artworks. Snowflakes cling like stars to Emma's curls, dark as deep space.

The sky is this rust orange tint it takes so often during winter nights, when the streetlights reflect on the snow.

David walks between us, beaming like a kid on Christmas day — or like a guy in love on New Year's Eve. His eyes are bright as the snow in Emma's hair.

"Remember last year?" I ask. "It was just the two of us. Things were definitely not this good in my life."

"But then we met you," David tells Emma, "and it became the best year of our lives."

"Last year at this time," Emma says, "I think I was hunched over a toilet after too many shots with my derby girls. Fun, but y'know. I prefer being slightly tipsy, with a stomach ready to burst, holding the hands of my loves."

She stops in the middle of the empty street and pulls us close. The three of us try to kiss all at once, a feat we've never achieved — not for a lack of trying. With all our scarves and coats in the way, it is pretty inconceivable, but we're just so full of love we'll never let it stop us.

From the open window of a nearby apartment, we suddenly hear shouts and cheers.

"*Trois! Deux! Un!*"

"*Bonne année!*" David cheers with them, kissing us both in turn. Emma has to stand on tiptoes to reach his lips and it never fails to make me smile.

"Oooh, say it again?" she asks, a glint in her eye.

"*Bonne année,*" he whispers in her ear.

"Happy New Year," she answers, almost in a growl. "Now, let's go back." She takes his hand and guides us back home.

"You're so adorable when he speaks French." I laugh and follow them.

"*C'est même pas si sexy que ça,*" David notes.

Emma all but starts running with us in tow.

"Careful, *amour*. You don't want us to —" David slides on a sheet of ice hidden under the snow. He falls flat on his back. Emma and I fall on top of him, cackling.

"Any of you hurt?" I ask.

"No, the layers of coats cushioned the fall," David says.

"You should be careful when you speak French. One of these days you're gonna get us killed," Emma mumbles against David's coat.

"*Je t'aime.*"

FIFTY-FOUR

"So, how's your mom?" Mitch asks, handing me a London Fog in a to-go cup.

"Getting better every day. She's going on walks daily, and she says she can go for longer without getting out of breath now."

"That's great!" Cory squeezes my shoulder.

Two weeks into the new year, Georgie, Cory and I are crowding around the counter at Le Trèfle, waiting for Mitch's shift to end. We end up going for dinner in a tiny Chinese restaurant down the street.

"Guys, I need your advice," I declare, once we're seated around various baskets of dim sum. "I decided to come out to my parents."

"As bi?" Georgie asks, struggling to grab a dumpling with his chopsticks.

"As the whole deal." I exhale and rake a hand through my hair. "Bisexual, polyamorous, in a triad."

Cory winces. He had a pretty rough time coming out to his parents — years later, he still only sees them at Christmas. I doubt they've even met his boyfriend.

Georgie angrily skewers the unruly dumpling with a chopstick and shoves it in his mouth. "Yeah. Our folks aren't exactly the spokespeople for acceptance."

I suddenly realize I've never heard Georgie talk about his family.

"That bad, huh?"

"Let's just say I haven't seen dear Mom and Dad in six years. The day I turned eighteen, I bolted out of there and never looked back."

Cory rubs his back soothingly.

"I'm so sorry — I didn't mean to bring back bad memories." I squeeze Georgie's hand.

He shrugs defiantly. "I'm mostly over it, really. I've never felt at home in that family, so it's not like I miss them."

"I don't think it'll be this rough for you, Amy," Mitch says. "You have a good relationship with your parents."

That's what I'm afraid of. I'm scared I'll ruin it. I love them so, so much — I couldn't take it if they rejected me.

Mitch must see the terror in my eyes — she takes my hand and tilts my chin up to look at her.

"Let's make a pact. We both come out to our parents this weekend, and we'll weather the storm together, alright?"

I look around the table at Cory and Georgie, who have both been hurt so badly by the same decision I'm about to make. Cory nods, a soft smile on his face.

"Whatever happens, we'll be here for you. We're a family."

339

FIFTY-FIVE

"Can you help me with this?" I hand David a necklace. "My hands are shaking, I can't work the clasp."

David pulls me close. He quickly fastens the chain around my neck before hugging me.

"I'm sure it'll be okay," he tries to reassure me.

This is it. The big coming out. David and I are invited to my parents' for dinner.

I can't stop thinking about the resigned look on Georgie's face yesterday. The look of a guy who'll never see his parents again and who's okay with that, even though he knows it sucks.

I try to picture myself, knowing I'll never again see Mom's smile, or hug Dad. Knowing I'll never hang out with Charlotte again.

Tears well up in my eyes as panic rises inside me.

I know I'd still have Mitch and Cory and Georgie, and, most importantly, David and Emma, but it's not the same. It could never replace my parents' love.

My hands shake with anxiety. Tears fall freely down my face — in a stupid non-sequitur way I thank whoever's listening that I didn't do my makeup yet, and I feel dumb for holding on to such a silly matter.

David grabs the box of tissues from my nightstand, guides me to sit on the bed.

"Hey, look at me. Your parents are good people. Open-minded. They love you and will accept you no matter what."

"They won't understand. They'll think we're weird and depraved."

"No, they won't. We'll explain that it's just love and that we're the same people we always were, except now they'll have to pull up one more chair at family dinners."

"Are you sure?"

"Have you *met* Emma? It's impossible not to love this girl. They're gonna fall under her charm in two seconds, tops. But, tonight, they don't even have to like her. They just have to get used to the idea that she exists."

"I hope you're right."

"I always am." He winks and kisses the tip of my nose.

Although I'd rather have it all over as soon as possible, I wait until after dinner to breach the subject. It's easier to be open-minded when you're relaxed and have a bellyful of bœuf bourguignon.

"Mom? Dad?" I begin, when the dishwasher is loaded and we're all sitting comfortably with a fresh glass of wine. "We have something to tell you."

"What is it, honey?" Dad looks wary — he's had his fair share of bad news lately.

Mom puts a hand over mine, beaming. "Are you pregnant?"

"No, but if I was, way to beat me to the punch!"

Mom chuckles. "Sorry."

This quip, at least, manages to distract me from my stressful news. I take a deep breath. No use wasting time on preambles. Do it quick, just like jumping in a cold swimming pool.

"David and I are in a polyamorous relationship."

I watch my parents in apprehension. Their faces betray no reaction whatsoever. They have probably never even heard of this word.

"That means," I look at my clenched hands because the worst is yet to come, "that we're both in love with a third person. We're in what is called a triad — it's just like a normal couple, but there are three of us."

Dad's eyes widen. Mom's brow furrows. They both stay silent.

"Um, this person is a girl. Her name is Emma."

"A girl?" Mom finally says.

"Oh, yeah. I'm bisexual." This information, which used to feel like such a big deal, is now nothing compared to what I just announced.

"Oh."

Silence falls over the table. An awkward silence, heavy with unasked questions and unconfirmed fears. David takes my hand in his. His strength allows me not to get up and run far away from this kitchen.

"How long have you been — um — with her?" Dad finally breaches the quiet.

"About four months."

"So, it's serious, then?" Mom raises a doubtful eyebrow.

"Yeah, we're in love."

David nods his assent.

"Why did you wait so long to tell us?"

"Um, well, when it was just —" I can't say 'when it was just sex' to my parents! I clear my throat. "When it was nothing serious, I figured it didn't concern you. But now that it is — now that it's love, we want you to meet her."

Mom frowns, as if she knows exactly what I meant by 'nothing serious,', but Dad just nods.

"Actually," I continue, "we made the decision to tell you while you were in the hospital. I was scared you'd... leave, before meeting her." My eyes get misty and I take Mom's hand.

Dad looks at her with a fond smile. I guess he's still not used to the idea that she's out of danger and on her way back to health.

Mom clears her throat and presses my hand. "Well, this is a lot to take in. I'm not saying I understand how you can love two people at once. But I'm looking forward to meet this girl. Bring her to dinner next Saturday."

"If both of you fell in love with her, she must be quite something," Dad says.

I sigh in relief. "Thank you so much. I was terrified of telling you."

"Don't be," Dad says, reaching across the table for my hand. "We'll always love you."

"That's what I tried to tell her," David pipes up. "But you know her — she's a worrier."

David and Dad share a laugh and my dad claps him on the shoulder.

"Just like her mom. Thanks for taking care of Amy. I'm glad she has you."

"You'll be glad she has Emma, too. She's an amazing girl. They both are."

Mom drains the last of her wine and gets up.

"Go, now. It's getting late and I only have seven days to get used to this."

I laugh and hug her. "I love you, Mom."

¤

Amy Evans — I still have parents :D What about you?

Michelle Murray — same, although I had the 'what about grandchildren' talk

Amy Evans — ugh. That's always their first question isn't it?

Michelle Murray — coulda been worse :P

FIFTY-SIX

As soon as the doorbell rings on the following Tuesday night, a wave of anxiety slams right into me. I was calm and composed all day. I thought that if coming out to my parents went so well, telling Charlotte would be a cakewalk.

After all, she already knows about our open relationship, so I was certain she'd have no problem with polyamory. I was also pretty sure she and Emma would get along great.

But the sound of the doorbell pulls out some insecurities I didn't even know I had. A nasty voice in the back of my mind whispers stuff like *What if she hates you?*

Rationally, I know my sister won't *hate* me, but lately — since I told her the truth about our open relationship — we've been so much closer, and I'm scared this might drive a wedge between us.

The same voice pulls at every single insecure thought I've had about my sister lately.

Do you really know her?

She's changed so much in the past few years, how can you pretend to know how she might react?

After all, I might have known her when she was small and idolized me, but she's an adult now. We're on equal footing and I don't think I could bear her judging me, or thinking I'm weird.

I take a deep breath, do my best to shove these intrusive thoughts deep enough so I can't hear them, and plaster a smile on my face before opening the door.

"Hey, sweetie. Thanks for coming," I say as I take her coat.

"Won't say no to free food!" It's only been a few months since she moved out. I remember trying to get by without Dad's cooking; it wasn't easy.

"David's making homemade pizza: your favourite."

"Oh, that's so nice of him! Do you need any help?" she offers as we join him in the kitchen.

"Nah, I got it."

"Actually, we wanted to talk to you." I pour three glasses of red wine. Giving her alcohol is so weird — I'm still not used to the fact that she's an adult now.

"What about?"

"Well, you know about our open relationship agreement? It kinda morphed into something else."

Charlotte looks puzzled and turns to David for clues.

"We both met the same girl, by pure coincidence."

"And we really liked her," David adds.

"So when we realized it, we tried to date, like, the three of us together. And it went great —"

"We're in love, actually —" David clarifies.

"Yeah, so the three of us are in a polyamorous relationship. A triad."

Charlotte grins and raises her wine glass. "That's so great, you guys!"

I let out a relieved sigh. The invisible fist that squeezed my lungs since the doorbell rang finally relents.

"I'm so glad you think so!" I get up to hug her. "She's coming over after dinner so you can meet her."

"I can't wait!"

"We came out to Mom and Dad last Saturday, and —"

Charlotte's jaw drops. "You came out? Oh my god, that's so huge! How did they take it?"

"Pretty well, considering. Mom invited the three of us for dinner next Saturday. She wants to meet Emma. And I think it's better if you meet her tonight, so she won't have to meet all of you at once. You'll be one more familiar face for her."

"Count on me."

David pulls the pizza out of the oven and sets it on a serving plate at the centre of the table. After we've all taken a bite and exclaimed on the deliciousness of it, Charlotte looks at me with wide, expectant eyes.

"So? How d'you meet her?"

"Oh, you're so gonna love this. I was at karaoke with my friends, and Emma and I chose the same song. When it came up, we decided to do a duet, and we just clicked."

"What song?"

"'Don't You (Forget About Me)'."

Charlotte lets out a squeal. "That's perfect! What about you?" She turns to David.

"Her roller derby team hired me to shoot a calendar for a fundraiser. We flirted through the whole shoot, and, at the end, she asked me out."

Charlotte sighs contentedly. "These are such great stories. I can't wait to meet her."

"You're gonna love her," David says.

Emma gets here around eight, with blueberry pie. Charlotte's immediately won over by the bringing of dessert — free food, you know.

"Did you make this yourself?" she asks between two oversized bites.

Emma nods.

"It's amazing. Amy and David are pretty lucky to have you."

"She does more than just feed us," David points out.

"Ew, I don't need the details!"

I playfully swat at Charlotte's arm. "Don't be silly — David only meant that she's amazing in so many ways, not just because she can cook."

"Stop it, you're making me blush." Emma hides her smile behind her hand, but I can still see crinkles at the corners of her bright eyes.

The conversation turns to books and school. Emma and Charlotte realize they went to the same cégep and they exchange anecdotes about teachers. David uncorks another bottle of wine.

Emma and Charlotte are getting along great; my anxiety melts away. I know that whatever happens when Emma meets our parents, Charlotte will have our backs.

The night passes by so quickly that when Charlotte looks at her watch she only has time for a quick goodbye before running out to catch the last train.

David, Emma and I snuggle up with one last glass of wine before bed.

"I think that went well," Emma says.

"She really likes you." I nod and kiss her wine-stained lips.

"So will Amy's parents," David says.

Emma lets out a sigh. "I hope so. I was so nervous to meet your sister."

"Really? But you looked so calm!"

Emma winces. "I've gotten so used to being alone — I live by myself and my last long-term relationship was years ago — I guess I'm not used to have people I can open up to."

David holds Emma close, soothingly rubbing her back.

"Oh, sunshine." I press a kiss to her head. "You can tell us anything. I know it's not easy when you're not used to it, so you can take your time — you can tell us as much or as little as you want — just know that you can trust us."

"Plus," David adds with a mischievous grin, "I've got years of experience cheering Amy up."

"I love you," Emma grins, pulling David and me into a hug.

FIFTY-SEVEN

Emma lays spread-eagled on her bed, surrounded by books. She picks one up, reads two lines, heaves a deep sigh, and trades it for another one. She does this over and over for a good ten minutes, while I try to tame my curly hair into an acceptable bun. She throws the last book on the floor with a particularly loud and long sigh.

"Is everything okay, honey?"

"No," she groans. "I'm meeting your parents in less than two hours. They're gonna hate me."

"No, they won't."

"We should just go back to pretending I don't exist."

I put down my handful of bobbypins and sit on the bed next to Emma. A few books join the one already on the floor.

"Emma. You're one of the two most important people in my life. I can't ever pretend you don't exist." She sits up and I take her hands in mine. "But I don't want you to do anything you're uncomfortable with. You don't have to meet them if you don't want to."

"I want to. But I'm just... so fucking scared. Amy, I've never been in a long enough or committed enough relationship to even get to the meet-the-parents stage."

I raise my eyebrows in shock. I had no idea.

"But this?" she continues. "This is the boss battle of meet-the-parents dinners. I can't imagine them being thrilled to meet me."

"Everyone you meet loves you. You're an amazing person." I lean in to kiss her softly. She looks away.

"I'm not scared they won't like me as a person. I'm afraid they won't like me as a concept. The fact that you have two lovers. I'm the manipulative stranger who corrupted your perfect monogamous couple. No matter how charming I am, if they can't get past that, there's nothing I can do."

"Mom called yesterday. She asked me if my girlfriend had any food allergies. She was perfectly sweet about it. Trust me, if she had a problem with it I would have heard it in her voice — in the way she'd say 'girlfriend'."

"You sure?"

"Look how scared I was before I talked to them. I was convinced they would hate me, disown me. Look how well it turned out. They were shocked, sure, but none of my worst fears came true. It might be awkward, of course, but I promise they won't hate you."

"Okay." She nods and gives me the tiniest smile. "Can't wait for it to be over, though."

I hug her tight. "It's gonna be okay."

David comes back from a shoot and walks in to see us locked in a tender embrace. He jumps on the bed to join the fun, his camera bag still slung over his shoulder. Emma's too small double bed creaks and a few more books fall to the floor.

"My books!" Emma protests from underneath me.

I pull out a crumpled copy of *I Know Why The Caged Bird Sings*. Emma's eyes widen and she pouts.

"I'll buy you a new one," I giggle.

"Come on, girls," David says, struggling to get up. "We don't want to keep Phillip and Geneviève waiting."

¤

Mom decided to make fondue for dinner. The perfect kind of meal to get to know someone, since we're all sitting around a pot of boiling cheese for at least an hour. The first half-hour is pretty awkward — the obligatory 'So, what do you do?' and the likes — but no more than when I brought David home for the first time. I have to give it to Mom and Dad, they're taking it really well, acting as if meeting their daughter's second lover was a common occurrence in their lives.

Charlotte also helps, talking about school to take the spotlight off Emma.

"So, this really works, doesn't it?" Dad asks, spearing a cube of bread with his fork.

"Absolutely." I nod, beaming. "We're in love."

"What about children?" Mom asks.

"Well, we don't know if we'll ever want some, but if we do, I'm sure a kid with three parents will turn out just as well as one with two. That kid would have so many people to love and care for them."

"Yes, I suppose so." Mom smiles reluctantly. "Well, I guess I still have lots of time to get used to *that* idea."

"Definitely," David answers. A glint in his eyes, however, tells me he's already imagining the three of us raising a family together.

"If you'd like," Emma suggests, "we have a few volumes on polyamorous families at the bookstore where I work."

"That would certainly help us understand, wouldn't it, Geneviève?" Dad squeezes Mom's hand and she nods, a beam on her face I didn't expect to see tonight.

After dinner, Emma offers to help Mom with dessert. They come back twenty minutes later, laughing so hard they almost drop the plates. David and I share a tear-filled look. I knew they'd like her. Charlotte gives me the less subtle thumbs-up and grin ever.

"Amy, you didn't tell me Emma was such a great cook!"

"Mrs. Evans, I'm not —"

"Please, call me Geneviève. I'm telling you, next time, we *have* to cook together."

I'm grinning so hard my cheeks threaten to burst. David takes Emma's hand and looks at her lovingly.

"I'd love to." Emma beams.

FIFTY-EIGHT

I hurry back home from the subway station, bracing my umbrella against the unseasonable rain and wind. That kind of weather should be illegal in March. The remnants of snow are grey and depressing. I finally reach home, only to find a tall, lanky figure huddled under the tiny porch roof.

He straightens up when he sees me approaching. His overgrown, blonde hair is drenched and hangs limply before his ghostly white face. The rain has soaked through his clothes — his teeth are chattering.

"Jeff?"

"Hello, Amy." He tries to smile, but his shivers turn it into a grimace.

"How long have you been waiting?" I ask as I unlock the door.

He shrugs. "A few hours."

"Are you insane?" I let him in and instruct him to take a hot shower while I throw his clothes in the dryer.

I dig up an old pair of David's sweatpants and a T-shirt and leave them by the bathroom door.

What the hell is Jeff doing here?

I haven't heard from him in six months. I got the occasional J-Walkers update from Mitch when she tells me about Justin, but Jeff hasn't made any effort to contact me since we broke up.

Didn't he think a text message, an e-mail, or even a phone call would be better-received than — than whatever *this* is? I mean, big romantic gestures in the rain are all well and good in rom-coms, but who does that in real life? How could he think this was a good idea?

I put the kettle on. A cup of tea will calm my anger and my nerves. And might warm up Jeff. I'm not an animal and, regardless of my other feelings towards him, I don't want him to freeze to death.

Even though it would totally be his own fault.

When I hear the shower turning off, I freeze in panic. The last time I saw Jeff, I asked Hugo to come along for my safety. Jeff didn't do anything, but my arm still burns and my stomach still churns at the memory of the time before that, when he got aggressive and grabbed me. Not a great track record, and I suddenly realize I'm alone with him. And no one knows he's here.

What if he doesn't get whatever he came here for? What's he going to do then?

I grab a chef's knife and set it out on the counter, easy to reach.

No, that's too obvious. He'll think I don't trust him.

Well, I don't, but he doesn't need to know that.

Next to the knife, I set out a cutting board and a bag of onions. I could be making dinner, he doesn't know that.

I take a deep breath and set two mugs of tea on the kitchen table.

"Why are you here?" I ask when Jeff is, at last, dry, warm, and dressed.

"I miss you."

"Jeff, it's been, like, six months!"

"A long six months."

I raise my eyebrows. You don't just show up to an ex's door and wait hours in the rain because 'you miss them.'

"Amy, I've always been too afraid to tell you what I want. All the time I spent in London was lost in regrets. Regrets that I never told you what you mean to me. I was losing my mind. So I did what I had to do — the only thing I *could* do. I left the band in Dublin and came back home."

I stay silent. None of this makes any sense and nothing I can say would make this any easier.

"I want you, Amy. I know you're the one for me and I wanna spend the rest of my life with you."

"Jeff —"

"I know what you're gonna say. But remember how we used to be. We were so good together. I know Dave's not the one for you. I will wait. Forever. One day, you'll be with me."

I stand up without a word and shove Jeff's half-dry clothes in a plastic bag, storming towards the front door.

"You need to leave. You can keep *David's* old clothes."

"But, Amy —"

"David, *Emma,* and I are perfectly happy. You have to forget me." I hold the front door open and he reluctantly steps out.

"Who the fuck is Emma?"

"Our girlfriend." I slam the door in his face.

FIFTY-NINE

On a rainy Friday night late in April, I join my loves after work at Emma's place. We spend most of our time at mine and David's place, because it's bigger — and also because we have a queen bed, while she only has a double. I love going to Emma's once in a while, though. Her flat is super cozy and really feels like her — as soon as you walk in you know she lives there. Also, she doesn't have a dining table, so we sit at the kitchen island on bar stools, which I've always loved.

I chop vegetables while Emma mixes up a marinade for a ceviche. She always makes fish because she knows how much David loves it. He pours three glasses of rosé wine. I stop for a second, marvelling at how easy and natural this feels: the three of us, in a kitchen, working as a team. We've only been together for seven months, yet I feel like we've done this for years. I let out a contented sigh.

"I am so in love with you." I put down my knife on the cutting board and lean over the island to kiss David, and then I turn around to kiss Emma.

"Me too," they reply at the same time.

After I've chopped everything up, Emma tosses it all in a bowl with the fish and the marinade and sticks it in the fridge.

"This has to rest for an hour, which gives us plenty of time to talk." She pulls up a stool and sits at the island in front of David, taking a sip of wine.

"Anything in particular?" David asks, frowning.

I sit down with them after clearing out the island.

"Yeah, actually. But nothing bad," she adds, seeing the alarmed looks on our faces, "just serious. My lease is up soon, and I have to decide whether or not I renew it."

"Where would you go?" I ask, wondering why she would leave this cute apartment.

Emma takes a deep breath. "I mean, at this point I spend one, maybe two nights a week here. Half my clothes are at your place. It's the first time in my life I actually like living with other people. I guess what I'm asking is: should I keep a place to myself? Or do you guys want to make me some room in yours?"

My eyes widen in surprise, but I'm beaming. I whine every time she spends the night at her place, and I call her as soon as I know she's up, just because I missed her during the night. David looks at me, a grin as wide as mine illuminating his features.

"I would love to live with you, and judging by Amy's face, I can tell she's not totally opposed to the idea. However —"

My smile turns into a sulk. "No *however*!" I interrupt. "We love her and living together is the best idea!"

"*However*," he continues pointedly, "our place may be bigger, but I think we should start this new chapter of our lives from scratch. Get a new place, even bigger, and make new memories."

"Yes! This way it will truly feel like *our* place —" I motion at the three of us, "instead of trying to cram you into ours."

"And Jeff wouldn't know where we live," David adds. I've told them about his big comeback and they both agree he crossed the line between cringy ex and creepy stalker.

"I think I'd like that." Emma nods. A smile slowly graces her face as she considers the idea.

"So, can we look up apartments, now?" I ask excitedly.

David and Emma chuckle. "You are the cutest." Emma tilts my chin up for a kiss.

SIXTY

Excitement seems to electrify the air, as Emma gets ready for her first roller derby bout in a year and a half. She's wearing her usual derby uniform — her team tank top, hot pants, and thigh-high pansexual-flag-striped socks.

I splay a hand across the expanse of skin spreading between shorts and socks. "Good god, your thighs look so strong. I wanna take a bite!" I growl at her like a predator ready to pounce.

Emma giggles and pushes me away. "Stop it! I can't be late!"

"And we have to meet Charlotte and Hugo," David says as he enters Emma's bedroom. "Although, that's one meal I can't refuse," he adds, ogling her other thigh.

"Y'all are the worst." Emma shakes her head at us, still laughing. "See you after the bout!"

"Break a leg!" I say after she kisses me.

"Maybe not." She winces and flexes her just-healed knee.

"*Merde*, then," David says.

"Don't you start with the French!"

¤

The host of the derby bout is a fabulous drag queen in a pink ringleader jacket and a purple tutu. She introduces the players, starting with the visiting team, the Toronto Tornadoes. When she gets to the home team, Les Chipies, the arena fills with cheers and shouts.

"And, last but not least, back on the track after an eighteen-month break, give it up for our very own number twenty-one, Emma Sculation!"

The tumult is deafening. You'd think Beyoncé had just walked in. David and I are no exception. We shout at the top of our lungs while Emma waves at the crowd, skating among her teammates.

Roller derby is always exciting — never a dull moment — but this bout? Exhilarating. The teams are neck-and-neck throughout the game, right until the very end. We're on our feet before the ref even blows her whistle, when Four-Leaf Klobber wins the final jam against Rainbow Roadkill, thus confirming a victory for Les Chipies.

David, Charlotte, Hugo and I high-five and hug each other, cheering along with the crowd, while Les Chipies take their victory lap past the elated crowd massed around the track.

We join the team at their usual dive bar down the street to celebrate their win. I share a pitcher of beer with Charlotte and

Hugo — David's off talking to some of the girls he met at the calendar shoot and Emma's surrounded by people wanting to congratulate her.

After a while, however, I start feeling a bit third-wheely. I know it sounds ridiculous, because this is my sister and one of my best friends-slash-ex-booty-call, but the vibes they're sending each other are off the charts.

I excuse myself to find Emma. I notice Charlotte giving me a vaguely guilty look when I leave, but then Hugo says something I don't catch and she turns back to him, a grin on her face like I've never seen.

I join Emma and she introduces me to her team. We drink, chat, and play a couple games of pool — that is, I play and Emma gives up after her first shot, where she manages to sink the eight ball.

"Give it up for Emma Sculation!" Glitter Bomb hollers. "Good thing she's better at skating than playing pool!"

Someone taps on my shoulder and I turn to see Charlotte, twisting the hem of her shirt and bouncing on the balls of her feet, full of restless energy.

"Can I talk to you outside?"

I follow her and sit on some neighbouring shop's staircase. Charlotte stands in front of me, swaying from side to side, like she has no idea how to start.

"You like Hugo," I state simply. I know Charlotte — whenever she wants to tell me something, she always skirts around the issue, never knowing how to breach the subject. A little prompting is often just what she needs to get started.

Her jaw drops. "How did you know? Is it that obvious?"

"Oh, honey. You think I don't know flirting when I see it? You two are obviously into each other. I've known since my birthday last year."

Charlotte gives a sheepish smile. "We really hit it off that night. We've been texting since then. We started out being just friends, because I was seeing someone back then, but it slowly developed into something more. We didn't want to do anything before I talked to you, though." She looks away and sighs, her shoulders sagging. "It feels kinda shitty doing this with someone my sister used to —" She shrugs away the rest of the sentence, obviously feeling awkward about the whole thing.

"Oh, Char, don't worry about it. My relationship with Hugo has always been about so much more than just sex. He's a great friend of mine and he'll continue to be, whether or not we sleep together. And I want to focus on what I have with David and Emma — that part of my life is over."

Charlotte fiddles with the owl-shaped pendant of her necklace. Everything about her screams 'unsure.'.

I take her hand in mine. "Hey. I'm not doing it as a favour to you. I genuinely don't mind, and I truly believe you two would be good together."

At last, she meets my eyes. A smile slowly stretches the corners of her mouth.

"Now, go! Enjoy!"

Charlotte disappears inside the bar. Two minutes later, Hugo comes out. He walks up to me, hands in his pockets, an amused smile on his lips. He nods at me like 'sup?'

"Thanks," he says. "That's a pretty nice thing you're doing."

I shrug. "You two are so smitten, how could I stand in the way of that?"

A mischievous glint lights up his eye. "But are you certain you'll be able to resist all this?" He gestures at his entire body, wriggling for good measure.

I push him playfully. "I think I'll have my hands full with these dorks." I motion at David and Emma, walking out of the bar and recreating the best bits of the bout.

Charlotte follows them out, and looks expectantly over at Hugo.

"You should go," I tell him. "Evans girls don't wait."

He chuckles. "Thanks again, seriously."

"No problem. I think I'm gonna like having you in the family."

He hugs me tight. "See ya, sis."

SIXTY-ONE

Julia's wedding takes place in Mont-Tremblant, where Jason's parents own a country house with acres of land. David and I have to get there for the rehearsal dinner on Friday. Mitch and Emma aren't invited — it's a small affair, strictly for the wedding party, as Julia drilled into our heads when her bridesmaid Brittany wanted to bring the dude she's been banging for three weeks. However, Emma and Mitch drive up with us for rental car logistics. The four of us got a suite so Mitch would get her own room. Cory and Georgie are joining us tomorrow, before the wedding.

At the rehearsal dinner, Julia is in her now-usual bridezilla state, freaking out at the smallest detail and fake crying to get what she wants. Her wedding planner, Heather, is basically a drill sergeant. She makes us practice walking up and down the aisle eight times because we're not walking slowly enough. We're dragging our feet at a zombie pace when she deems it passable at last. It's especially excruciating because I can't even make fun of her with David; since he's the best man, he's paired with Olivia, the maid of honour, while I'm stuck with one of Jason's douche friends from business school, Mathieu.

Mathieu keeps flexing and watching to see if I'm checking him out. He clearly thinks he's God's gift to women. I cope by reminding myself that, tomorrow, we'll just walk up and down the aisle once, and then I can run away from him for the rest of the night.

But then, of course, Julia unveils the seating chart for the honour table and, while she magnanimously seated me to the right of David, Mathieu is on my right. And, of course, Mitch, Emma, Cory and Georgie are far away at a 'not-so-close friends' table. I plan to stuff my face lightning fast so I can join them on the dance floor ASAP.

Tonight also marks the first time I've seen Julia's parents in forever. I was constantly over at their home when we were kids, but, ever since Julia moved out, we lost touch.

"Amy, sweetheart, you look wonderful!" Mrs. Tyler kisses the air around my cheeks, a greeting reminiscent of the soap operas she's so fond of.

"How are you?" Mr. Tyler asks, clasping my hand between his.

"I'm great, thanks. Have you met my boyfriend?" I pull a relieved-looking David from a conversation with Olivia.

"David, come meet Julia's parents. Mr. and Mrs. Tyler, here is David Paradis."

They greet each other and Mrs. Tyler pulls me aside.

"He seems such a nice boy. How long have you two been together?"

"Four years."

Her eyes dart to my naked ring finger and I know exactly what she's about to say.

"Don't worry, dear. I'm sure he'll ask soon."

I smile politely and I'm saved from having to answer by Mr. Tyler's booming voice.

"If I were you I'd pop the question soon, my boy! A pretty girl like Amy won't wait forever!"

David and I chuckle awkwardly and walk away, pretexting a wedding-related emergency.

"We have got to get you a ring to wear on these occasions," David whispers in my ear.

"Or maybe we should just explain our life choices in detail, see how shocked they would be?"

David laughs, but reminds me of Mr. Tyler's heart problems, so I drop it.

During dinner, I notice David squirming in his seat in front of me, but I don't pay much attention: I'm caught between Mathieu trying to explain his fitness routine and Brittany bitching about her date not being allowed at the head table.

The night finally ends, with Julia's reminder to meet in Olivia's room at eight sharp the next morning to get ready. David and I can finally join Mitch and Emma back in our room. They're playing board games and have opened a bottle of wine.

"Good god, I'm so jealous of you guys right now!" I drop down on the couch next to Mitch, taking a swig straight out of the bottle.

David sits on the floor at Emma's feet, resting his head against her thigh.

"It was fucking horrible," he mutters. "Douchebags, stuck-up parents, overall just shitty people. And don't get me started on Julia's sister — Olivia? She dropped hints all night. And when that didn't work, she tried giving me a hand job under the table!"

"What?" the three of us exclaim. Mitch chokes on a potato chip.

"That's why you were squirming!" I realize as I rub Mitch's back so she can recover.

"Yeah. I managed to stop her, but how insane is she? Her parents were, like, two seats down; you were right in front of us!"

"I think she's mad because her little sister is getting married and she's still single."

"What a shitty family," Mitch croaks, her voice still hoarse from coughing.

"Why did you agree to go to the wedding if you don't like them?" Emma asks.

"Well, on his own, Jason's a great guy. He's my best friend, so of course I agreed to be his best man."

"But, Julia, man! I mean, she's my oldest friend, but damn! I can't wait for this to be over so I can slowly phase her out of my life."

"Alright, so if I understand correctly, that means tomorrow will only be survived with copious amounts of alcohol?"

"You got it," Mitch says, refilling her glass. "David, you got your flask?"

"Of course!" He pulls out four flasks from his nearby suitcase. "And I brought some for my favourite ladies!"

"Oh, bless you!" I unscrew the top of the flask he hands me and take a sniff. "Scotch? You went all out!"

"Nothing's too good for my girls." He grins and it's still the sexiest thing in the world, even after all these years.

"Well, I'm going to bed, because '8 o'clock sharp, don't be late, girls!'" I say in my best Julia impression.

"The ceremony's at four. What the hell are you gonna do from eight to then?" Emma asks incredulously.

"Hair and makeup. Drink mimosas. Gossip. Probably take care of many bridezilla emergencies."

"Good thing we brought board games, eh, Emma?" Mitch says.

¤

Olivia Tyler — WHERE ARE YOU????????????

Amy Evans — Calm down, she said 8, on my way

Olivia Tyler — IF SHE'S HERE AT 8 IT MEANS WE HAVE TO BE HERE BEFORE HER TO BE READY FOR EMERGENCIES.

Amy Evans — Geez she's not the president

I'm so psyched to spend the whole day with them, yay! If they don't have mimosas ready as I walk in I think I'm going to scream. I knock on Olivia's door, hear "It's open!" and let myself in. Olivia, Sophie and Brittany are running around with curlers in their hair, all in various states of undress. The room looks like a toxic wasteland. Clothes, makeup and hair accessories are strewn about. The remains of what looks like a highly inebriated party are on every surface: empty glasses, several bottles of wine, and half-empty bags of chips.

Brittany still has last night's makeup smeared across her cheeks; Olivia has a run in her pantyhose, and Sophie's holding her head like it might explode. I set down my garment bag and my makeup case on an ottoman — pretty much the only free surface in the room. I'm tempted to watch them freak out for a while as I sit there calm and collected, but I don't want to witness Julia going berserk if she sees them and the room like that.

I have to do something. I take a deep breath and summon my inner-Julia — I've seen her boss her way through high school, surely I can do it too.

"Alright, ladies, the cavalry has arrived. Stop messing around. First order of business, coffee. You all obviously need it more than mimosas right now."

The girls look at me with a mix of relief and *how dare she?* as I start up the coffee maker.

"Sophie, take some Advil." I pull a bottle out of my purse and fill a cup of water in the bathroom. "Anybody else needs some? Brittany, for god's sakes, wash your face." I hand her a bottle of makeup remover.

"Yeah, guys, look at yourselves, flipping out and clearly not ready," Olivia jumps in, ignoring the fact that not two minutes ago she was one of them.

She starts making the bed while I pick up some trash, deliberately ignoring me and the fact that I just saved their sorry asses. Britt and Sophie come back from the bathroom with clean faces, coffee mugs in hand, as we finish cleaning up the room.

"So where's the bride?" Britt asks.

"Relax," Olivia says, pouring herself some coffee. "She's always late. We'll finish cleaning up and setting up everything we need, and then I'll call her."

"So, of course, it was vital that you text me in all-caps because I wasn't here at 7:54?"

"I panicked because these guys were a mess."

"Bitch, it's your room!" Sophie exclaims in outrage.

Olivia takes a deep breath, eyes closed, and pinches the bridge of her nose. "Just drink your coffee. It'll all be over in sixteen hours and thirty-six minutes."

Apparently, Olivia doesn't know the word 'sorry.'

We set up everything in 'stations,', as she calls them: makeup, hair, clothes and refreshments.

"Alright, I'll run to the Starbucks down the street — you know Julia, nothing but a *venti* soy latte with two pumps of vanilla will do!"

Somehow, Olivia manages to smile while saying this, but you can tell she's had enough of this shit. "I'll be back with the bride in fifteen minutes. Make sure the mimosas are ready when we return."

Thirty minutes pass before the bride-to-be finally arrives, followed by Olivia, who's clearly trying to talk herself into not killing her sister on her wedding day. Julia walks in with the brightest of smiles, but I can tell this won't last. At the first hint of a glitch, she might explode.

As it is, she manages to passive-aggressively put down each of her bridesmaids — backhanded compliments have always been her strong suit.

"Mom and Dad are so happy — as their youngest daughter I was kinda their last hope, you know?"

In the bathroom, Olivia keeps her teeth clenched, but I see her, seconds later, frantically rubbing at an eyeliner streak across her cheek.

We eventually manage to get ready, in the matching light pink — sorry, *honeysuckle* — dresses and gold pumps Julia chose for us. We solve a few bridal calamities, help Julia get dressed, and do each other's hair and makeup. Around one, I leave to get lunch for everyone, and we force Julia to eat at least a little.

All through the day, we have to liaise with Heather, the wedding planner, to make sure everything's going according to schedule. When it's finally time to leave for Jason's parents' place, I'm exhausted. I'd rather take a nap than stand through an entire ceremony, followed by a lengthy party.

¤

I have to admit, Julia, Olivia, and Heather did a pretty amazing job. The happy couple are getting married under a huge oak tree decked out with garlands to make it look like it's in bloom. The aisle is covered in pink petals. Very fairy-tale chic.

Mathieu manages to be almost decent while we walk down the aisle together. I guess Julia's shriek of *Just shut up and smile!* last night must have worked. He stared lewdly when he saw me in my butt-hugging dress, but that was it.

David looks gorgeous in his tux — Olivia seems way too happy to have him as arm candy. She smirks at me in triumph as they walk up the aisle. I ignore her — she doesn't know she chose the wrong couple to start drama with.

I cheer with everyone else when the minister finally declares that Jason can kiss his new bride. I'm happy for them, but honestly? I'm mostly cheering because it's finally over — the worst part of the day is, at least. The rest might be a bit boring and eye-roll inducing, but at least I won't have to get through it while standing for half an hour in front of two hundred strangers, a fake smile pasted on my face as I try not to fall asleep or groan out loud.

I have nothing against weddings per se. I'm all for celebrating the love between two — or more — people, but Julia's wedding is the epitome of these huge, pricey, too elegant weddings. Those weddings that seem to be more about 'Look how much money we have and how perfect our couple is!' than about sharing the love with their loved ones. But, then again, I should have expected that from the start, knowing Julia.

We finally make our way to the reception tent, where waiters are serving cocktails and hors-d'oeuvres. I grab a bunch of canapés and an old-fashioned, because the other option was a strawberry daiquiri — of course, Julia and Jason chose the most stereotypical and heteronormative signature drinks. I take advantage of everyone mingling to join Emma and our friends. They pull me into a group hug and David piles on.

"Survived okay?" Emma asks with concern.

"As much as I could."

"How was your morning?" David asks me, since we had no time to catch up before the ceremony.

"Bitchy remarks, gossips and emergencies. You?"

"Smoked cigars, played video games, got dressed thirty minutes before we had to leave. If you ignore the racist and sexist remarks from Jason's bros, it went great."

"As for us, we slept in, ordered room service waffles, and played the Game of Life. We changed the rules to accommodate poly weddings, and I won!" Emma says, beaming.

"She actually just took my spouse," Mitch fake complains.

"I'm so glad to finally be with you." I heave a relieved sigh. "I feel like I lived three whole days since I woke up this morning. Somebody bring me a bed."

"Come, let's sit down."

After dinner, David makes his best man speech and I'm impressed. After this whole weekend, I couldn't possibly manage to say two minutes worth of good things about Julia and Jason. Good thing I'm not the maid of honour.

The happy couple dances their first dance — to "The Way You Look Tonight," of course — and then the party can finally start. I run away from Mathieu and his creepy remarks, and make a beeline for the bar. Two beers in hand, I meet David at our friends' table. We sit down, enjoying a moment of peace while the rest of the guests invade the dance floor. We talk for a while, until we've had enough drinks to feel loose and get dancing. Emma looks like a ray of sunshine in her yellow dress. She went shopping for it with David and I wasn't allowed to see it before today. They both said I would adore it and they were right. The brilliant colour sets off her dark complexion perfectly, reminding me of the way she was dressed on our first triad date. She dances like she's alone in the room. Her dress fans around her as she twirls and her face is animated with a smile made of pure light.

The temptation is killing me. It's so hard to see her like this, looking lovely as ever, without being able to touch her — to kiss her.

A slow dance comes up. David pulls me close, and I can see in his eyes this is just as hard for him. Unabashed, Emma extends her hand to Mitch and they share the dance. Emma and I exchange longing glances above David's shoulder. She makes sure nobody's watching before blowing me a kiss.

When the song ends, Mitch pulls me aside.

"You guys should find somewhere private for a little while. I mean, it must suck to go to a wedding and not be able to kiss your date, right?"

I look around and find Cory and Georgie, looking perfect together, dancing in a tight embrace. They've obviously forgotten about the rest of the world.

"Mitch, we're not going to ditch you," I scoff.

"I'll be fine — look, they're starting a game of musical chairs!"

I tell Emma and David to follow me, discreetly, and make my way out of the tent, feeling like a spy. I spot a tool shed in a corner of the yard and notice there's plenty of room between the back wall and the hedge behind it. I slip in and make sure the hiding place is out of sight. The others join me shortly.

"Were you seen?" I ask in a spy voice.

"Negative," Emma answers seriously.

"I was, but managed to shake 'em off," David adds.

"We're such dorks."

"I love us." Emma grins.

I pull her closer and bury my face in her neck. She smells of spices and pears, and a bit like the flowers that covered every inch of the marquee. David presses his body against her back and we share a kiss above her shoulder. Emma's hand is on my thigh, making its way up, under my skirt, when suddenly I hear a shriek.

"Oh. My. God!!!"

The three of us jump at the sound and look up to see Julia, her mouth wide open in shock, champagne flute dramatically dropping on the grass at her feet.

"You didn't shake her off," Emma whispers to David.

"Seriously, Amy? This is *my day*! You're making it all about yourself, AGAIN! You're ruining everything, with your perverted ways!"

"What's ruined? Nobody saw us," David says diplomatically.

"Only because I followed you when I saw you leaving with Mitch's date!"

Julia's voice is so loud now, I'm pretty sure people in the marquee can hear her above the music. Talk about making a scene.

"Stealing your best friend's date, now?" she continues. "That's a new low, Amy."

"Actually, the three of us are together," I say calmly. I can see Julia get increasingly worked up, and, frankly, I'm not here to fight. I came to this wedding to show support for an old friend, even though our paths split a long time ago. I see now it's hopeless to try mending this frail connection.

"We're in love," I continue, voice steady. "Mitch brought Emma as a plus one to help us out."

"What the hell?" Julia mutters. I've never seen her this confused before.

"Look," David says coolly, "this is your day. Nobody else saw us. Go enjoy it — forget what you saw, and we'll just leave, alright? No need to make a scene."

"This is disgusting." Julia turns and walks away, head held high.

I text Mitch, explaining what happened. She and the boys join us and we decide to find a bar where we can spend the rest of

the night and unwind. I think phasing Julia out of my life won't be
necessary.

SIXTY-TWO

The early July sun shines bright on our new patio table. On it, delicious food waiting to be eaten. Around it, my friends, the people closest to my heart, here to celebrate a new start in my life with David and Emma. I stand up and raise a glass of champagne.

"I want to thank all of you for being here for our housewarming party. You're all so great, so important to my life, I could never be where I am without all of you by my side. We all grew a lot in the past few years." I pause, looking through misty eyes at all of them.

Cory and Georgie, closer than ever, a new ring glinting on Cory's left hand.

Mitch and Justin, who's finally back from the UK, taking their platonic soulmates thing to the next level by moving in together.

Charlotte, my beautiful sister, who's not so little anymore, who arrived together with Hugo. No matter where this takes them, I know they'll make each other happy.

I clear my throat and continue. "I guess I just want to thank you all and hope we'll all be together, through the good and the bad, in five, ten, or twenty years."

"Hear, hear!" David cheers, and we all clink our glasses together.

We eat and drink, and I give everybody tours of our new place.

Mitch takes me aside. "Alex says hi."

I stop in my tracks. "Really?"

"Yeah, she stopped by Le Trèfle. She looks well."

"I'm so glad. She deserves it." I mean it. We've been through a lot of bad stuff, but I'll always love her. She was my best friend, and if cutting me out of her life was the right thing to do to heal, I'm glad she did it.

Mitch bites her lip, looking unsure. "There's something else. She's going out with Marie-Ève."

"Marie-Ève from Gaspésie?"

Mitch nods. "They met at some circus-themed art exhibit."

I take a second to process that fact. The more I think about it, the bigger my smile gets.

"Holy crap, that's perfect!"

¤

At the end of the night, when everyone's gone, David leads Emma and I to our new bedroom and sits us on the bed — king-sized, of course. At the place of honour, above the bed, hangs a framed outtake from David's mermaid series: Emma and I, underwater in our mermaid costumes, hair flowing around us, hugging David in his scuba gear.

He comes back with three champagne flutes. "There was just enough left for one last toast. To our new life."

He raises his glass, and we clink ours against his.

"To our new life!"

THE END

ACKNOWLEDGEMENTS

OPEN: A Tale of Love, Mermaids, Bassists, & Creepy Dudes wouldn't be the novel it is — hell, it wouldn't even be in your hands today — without my team, my crew, my family. If this book is my baby, then they are its godparents, weird uncles, cool aunts and that one family friend you're not sure why is there but always has a fun anecdote to tell. I could never thank y'all enough and I love every single one of you.

The most special of thanks to Bobby Lacroix, my husband, my best friend, my assistant, the one who takes care of my heart and my mind and walks with me every step of the way to fulfill my dreams. I love you.

Very special thanks to François Tousignant, a wizard who gave me more meaningful advice than I can remember, who helped me grow from someone who wants to tell a story to an actual author, a guy who cares just so damn much.

To Marie-Ève Bart and Ariane Préfontaine (the real Glitter Bomb), my favourite Hufflepuffs, who gave me their time and precious advice: you two are the best readers a girl could ask for and I can't thank you enough.

To Em Trencher, for your unwavering love and support, for being you, and for providing the inspiration to make the final draft of this book what it needed to be.

To Lauren West, who *gets it*, and who showed me people care when I needed it the most. You're a generous soul and I'm forever grateful I met you.

To Julie Desrosiers and Katherine Delorme, my work mom and work wife, who make having a day job okay and even fun most of the time, and who never fail to cheer me on (or up!)

To Cassandra Fountaine, who designed a cover more fantastic than I could have ever dreamed of.

To my long-time friends, Thomas Deshaies, Thomas Mongeau, Anne Reigner, Mariane Ménard, Gabrielle Ménard and Annie-Claude Bertrand; and to my family, Maman, Papa, Brigitte Nantel, Denis Blais, René Nantel, Julien Blais and Estelle Blais, for shaping me as a person. I truly wouldn't be who I am today without the experiences we lived together, and without your love and support. I couldn't dream of a better family.

To Laury Lacroix, the real Four-Leaf Klobber, for your friendship, your support, and for introducing me to roller-derby.

To a bunch of creepy dudes who gave me enough writing material for a whole novel. I won't name you but this was cathartic.

To everyone whose face lit up when I said I was writing a queer, polyamorous romcom — you helped me keep going when it felt like nobody cared.

To my counselor, Maga-Li Monteilhet-Labossière, who helped me get my shit together enough to decide to publish this book myself.

And finally, thank *you*, reading this, for being there, for caring, and for giving a shot to an unknown queer author who writes stuff that's a bit too niche.

AUTHOR PHOTO: SIMON BONNALLIE

Emilie Nantel is a queer fiction writer driven by the need to break the allocishet, monogamous mold and lend her voice to underrepresented communities.

Emilie developed her casual, witty voice writing fanfiction, always seeking the different, the underground, and she still carries that in her original fiction.

As a bilingual Montrealer, it's important to her to showcase the heart and soul of this vibrant and diverse city and its people in her writing.

You can usually find her curled up with a good queer book, or dreaming of the day she owns a cabin in the woods with her husband.

OPEN: A Tale of Love, Mermaids, Bassists, & Creepy Dudes is her first novel.

Visit Emilie at **emilienantel.com** and join the newsletter to access some exclusive prequel short stories.

Twitter, Instagram, & Facebook: **@emnantel**

Tumblr: **emilienantel.tumblr.com**